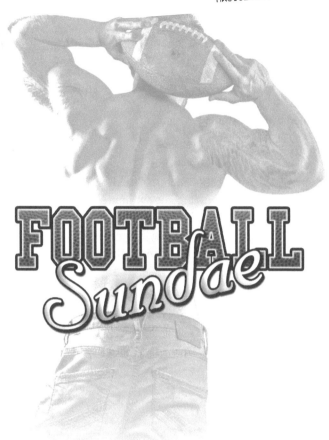

FOOTBALL
Sundae

DARYL BANNER

Football Sundae

Cover Model / Photographer
Nathan Hainline

Cover & Interior Design
Daryl Banner

Background photo on cover provided courtesy of
Jan Behrens

OTHER BOOKS BY DARYL BANNER

The Brazen Boys (M/M Romance)
Dorm Game ·
On The Edge ·
Owned By The Freshman ·
Dog Tags ·
Commando (Dog Tags 2) ·
All Yours Tonight ·
Straight Up ·
Houseboy Rules ·
Slippery When Wet ·

A College Obsession Romance
Read My Lips ·
Beneath The Skin ·
With These Hands ·

The Beautiful Dead Saga
The Beautiful Dead ·
Dead Of Winter ·
Almost Alive ·
The Whispers ·
The Winters ·
The Wakings ·

The OUTLIER Series
Rebellion ·
Legacy ·
Reign Of Madness ·
Beyond Oblivion ·
Five Kings ·

FOREWORD

Born and raised in a small Texas town myself, I know how unfriendly some can be with regard to gay people. I know not everyone understands us. I know I'm judged by some before they even get a chance to taste my mama's homemade pies. Really, they're the ones missin' out.

But this book is a departure from that. The small fictional country town of Spruce is a slightly idealized, friendly one. I believe this is how the world *should* be, and so dang it, this is how the town of Spruce is, where you'll be spending the next twenty chapters.

This is a book that's simply about love in all its clumsiness and hopefulness. I really hope the story melts your heart and touches you the way it touched me to tell it.

Rest assured, this dedication is all the "preaching" you'll find in these pages. It's not my job to tell you how to feel; I'm just here to tell a story and leave all the feeling up to you :-) Beyond this point, there's no political soapboxes. There's only Tanner Strong and Billy Tucker, two young men from Spruce who can't wait to tell you their story.

Thanks for picking up this book. From the bottom of this boy's heart, I hope you enjoy it.

And as always, happy reading!

XXOO
Daryl

CHAPTER 1
BILLY

Just when I thought my day couldn't get any worse, Tanner Strong struts through the diner doors with his entourage of jock buddies.

Tanner Strong. Let's take a minute to appreciate the lean slab of meat that was the high school quarterback of my horny, teenage wet dreams. When Tanner Strong enters the room, everyone turns their heads—and it's not just because he's something of a town hero. Tanner's body is built to order—straight from the sex fantasy factory, apparently—and his crushingly adorable face matches the goods, framed by short, dusty brown hair that pokes and jabs in all directions. He has this chiseled nose with a tiny scar across it that gives him this tough *I-beat-people-up-for-a-living* look. His full, plush lips half hang open as he turns in circles, ignoring the loud shouts of his comrades as he drinks in the sight of my family's diner, likely noting how much it's changed in the past three years.

He hasn't changed much. I could watch that dang face for hours. Those muddy brown eyes can still pull all my focus, just like they used to in the middle of history class when I should've been learning what year prohibition was repealed. It was 1930-something, by the way.

And please, let's not spend another hour discussing Tanner's broad, muscled shoulders that have obviously rammed into countless firm, hard-bodied rivals during his time on the field. Or the thick, bulging arms that come from those shoulders, the muscles of which make a stretch rack of those poor, tortured sleeves of his too-tight shirt. Or the pecs underneath said shirt that show through in perfect, distracting detail.

This is the first time I've really seen Tanner since high school. He scored some football scholarship and took off to Oklahoma, which is a twelve hour drive north from our little country hometown of Spruce. Every time he's come home since, the whole dang populace seems to throw a parade, even though he spends all his time out on his family's big ranch. Hell, the first summer he came home, I think he was sent off on some luxurious trip to Europe, or so said half the gossips that run through our diner.

But the sight of him and his buddies crashing through our door does not inspire the same wave of joy in me that it does in all our sports-loving, cheer-happy patrons. All four years of my high school career, I had suffered when, after every football game, win or lose, the whole team would burst through the doors and make a mess of our diner. Sure, it was great for business. Sure, my pa's a big fan of football and loved every second. But having to serve upwards of twenty-five to forty rowdy, cocky, Coke-guzzling, burger-chomping athletes and all their adoring fans after every game quickly became my Friday night hell. While they were here, it was a headache of nonstop noise, and after they left, it was hours of cleanup.

And it was always spearheaded by the great football hero and legend-in-the-making that is Tanner Strong.

Now, after three years of peace, he's back. And he brought a few former teammates. And the sight of him is making my insides turn over with a mix of horniness and dread, even as I stare at him from the window of the kitchen, a wet bowl in one hand and a rag in the other. I've apparently forgotten whatever it is I'm doing.

"Well, Junior, if your mouth was hanging open any more, you'd be washing your jaw instead of that bowl."

I flinch at the sound of my ma's voice, giving her thin, weary figure and frizzy brown hair half a glance before returning my attention to the bowl—and *not* to the guys who just piled into the booth by the TV. "I thought we close our doors at eight."

"It's ten 'til," she says back, "and it's Friday. You know dang well we stay open 'til eleven Fridays and Saturdays. Now get your booty out there and take their orders."

I lift my tired eyes to her. "Me? What about Mindy?"

"She's on break."

I gawk. "She just got here an hour ago!"

"And I just sent her on break. Skidoo!"

I give the bowl and rag a shake, lifting my eyebrows defiantly. "I'm in the middle of—"

She swipes them right out of my hands like they were never there, taking over the dishes. "Any other excuse you got not to hop on out there and take them sweet boys' orders?"

I scowl at my unbearable ma, then glance through the kitchen window, watching as the patrons cheer and laugh and give Tanner high-fives and slaps on his back as he makes his way to the booth his buddies have swallowed up. "Ain't nothin' *sweet* about them."

She smirks knowingly. "I know you all went to high school together. You might've—"

"What's it matter about high school??" I cut her off. "That was three years ago!"

"Exactly my point, Junior! Three years! Might be you were on opposite sides of the track back then, but I heard college really changed that Tanner boy. He ain't the same as he used to be. Maybe you got more in common now."

Me? More in common with the town football star? "You hit your head or somethin'?" I ask her.

She nudges me with an elbow. "Don't forget to tell them about the daily special. It's your pa's pride and joy."

The Touchdown. Just the thought of having to sell a special burger my pa came up with called *The Touchdown* to a quartet of obnoxious football-playing jocks turns my face a color that rivals the cherry pie I'll no doubt be gorging on later.

But I'm not built to whine. Hard work and sweat has kept my parents' diner open all these years, and it's put food on the table and a roof over our overworked, messy heads of hair.

"Maybe you can entice them later with your little dessert menu," my ma keeps on. "That might be all the endorsement we'd need, if Tanner takes a liking to one of your *culinary concoctions.*"

I feel the corner of my mouth pulling up. She's right, and she's set my mind back on track. No matter the hell I might have to put up with this summer, come the fall, I'm kicking it out of here at long last to chase my dream of culinary school and someday opening my own place. My father's heart attack might have hindered me leaving right out of high school, but now I have an associate's degree in business under my belt before I head off to become a real dessert chef. *Billy's Confections. Billy Bakes. Billy's Sweet Tooth Tastery.* All the possible names of the business I'll eventually open and operate race through my head like ice cream flavors.

My dreams are just a summer away. And I'm sure as hell not gonna let a hotshot college athlete scare me into the kitchen. I grab my apron, then puff up my chest as I tie it on. *You can do this, Billy.* I glance into the side of the fridge, which is basically the kitchen's version of a body-length mirror, being polished so shiny that I can see my slender shape, my short, messy brown hair, and a smudge of dark grease on my forehead—which I wipe away. Under my black apron with the diner emblem across the chest, I'm wearing a fitted navy blue plaid shirt rolled up to the elbows. Worried I look a bit uptight, I let pop the top button, then give my disheveled brown hair a push of encouragement in the right direction before slipping past the swinging doors.

The noise of our rowdy guests reaches me long before I reach them. Despite my little pep talk a second ago, my feet don't seem to move properly, as if they're trying to drive me back to the kitchen. When I reach the table, they don't notice me. I try to speak, but they all suddenly burst out laughing at some joke one of the guys was finishing. I only need to catch the punch line—"And that's why you call it *pussy!*"—to know what sort of hell I've walked into.

Just get their orders. Quicker served, quicker gone.

"Welcome to Biggie's Bites," I state over their laughs. "I'm William. Can I start you guys off with—?"

"This, right here," announces Kirk, the one across from Tanner, a beastly guy with a buzzed head wearing a sleeveless green jersey that shows off his thick shoulders. He jabs a pudgy finger at the menu. "That big ol' juicy thing. Put it in my mouth."

"Fag," teases Joel, the blue-eyed blond at his side in a grey shirt, stained with grease from working at his pa's auto shop two blocks over. He's got an unfortunate pox of acne on his cheeks that's festered there since his thirteenth birthday. I'll call him Zits.

Oh, and a word about the word "fag": Growing up gay in this small country town of Spruce that no one in the world's heard of, even with as "friendly" as it is, you still hear the three-and-six-letter F-bombs thrown back and forth twenty times a day between boys at school who can't be bothered to broaden their vocabulary. I guess I've either grown a thick skin or become so desensitized that I don't even associate it with "gay" anymore.

Maybe that's what inspires me to make light of it. "That would be *me*," I interject with a smile, "though my nametag reads 'William'."

The four boys shut right up and stare at me. Zits tries to say something twice, sputters and fails both times, then finally manages to get out, "B-But you're not a fag. You're just gay. There's a difference."

Now it's my turn to stare. "By all means, enlighten me of this difference."

Tanner swallows a chuckle of amusement, his face going red. The fact that my words might have had anything to do with his reaction gives me such a rush of private joy, I can't even begin to describe it.

"A fag's, like ... just a stupid person," explains Zits.

"Oh. That explains it so much better," I remark.

"Yeah, see? Totally different," exclaims Zits, missing my sarcasm completely, and the third one at the table sitting next to Tanner—a thinner guy named Harrison with blunt black eyebrows, russet skin, and wearing a t-shirt with grass stains on the arms—grunts his agreement.

This is how I'll say I spent my Friday night: getting a lesson in etiquette from a bunch of rowdy jocks who, just seconds ago, shared jokes about pussy and called each other fags. Jeez, who smacked me with the lucky branch?

I know these guys from high school when they used to play football alongside Tanner. Kirk, who still bags groceries down at the market and lives in a trailer by his grandma's house. Joel/Zits, who gets greasy tinkering under cars at his pa's shop. Harrison, who works as a farmhand for an aunt or uncle of Tanner's, far as I know.

"Can I get you guys anything to drink?" I ask politely.

"Gimme a Coke. And this juicy thing," says Kirk. "Cook it medium-rare. Double cheese. Toast the bun, too. Fuck, I'm hungry. This come with fries?"

If you read the menu ... "Yes, or coleslaw, your choice."

"Coleslaw's gross," Zits interjects, face wrinkled.

"Your *face* is gross," returns Kirk.

Zits ignores him and lifts his menu. "I want this one. No pickles. Lather mine up in mayo ... extra mayo."

"He likes lots of white, creamy stuff in his mouth," Kirk explains.

The others laugh, but Zits punches him so hard in the shoulder that Kirk jerks forward, kicking the leg of the table and causing the salt shaker to fall over.

"Burger of the day?"

The words come from the one person at the table I've been trying hard *not* to look at. The one who might or might not have already stolen enough of my attention in high school. The one I secretly pined over ever since I was thirteen and first discovered how my cock works. The one who's always flocked by cheerleaders and flanked by buddies—and never once looked my way.

But now he's looking my way. *Tanner Strong is looking my* way. *The* Tanner. Tan the Man. Quarterback of Spruce High School. The hero who's returned home from college and flipped the whole dang town upside-down. The star.

And he's asking me about my pa's damned burger.

"Yes," I state, staring at the fallen salt shaker instead of him. "Burger of the day is called *The Touchdown*, and it contains—"

"TOUCHDOWN!!" shouts Zits with enough volume to fill the whole diner, throwing his big hands in the air and waving them. "TOUCHDOWN!!" joins in Kirk, his voice roaring and booming. Harrison and his blunt black eyebrows jump in, too. To my surprise, other tables fall in line as well, throwing their hands up and shouting, "TOUCHDOWN!!"

"Okay, I want one of those," decides Tanner.

"Scratch my last order," blurts Kirk. "I want one too." Zits shouts, "Me too! I don't care what's in it." Harrison raises his hand. "Gimme one of them, too! Big and juicy! Double-everything! *Score!!*"

After recovering from laughing at his buddies, Tanner hands over his menu. When I take it from him, our fingers touch. I feel a surge of enjoyment thunder up my arm just by the little flirt of skin my fingers feel when they graze his. I keep my eyes on the menu knowing full well that his deep eyes are on me and are guaranteed to melt me to a puddle of nothing right here in front of him and all the rest of the world. *Don't look at him. Don't you dare.*

And then he has the audacity to say, "Thanks, Billy."

Billy. He remembers my name, the one I actually go by, the one that's not on my nametag.

I look up at his face.

Big mistake. His rich brown eyes smolder me. His eyebrows are pulled together with just the slightest pinch of concentration. His mouth is barely parted from the words he just spoke, which invite me into a whole library of fantasies I thought I'd locked up in my all-too-horny teenage brain when we graduated years ago—ridiculous and unlikely fantasies of under-the-bleachers make-out sessions, sweaty locker room jockstrap-clad meet-ups, and maybe a carefully orchestrated sleepover which always ended with him sleeping right by me, except in my fantasies, neither Tanner nor I were sleeping at all, each of us excitedly waiting for the other to make a move.

"Oh, and a Coke for me, too," adds Tanner.

I swallow down my horny teenage sex fantasies, trying with all my might to shove them right back into that vault in my brain where they belong. With just a quick nod, I take the menus and head back to the kitchen while dodging a chorus of diners who are still chanting, "Touchdown! Touchdown!"

When I return to the back counter by the kitchen, I head straight to the POS and put in their orders. I have to do it three times because the machine's been possessed since two Halloweens ago and keeps canceling the whole dang order when I try to add extra mayo to Zits' ticket.

"Piece of shit," I grumble at it.

"Hey now," warns my frizzy-haired ma who appears by my side to see what the hell I've gotten myself into.

"That's what it's called, ain't it? POS?" I tease.

She chuckles as she continues on her way. Then, my pa, his salt-and-peppered brown hair smashed down by a cap and his mustache looking particularly out of control tonight, pokes his head out of the kitchen in a smoky cloud of grill steam. "Am I hearing a bunch of excitement out there?"

I lift a brow. "We gettin' the ventilation checked any time this year? Or is it your plan to run outta breathable oxygen by ten o'clock?"

"Never mind the dang ventilation. Are the diners likin' the special tonight? Is that what I'm hearin'?"

"Yeah, Pa. Over the moon."

"They lovin' the Touchdown?"

"It's a total hit, Pa. Everyone wants one."

"Score!" He disappears into the back again.

After taking out an extra plate of fries to the Kimbles and refilling glasses at the table of ladies who meet here every Friday to eat chicken fried steak and play dominos, I bring the boys at table 12 their Cokes. They hardly seem to notice me anyway, bellowing out with obnoxious laughter and shouting at the game on the TV. Kirk nearly elbows me in the nuts when he throws his hands up at something his buddy across the table says. When their order is ready and I bring them their burgers, the four of them shout, "TOUCHDOWN!" yet again, and then I get to enjoy another loud wave of the word coursing through the diner from every mouth big and small, young and old.

While I'm at the kitchen sink again washing cup after greasy cup and thinking about which delicious treat I'm going to serve up for Saturday's Sweet—an item my pa lets me add to the dessert menu every Saturday to show off my pastry skills—I can't help but stare at table 12 through the window, even though it's across the length of the diner and Tanner's backside is all I see. Here in Spruce, football is the beginning and the ending to everything. All it takes is for Tanner Strong to waltz into town from college and it's like Reverend Arnold himself is calling a holiday in the name of the Father, Son, and Holy dang Spirit. I'm sure I'll hear all about it on Sunday, when every business closes and half the town piles into the church at the end of Apricot Street.

And really, can I blame them? Tanner is a walking, talking wet dream. He's got it all. He's handsome. He's built. He's well-off and sitting pretty in that big ranch his family owns at the edge of town. The Strongs own a number of businesses around here and pretty much run the town, along with the Evans, Whitman, and McPherson families. They also throw the biggest most extravagant parties out there on the ranch that the whole town's invited to, so of course everyone loves them.

Meanwhile, I'm still scrubbing cups in the kitchen so feverishly, I might rub the poor things out of existence. I'm usually the guy who does the books and waits on a table or two, but I'm having to pull double duty since Dane, our busboy, called in sick. To make matters worse, I can't peel my eyes away from the back of Tanner's head, wondering how much the last three years of college really have changed him. Apparently not much, despite what my ma heard. He's still loud. He's still the spotlight of the whole populace of Spruce. He's still hot as fuck.

Not that it should matter. He'll have every girl from here to the edge of Spruce all over his tight-jeans-wearing ass the second news spreads that he's back. He'll have all the attention he craves. Why should I add any more to it?

"My, my, can those boys put down some food," Ma mumbles when she sees me later at the POS adding more to their total. While eating their Touchdown burgers, they order two big appetizers and three extra baskets of fries, which they finish every bite of. By the time we get to the dessert menu, I feel fifty pounds heavier.

Apparently to prove that their stomachs really are bottomless pits, the boys order a huge lava brownie apiece lathered in hot fudge. But just as I leave to put in their dessert orders, the twang of Tanner's deep, gravelly voice stops me cold. "Hey, what's that 'Saturday's Sweet' thing on the back?"

I swear I could listen to Tanner read a dictionary on a hot sweaty porch pestered by flies. "Every Saturday, my pa lets me come up with a new dessert."

"You?" Tanner lifts an eyebrow. "Like, you actually make them?"

"From scratch, pretty much."

"Well, shit." Tanner smirks at his buddies, then lifts his chin at me. "Gimme one of them Saturday Sweets, then. Whatever it is, don't care. I wanna try it."

I swallow hard. *Today's not Saturday.* But instead of protesting, I tell him, "I-It'll take twenty minutes, about."

Tanner gives me his soft brown eyes. "I got the time."

Lord, what those eyes do to me.

"Dude, c'mon," blurts out Kirk. "You really wanna wait twenty dang minutes for some fruity-lookin' dessert? I thought we were gonna hit up the bar after this!"

"The bar can wait. And besides, it's open 'til three. I got all the time in the world to try out this ..." Tanner lifts his gaze to me yet again. "... *Saturday Sweet.*"

I swallow hard, give him a curt nod, then whisk my way back to the kitchen. Every footstep seems to chant the words in my ear:

It's not Saturday. It's not Saturday.

"Whatcha doin'?" asks my ma over my shoulder as I'm hacking away at a pair of defenseless apples.

"Saturday Sweet on a Friday, that's what."

"Mmm." She gives me a nudge. "Tryin' to impress the boys, are ya?"

I snort. "Like hell."

"What'd you decide to make?"

"An apple pastry vanilla thing."

"An apple say-what?"

"I haven't had time to name it yet."

I already have my puff pastry dough sitting pretty in the cooler, so I pull it out. After mixing up my apple filling spritzed with a pinch or five of my secret spices, I put it all together and toss one into the oven, then go check on my homemade vanilla bean ice cream in the deep freeze. It's still a bit soft, as I'd intended for it to thicken for tomorrow, but I guess it'll have to do. It's pairing with molten hot apple anyway.

After all the prep for my Saturday Sweet, it's almost comical tossing the three bricks of frozen brownie into the microwave and watching them get nuked through the glass. My parents insist on buying them because they're quick to make and cheap, even though I could whip up something better in five minutes. *No one appreciates fine culinary art anymore. They just want nuclear chocolate and calorie-packed filler.*

Ding.

I plate the lava brownies and start nuking the fudge topping while the scent of apple cinnamon heaven fills the kitchen. I catch my ma through the window chatting it up with the domino ladies.

She meets my eyes and gives me a wink, then is pulled back into conversation.

My gaze drifts to table 12. I find myself thinking of all the times my pa dragged me to the football games. Really, in a town like this, there are only so many options you have for entertainment, but this particular one had a few unintended perks in this gay boy's longing, gear-and-spandex-addicted eyes. As my pa kept trying to point out the intricacies of football, my eyes were glued to Tanner's *tight end* as he crouched low behind his teammate and reached between his legs, ready for the ball. I'd never admit any of this out loud, but I hardly ever had any idea who was winning or losing. It didn't matter to me. As long as I kept my eyes on Tanner, I was winning. And right now, staring through the window at table 12, I'm winning.

Ding.

I bring out their lava brownies and set them on the table, making sure to save Tanner's Saturday Sweet for last. His eyebrows lift at the sight of it before him.

"It's a ..." I freeze. What in jock hell was I going to call it? "A flaky ... apple thing," I say, "with m-my homemade cream on top. Er, *vanilla bean* cream on top. *Ice* cream."

Kirk and Zits turn to each other and stifle laughs while Harrison sucks in his lips and looks away.

"Well," says Tanner, observing my creation, "that's ... quite a dessert."

His buddies burst into laughter, unable to contain themselves anymore. Tanner elbows Harrison, joining in the laughter and giving him a shove, telling them to shut the hell up. "It's got his cream on it," Kirk spits out, laughing so hard he looks like he's choking. *"And it's homemade!"* wheezes Zits, unable to even draw breath he's in such hysterics. "I make homemade cream too! With my right hand! Every night!"

Doesn't matter much, because the second I feel my face flushing red, I decide I've had just about enough of high school fantasies and humiliation for one damn night. Bidding them good riddance without uttering a word, I leave them to their desserts— *with or without my dang cream*—and head back to the kitchen.

Sometime later, Joel/Zits makes a pass at Mindy, who's back from break, and so when she's in the kitchen to refill his Coke, I give her the bill and tell her she can finish them. "He's not really my type," says Mindy with a loose, careless shrug, but takes the bill anyway and heads to their table, leaving me finishing up with the dishes.

After paying, the boys stay awhile longer to finish out whatever game's on TV while cracking jokes, hitting on girls that pass by, and talking to folk who stop by their table to see how Tanner's been. I'm stewing in my own fury at the sink, waiting to clear off their wreck of a table provided they don't suddenly decide to order four large pizzas to top off their brownie-and-burger-filled bellies.

I stare despondently at the crumbs of pastry shell that still remain on the back counter, waiting patiently to be wiped away, which is really what I'd like to do to this whole damn night. I just can't stomach going to the front of the house to finish my closing duties, worried that Tanner or his buddies might say something. I don't even want to think about the conversation that probably ensued at the table after I presented Tanner's dessert. Who the hell am I kidding? Is this some fancy French bistro? After listening to his buddies' laughter all night, I know *exactly* how it'll sound when they're in Tanner's pickup driving back to his big ol' ranch, having a laugh at my expense. Their hearty guffawing rings in my ears, even if it's partly imaginary. If I'm lucky, I'll be the talk of the town by morning: *Tanner Strong gets a polite welcoming back to Spruce by the town homo, who bakes him an apple-something with his homemade "cream" on top.*

After I peek through the window to find them gone, I finally allow myself out of the back and make my way to the boys' table to bus it. Piling all the dishes into my grey tub, it's under Tanner's drink that I find my tip, neatly folded and crisp. I open the single bill up.

It's a fifty.

I stare at the bill, unable to close my mouth. But that's not all. When I flip the fifty over, a message is written at the bottom: *Thanks for putting up with me and my buddies. The apple thing was seriously delish. Even the cream. I'll be back for more—Tanner.*

Well, I'll be damned.

CHAPTER 2
TANNER

"Peach tea," announces my mama as she sets a heavy glass on the coffee table. Her smooth, blonde beehive hairdo shows off two gold hoop earrings that dangle at either side of her neck, which you hardly notice with all your attention pulled to the thick makeup on her face.

"Thank you, Mama," I say back, giving a little grunt of thanks as I pick up my drink and start gulping. I throw an arm over the back of the couch, feeling the afternoon sun washing over my skin through the big floor-to-ceiling windows at my back and side.

She lifts a hand up to rest her chin on as she crosses her long, blue leggings-clad legs. She's got a ring adorning every dang finger, her hands so cluttered you can barely distinguish a wedding ring in all that gold. "I'm throwin' you a big ol' party in a month. I want you to—"

"Mama, c'mon," I say, cutting her off and setting the glass down with a sigh. "I just got in. And I—"

"Don't you go tellin' me no one cares about you being back in town. Spruce ain't nothin' without you. You're the shining star in everyone's sky, sweetie! Get it in that thick skull of yours! I want you to invite all your old friends. Think of it like a football team reunion."

"None of them even play anymore except for maybe Toby, and he's got two kids and doesn't have time to even throw a ball in the fields with me no more."

"Ain't none of them got the scholarship like you did. To them, football's just a dream—but you're *livin'* that big dream. Share it with them, son! Give the town somethin' to believe in, for Christ's sake. You're an inspiration!"

"Oh, cut it with all that, Mama," I spit out, then give her a teasing smirk. "You know dang well the only reason you wanna throw me a big ol' *anything* is to show up the Evanses and the Whitmans for the wedding they planned back in March."

Her face straightens at once. "We are *not* going to talk about the Evanses or the Whitmans or that ridiculous *joke* of a wedding they threw Denise and Larry. Lord help me, if you were here and saw the cake ..."

"I know. You wouldn't shut up about it on the phone."

"It was yellow! The whole dang thing was *yellow*! Was it some sort of funky, off-putting cream-colored look they were goin' for? It looked like the baker done peed in the frosting, for cryin' out loud. Oh, and that extravagant DJ and the silly ponies? What was that wedding? A circus?" She huffs and crosses her arms as tightly as her legs, all the bangles on her wrist clattering together. "The Evanses and the Whitmans better stand back. Those McPhersons, too. I'm the one who throws the best parties."

I withhold a sigh, staring at my mama's distressed eyes that are full of neighborly competitiveness. She's been at war with those ladies ever since grade school when they were part of a clique and my mama was ... well, she was the outcast back then. Fifty pounds heavier and frizzy blonde curls that were so out of control, no salon in three counties could tame them—or so is evidenced by the pictures she's shown me in her albums. The girls were mean to her until they all grew up and started popping babies out. Then my mama got a pretty coin or two in her wallet and suddenly they started to pay attention to her. It's been a lifelong competition between all the big wigs of Spruce. Trouble is, it feels like they all lose in the end.

But I guess I kinda have to give her this one. It's really as much of an ordeal for me as it is for her, this party she wants to throw me. I don't know what my mama and papa do with all their time while I'm away at school, as I don't imagine it's just spent sitting around watching their businesses make money while they kick back and drink tea all day, but the second I come through that door, my mama's eyes light up and my papa sucks in his lips and pretends not to be all teary-eyed and proud.

"I heard Jimmy's starting football this year," I say.

"Your baby brother's always been trailin' right behind you all your life," my mama says with a twinkle in her eye. "He wants to grow up to be just like you."

Almost eight years younger than me and just starting high school, my little brother Jimmy is what my parents used to lovingly call their "oops" baby until Cassie Evans made some remark about how insensitive that sounds. I don't think my mama's ever quite forgiven her for that.

She rises from her cushy armchair and makes her way to the kitchen while asking, "So you gonna do anything special with your summer?"

Staring at the last gulp of peach tea bouncing around in the bottom of my glass, I pick it up and find myself thinking about Billy Tucker at the diner. I'm still having serious doubts that he's really the same Billy Tucker I went to high school with—the Billy who kept to himself, the Billy who was arty and sat in the back of all the classrooms and who everyone said was gay, but no one was actually close enough friends with him to know for sure. Maybe all of that's changed since we left school. Maybe he *is* gay and everyone knows now. All I'd have to do is keep my eyes and ears open to find out.

The sound of the blender rockets from the kitchen and fills the house. I smirk, recalling how red Billy's face got when he presented his dessert. *He made that dessert just for you, Tanner.* I knew damn well that he only serves his special desserts on Saturdays. I was ready for him to shoot me down, but he didn't. He actually put together a whole apple dessert for me, complete with homemade vanilla bean ice cream. It was the best damn thing I'd ever tasted, and I've been to Europe and had some of the finest pastries Paris had to offer just a summer ago.

I have to see him again. This town is only so big. I'm bound to run into him again, or else I'm gonna have to find an excuse to go back to Biggie's Bites. *Who am I kidding? Every time my stomach growls is an excuse.*

And I'm *always* hungry.

I down the last splash of my tea, then shout, "Yeah," over the sound of my mama's blender. "You can say I'm gonna do a thing or two with my summer."

CHAPTER 3
BILLY

The selection of onions is pretty pitiful for a Tuesday. So are the tomatoes, three of which have big, ungainly dark spots on them. It's just a big ol' summer crop of wimpiness by the look of it. I try to make do with what the Marvin brothers have for sale and pick the best I can find from the bins, bagging them one at a time.

"I kinda expected you'd own the place by now."

It's Lee, the younger of the Marvin brothers, a blond tall fellow in his late twenties—*or is he thirty by now?*—with his hairline already receding pretty deeply at the temples. He always looks sweaty and worn out, like he just crawled out of a barn he was forced to clean with a toothbrush on his hands and knees. His older brother Gene is the stern, cold type who is all business where Lee is all heart.

"Nah," I say back. "It's my pa's thing. I wanna open my own place someday."

"Yeah? What'll you call it?"

I turn over a tomato, checking it for spots before I bag it. "I can never decide on a name, truthfully."

"It'll come to ya." He gives a nod at my bag. "Hey, I know the crops ain't that great this week. Let me give ya a little discount or somethin'. Ten off sound fair?"

"No, no, it's fine. Your brother will be all over my ass and yours if you do that. But thanks, Lee." I smile, then give a nod across the room. "How's the greens?"

Lee bites the inside of his lip, then slaps me on the back. "Come. I'll show you the less wilty ones."

Twenty minutes later, I'm leaving the market with two bags of produce that should get us through the next couple of days. I already know my pa will complain about the lettuce, but Lee did his best, selling me the greens his older brother probably would've saved for some other favored customer.

It's no secret that my parents' diner is looked at as the hole-in-the-wall of Spruce. There are far nicer restaurants that people can eat at, the nicest of which is owned by the Strongs called Nadine's—which is named after Tanner's ma, probably as some kind of annoying romantic gesture from his pa. I like to think people come to Biggie's Bites for its charm and its finger-lickin' burgers. No one makes a big fuss over the Saturday Sweets except the regulars, but really, who comes to a burger joint looking forward to dessert? Half our customers skip dessert and head to the Cold Spoon, an ice cream parlor *also* owned by the Strongs. Not that they ever step through its doors more than once a month.

It's at the corner of 5th and Apricot Street that I catch sight of Tanner Strong's booty.

Yeah, that's right. It's his booty I see first. He's on his phone texting someone, from the looks of it, so all of his attention is pulled downward. And so's mine—right down to his ass in those tight, bun-hugging Wranglers. He's got on a loose sleeveless red tank with armholes that hang so low, the ridges of muscles all down his side show, and the red material bunches up at the top of his big, plentiful ass like curtains on a windowsill.

God, I want to be resting on top of that sill. I want to be the cat perched there, purring and in heaven.

Not a good time to be stiffening up in my pants, but I am. Also, I think I'm choking.

Like, literally, my whole pattern of breathing changes. I can't even bear to blink and miss a moment of him in those jeans. How is he not stopping traffic? How does he not have a flock of girls all over him right now, halted by the sight of his buns on display for the whole world?

Even *I'm* on a tight schedule and I'm standing here in front of Patsy's Pastries & Pies like an idiot, staring at the beauty that is Tanner Strong's backside.

I also notice for the first time that he has ink on his arms; one is thickly tattooed to the elbow while the other is just on his shoulder. He must've gotten them at college. *I don't imagine his ma's too happy with that decision.* I can't stop staring at all that sexy ink on his bulging arms. I wonder if I'd ever be brave enough to get a tattoo.

"Don't worry about it. Yours is gonna be way better," comes the voice of Mindy at my back.

At the sound of her voice, Tanner looks up and turns just in time to find me staring back at him. *Did he catch me staring at his ass, or was I already looking at his face?*

I spin to face Mindy, wide-eyed. "Say what?"

"Patsy's," she says with a nudge at the window next to me. "Whenever you open your own place, it won't have the vibe of someone's grandma's kitchen. Your pastry place is gonna be *way* cooler."

Too stunned wondering if Tanner's listening to this or still staring at me quizzically, I just give a short nod.

"I want to be your first employee, too," she goes on. "Not that

I don't love working for your parents. I do. But I want to see you succeed. Hey, can I ask you something? There's this musical playing at the movie theater. It's just tonight only. Arts appreciation night, or something."

I'm still trying to see Tanner through the corner of my eye, but he's too far behind me now. Has he walked away? *Fuck me three ways to Saturday.* "You haven't asked me something yet," I remark in half a mumble.

Mindy rolls her eyes. "I'm asking if you want to go with me, obviously."

I don't really want to go. I doubt my parents will mind since they're always excited at the prospect of me having even just one person in town to call a friend. Still, I start to squirm inside, wondering how I can gently let her down and evade going to the movies with her.

She leans toward me suddenly. "Listen. I've known you since we were, like, ten. I know you're gay. I'm not into you. The real reason I want to go is because there's a guy who's gonna be there too."

A guy? I lift my eyes up to Mindy. "Who?"

Mindy's face flushes when she says the name. "Steven Baker."

I gawp. "Steven Baker? Isn't he nineteen and, like, still having to finish his senior year of high school?"

"Don't judge me!" she blurts. "It's mortifying. I would never be caught dead admitting that to anyone. But you kinda have no friends, so you're safe and not gonna tell no one. And we work together, so there's coworker code."

"I do *too* have friends. Wait. Coworker code?"

"Yeah. You don't tell shit I tell you, and vice versa." She grabs my shoulder. "So you're gonna go with me. It's tonight at seven."

I sigh. The bags of produce I'm gripping with either fist are steadily growing heavier. "Alright. But, uh, if it's a musical they're playing and ... he's gonna be there ... are you sure he's straight?"

"Oh, playing stereotypes, are we?"

"Hey, you're the one asking the homo to see a musical with you," I point out. "Did your friends turn you down?"

"All of them but *you*," she says, then gives me a shove. Mindy really packs a punch, which is unexpected with her tiny build and elfin face framed with wavy brown hair. "He has to watch it for some summer school class. I'll ..." Her eyes flick to the side suddenly.

My heart jumps. I slowly turn my head. Tanner's still there and his eyes are flitting back and forth between us with curiosity. After one short moment, he gives a tight-necked nod, then returns his attention to his phone.

Mindy rolls her eyes and lowers her voice. "Listen. I'll help you stock the produce—"

"I don't need help."

"Not the point. I'm gonna ask your parents if you can come out tonight with me. They love me. They won't say no if I'm the one who asks."

I doubt they'd say no if I asked them myself, but ... "I think I have a headache," I lie.

Mindy isn't having any of it. "I'll owe you one," she lets me know, then grabs one of the bags from out of my hand before I can protest and starts off down the street.

For a fleeting moment before I go, I make eye contact once again with Tanner, who is already looking up from his phone again to witness my departure. He wears half a smirk of amusement, likely having heard most of that exchange. An adorable set of dimples push out from his cheek where his lips curl. *Oh, what those lips could do to me.*

Then I'm down the street too, my face burning, and it's nothing to do with the summer sun overhead.

Mindy doesn't even need to ask. This afternoon, the diner is so slow that my parents tell me to take the rest of the day off. "You can't just be here at the diner every day of the week," my ma tells me privately. "Get out there and have some fun. You've more than earned it, Junior." Every time she says something like that, I always wonder if she feels guilty that I still haven't gone off to culinary school. I never quite know what's really going on in my parents' minds. Sometimes I wonder if they've forgotten that I had dreams. Sometimes I wonder if they mistake me at times for just another employee in their diner.

Sometimes I wonder if they secretly expect me to just stick around forever, keeping my wings folded.

"Skidoo!" she says, swatting a towel at my ass with a light laugh, and then I have to wonder what my ma's dream is, or my pa's, and how close or far this life is to either of theirs.

As long as we're happy, I guess it doesn't matter.

I'm out of the diner an hour before I'm due at the movies, which gives me enough time to rush home and take a shower. Our house is a small white one on Wicker Street in dire need of a paint job. It's just a stroll down the road and around the corner from the diner, wedged between two other houses with nothing but quaint brown fences separating them. We have a little porch on which a stray male cat sometimes sleeps. The furry guy's there when I get home, but doesn't bother to lift his head. I'm sure I'll hear him outside through my window wide awake and hissing at something at three in the morning.

After a hot shower, I find a pair of worn jeans, which I give a sniff to before pulling on. A splash of water to my hair puts it all to one side and another to my face livens me right up. I push deodorant to my pits before slipping on a grey t-shirt and calling myself ready.

The sun is drifting away in a burning orange sky when I arrive. It's about a ten minute walk to the theater, but my back is still dripping in evening sweat when I meet Mindy at the front. "I said the movie *starts* at seven," she fusses. "Not to *be* here at seven."

"Seen your precious Steven yet?" I tease her, and she rolls her eyes and goes to the ticket window.

Ten minutes and a pair of Cokes and popcorns later, we're in the aisle of the narrow auditorium looking for seats. There are just about ten people scattered around them, but neither Mindy nor I spot the one she's looking for. "Fuck it," she mumbles, taking a seat halfway down and right in the middle. I follow, plopping into the creaky seat by her side.

I never even bothered to ask what musical's gonna play, but my question is answered after five previews and a "please turn off your cell phones" message flash on the screen. The thundering, bassy music of *Les Misérables* fills the auditorium and my skull. I chomp on my popcorn and watch, half-lidded and tired.

Light spills in from someone's late entrance. Mindy turns, curious if it's Steven, then taps me on the shoulder. With a mouthful of popcorn, I twist my head to get a look myself.

The silhouettes of four guys slowly turn into people as the doors behind them close and their faces get lit by the light coming off the silver screen.

It's Tanner and his trio of morons: Zits, Kirk, and the blunt-eyebrow wonder Harrison.

And his eyes fall on mine right away. He gives me a little superior smirk, then gets pushed and prodded by his friends as they loudly pile into the back row, snorting and whispering at each other.

I flip back around, facing front and shoveling popcorn into my mouth with five times the speed. I don't even know what's happening on the screen. Russell Crowe is moaning notes and Hugh Jackman is looking weary.

What the hell is Tanner doing here? Why did he bring *them*? I can't think of a type of movie a bunch of jocks like that would enjoy less than *Les-fucking-Misérables*. After a short breath, I decide to give it all a chance. I suck down my Coke, determined to enjoy the movie.

Then I hear a snicker. Then it turns into a full-blown laugh. An old woman way ahead of me turns around, then decides to pay it no mind, returning her attention to the screen. I hear little whispers and titters that never seem to end for a solid half hour. Anne Hathaway's looking sad and singing about dreams or something when another sputter of laughter comes from that back row, ruining the delightfully depressing mood this movie is trying to set.

I turn to Mindy, but she seems to be ignoring it all, her mouth tightened as she scowls at the screen with annoyance. *Steven's not here*, I remind myself. *Steven was the whole point.*

"You wanna just get out of here?" I ask her quietly.

"And waste my five bucks?" she retorts, likely with more attitude than she intended.

I sigh and slouch in my chair, my half-eaten bag of popcorn and watered-down soda forgotten. After another ten minutes of sporadic tittering and whispers behind me, I finally decide to grant myself a little break, since I feel like I'm holding a gallon inside me. "Bathroom," I hiss into Mindy's ear, then head down the aisle, ignoring the ongoing giggles from the idiots in the back row.

The doors slam shut on my way out. I squint against the bright lobby lighting and spot a female usher in a tight polo shirt with her hair bunched up in her hat, long blonde strands trickling down her face as she leans on her broom by the front doors ... and she's being hit on by none other than Steven, who apparently hasn't made it to the movie at all. The two draw silent and look my way as I pass by, but I pay them no mind, too annoyed even to say hello, and head for the restrooms.

The men's is mercifully empty. Unzipping my pants on the way, I head to the farthest urinal out of the five. Once it starts coming, I vocalize a deep sigh of relief.

Halfway through my business, the door creaks open and someone draws near. To my surprise, they come to the urinal right by mine. I smirk, annoyed at first, then lift my gaze slightly.

Holy fucking hell it's Tanner.

Still releasing the Nile from my dick, I turn my face away, wide-eyed, and stare at the wall at my side. I hear him unzip, and then a heavy stream smacks the wall of his own urinal. *Really, is this a competition or something?*

Side note: I can't help but wonder how big and strong one's cock must be to generate such *force* in their peeing.

I mean, okay, let me get weird for a second. This guy's stream is so damned potent and loud, I literally imagine him drilling a hole through the ceramic. We're talking jackhammer-caliber here. He could probably power-wash a sidewalk with that thing. And isn't it sort of logical that, due to what I'm hearing, he *has* to be hung? Really, how often can you say that someone's dick *sounds* big?

"Enjoying the movie?"

Lord in Heaven he's talking to me. And I'm still peeing. My "Nile" seems a lot more like a wimpy creek trickling through the woods behind my house compared to that *Leviathan* he's got in his hands, which I refuse to look at.

"Did I get it all wrong at the diner or somethin'?" he asks. "You *are* Billy Tucker, right?"

I speak to the wall in front of me. "Yep."

"The same one I went to school with?"

"The one and only. Unless you check a phonebook. Or Google. There's probably a million of me."

After a short silence, he says, "Well, you've changed, man."

I'm not really sure how to take that. We're definitely still peeing, by the way. "I'm the same guy I was."

"I dunno what you've been up to the past few years since high school," remarks Tanner, "but you look good. Healthy. Happy."

I wish I could say it's totally an everyday thing that I get complimented by my high school crush in the men's bathroom while we're sharing a side-by-side pee. It isn't. I might have just stopped peeing.

Or I'm getting hard. Here. At the urinal.

Next to my high school crush.

Who just said I look good.

This is sorta how half of my horny teenage fantasies began, by the way. Except with a less filthy setting.

Shit. I have to leave.

Deciding I'm done—even if I'm not—I pack away my fast-stiffening junk and zip up. "Thanks, you too," I say so quickly, I'm not even sure the words come out right, then slam into the counter and quickly wash my hands. In the reflection in the mirror, which I don't fully look at, I feel his face on me.

He's watching. I bet he's wondering what the fuck is up with me. He's probably regretting saying anything at all. *That weirdo Billy kid. Billy the weirdo. Billy the homo who had a hundred girls around him all the time, yet no girlfriends. Billy, the guy who's still stuck here in this town. Billy, the loser who didn't go to college.*

All those thoughts swirling in my head, I twist the faucet with so much force, the handle comes right off. I gawp at it as hot water hisses angrily out of the nozzle. After a moment of horror, I try to push the handle back in place ... only to succeed in spraying water all down my front and up into my face. When I decide I've gargled enough tap water for a lifetime, I start pummeling the damn thing using the dislodged handle like a hammer, determined to beat the faucet into submission.

Then there's a presence at my legs, and ever calmly, the water comes to a stop.

I peer down, horrified. Tanner sits back on his heels and looks up at me. "I shut off the water valve for ya," he explains, his gaze drifting to my shirt. "Damn, boy. You're drenched."

I can't move a muscle, staring down at the gorgeous face of Tanner Strong as he looks up at me, his rich brown eyes burning with what I daresay is amusement.

Tanner did this, I decide right then. *Tanner got me so flustered that I pulled the handle off. Tanner broke the faucet.*

Tanner got me wet.

He rises, coming up a foot taller than me, then smiles crookedly down at me, popping out a dimple. His lips are so full and perfect, plush and pink as lips can be.

"I, uh ... hope my buddies aren't being too loud," he says suddenly, lifting his eyebrows in such a way that all these adorable crinkles appear on his forehead. He leans against the counter, his biceps bulging and his proud pecs showing even through that skimpy red sleeveless *thing* he's still wearing from earlier. "I guess you can say *Les Misérables* isn't really their thing."

Soaking wet with my hair dripping over my face, I can't help but stand here and marvel for a second at how fucking sexy his voice is when he properly pronounces the title of the musical.

"I had to read it last year," he goes on, "for some kind of lit class I was required to take. Not a bad book. Kinda depressing as fuck, but y'know. The music adds a lot to the story, don't you think?"

His thighs are hugged so perfectly well by those jeans as he leans against the counter. I can't begin to describe how distracting it is, the way the material bunches up right at his crotch, lazily kissed just above it by the shiny buckle of his belt.

"You workin' tomorrow?" he pushes on.

I'm off. My parents told me to take the whole day off and relax. It'll be Wednesday. Nothing's going on. "Why?" I ask.

"Well, because I'm gonna want somethin' damn good for lunch, that's why," he says with a teasing smirk. "You gonna be there or not?"

"I'm gonna be there," I say at once.

Tanner smiles, flashing his teeth. "Then so will I."

Still holding the handle, hair dripping down my face, my nipples hardened through my shirt by the water, I cross my arms and lift my chin. I'm determined to grab any scrap of dignity I have left.

"Well, don't bother comin' if you're just gonna bring those ... obnoxious friends of yours," I say back, pulling the words out of my ass. "They're ... too dang loud. They made everyone in the diner upset."

Of course that isn't true. The four of them were the life of the party that became our Friday night at Biggie's, and everyone was having fun but me.

No matter, Tanner seems to see right through my words because he gives me a little shrug and concedes. "If you say so. I was plannin' on comin' alone anyway."

"Good." I make a quick, careless swipe of my wrist over my forehead. It does nothing to stop the dripping, only succeeding in spreading the water more and getting some in my eye, so I slap a hand to the air dryer button. Of course it doesn't turn on. I slap it three more times. No luck. "I think I ... need to head home to dry right up."

"I probably got a spare shirt in my truck."

"No," I blurt too quickly, my face flushing red. *He just offered you one of his spare shirts. Tanner Strong just offered you a spare shirt ... and you're turning it down??* "I'm fine," I insist, crossing my arms tightly and shivering from all of the wetness. I feel like some hidden AC vent is blasting right on me from somewhere just to spite and further punish me. "Just perfectly and awesomely well. Thanks. Have a great night."

I turn on my heel and push through the doors. In the echoey space of the restroom, I hear his deep, sexy voice call out, "Have a great night yourself there, Billy Tucker," before the closing door shuts him right up.

My wet feet slapping along the tile of the movie theater lobby, I rush to the front glass doors, deciding I've had quite enough for a night. Mindy will just have to forgive my sudden departure. On my way outside, I nearly crash into the usher. She turns away from Steven, who's still trying to woo her. They stare at my wet form with concern.

"Shit," grunts Steven. "You fall in?"

"Men's faucet needs fixin'," I say, slapping the handle into his palm on my way out of the theater.

By the time I get to my porch, I feel heavy and damp. The cat, sleeping in a new position on the steps, makes a weird sound when I pass, as if my presence offends him greatly. My shoes come off at the door and my sopping wet pants and shirt get balled up and thrown into the washer, since I'll do a wash sometime soon anyway.

I catch myself staring at my wet clothes as they sit atop the pile inside the machine. I remember way back when Tanner and I were in ninth grade—maybe tenth—and we were in the same gym class together. I was trying not to be obvious when I'd sneak a glance in his direction in the locker room. No one paid me any mind, even though a number of guys in my class confronted me about the rumors that I was gay. Tanner never confronted me, though. Only once in class when we were picking teams for basketball did he look my way, and our eyes seemed to linger on one another. I remember how strongly I fought my instinct to look away. It took everything in me to maintain that eye contact, and those five seconds were the most intense five seconds of my life. Even back then, I felt like he could see straight through me. He wore a size too small in his gym clothes, which was excruciatingly erotic (and annoyingly distracting) for me, since I could not stop staring at his butt in those gym shorts, which only came halfway down his thighs, hugging them all the way around. I don't know if he shaved his body back then or if he was just late to the puberty game, but I remember his legs being smooth and muscular, and as a teen who had just discovered what his dick can do, the sight of those legs and that ass and his broad shoulders squeezed tight by his heather grey, sweaty gym shirt filled my fantasies for months and months and months.

The way Tanner was looking at me in the restroom at the movie theater pulls me back to those high school days. How can someone's gaze be so intense? Is it some sort of observant football athlete thing? Is that why he's so damned good at what he does?

Standing here in my underwear in the laundry room thinking about him, it's making me feel very exposed to Tanner, as if I'm standing half-naked right in front of him.

Isn't that basically the definition of feeling exposed? Being drenched from head to toe, rendering half your clothes see-through, while standing in front of your high school crush who won't keep his annoyingly hot eyes off of you while you're at your most vulnerable?

I feel myself tenting in my briefs.

Tanner's staring at me in that restroom. His deep, muddy brown eyes. Suddenly he's wet, too. From head to toe, his body drips, that red tank clinging to his every rippling contour. His tats shine. His eyes are daring.

He bites his lip expectantly. *Oh, fuck.*

I rush into my bathroom and slam shut the door. I need to finish the imaginary scene in a bathroom right where we left off at the theater. When I turn on the shower, I don't know whether to make it a hot one to warm me up or a cold one to cool me the fuck down from the horny fantasies I'm enduring.

I decide on a hot one. Just outside the shower, I put a hand to my chest and slowly slide it down until I find the waistband of my underwear. *It's Tanner's hand,* I decide. Tanner's hand slips under the waistband, excruciatingly slow, then starts to pull my underwear down. His hand avoids my cock, knowing how hard it is, knowing how badly it wants to be touched. My underwear falls down my thighs, then slaps the floor. A hand is still placed teasingly on my inner thigh, and my breaths are long and uneven. My cock bobs as I step out of my underwear. *You have to touch it,* I beg Tanner. *Please, please touch it.*

But he doesn't.

My hand—*his hand*—slides around my hip and clings to my ass. I give it a little spank and then a squeeze. *What are you doing to me?*

His lips are by my ear. *"Get in the shower."*

When I step inside, the hot water pummels my back. It's a lot warmer than I'd prefer, but somehow I find that all the more erotic, like Tanner is making me do this and he's just a step away from joining me in this hot, steamy chamber. My heart races as the hand on my ass starts to rub in circles. I grab the soap with my other hand and slide it between my cheeks, lathering it up all slick and senseless down there.

Just that sensation is driving me insane. And I still haven't even touched my cock, which is throbbing so hard it aches.

"Hey, Tanner," I murmur into the steam.

"What?" he answers into my ear, standing at my back.

"You made me wet today," I tease.

I feel him grin against my neck. *"I sure did,"* he says, sounding all cocky and superior.

Soapy and slick, I spread my legs and slowly slip a finger inside. My body is so ready for it that it goes right in, all the way up to the knuckle.

I moan, pressing my face against the shower wall. My cock is still being ignored, but now its tip keeps poking at the shower wall down below, and it's being made all the more hard by the insertion of that finger in my ass. I twist and turn it, milking my body of every sensation it can possibly experience.

Then I add another finger.

Oh, fuck.

"Tanner ..." I moan. *Oh, fuck ...*

My stomach turns over with delight. Pleasure engulfs me as I start to work the fingers in and out. *Tanner ...*

I never do this when I masturbate. Ever.

And yet here I am, working my hole like a pro. I just chase the instincts, doing whatever I think might feel good. Somehow, it feels so good to ignore my cock and penetrate myself with these slippery fingers, in and out, in and out, while my cock throbs and begs. Just when I think I'm at max hardness, my cock swells more.

I feel close, and yet I feel like I can do this forever. I can ride the edge for hours in this shower with the steam dancing circles around me and the almost-too-hot water pounding on my back and sides.

"*Do it,*" Tanner urges me in a tough, growly voice. "*Do it right now.*"

I reach with my free hand and gently grip my cock.

It doesn't take much at all for the tingle of orgasm to arrive.

A third finger slides inside. I almost can't take it.

I'm only gripping my cock. I'm not even jerking. It's so sensitive and hard. The gentle rocking motion of my other hand finger-fucking me makes my hips move, just barely, causing my cock to slide in my firm, slick fist.

I'm fucking myself, and I'm fucking my fist.

I'm double-fucking.

"*Do it.*"

"Oh, Tanner," I breathe against the wall.

My pace remains slow because the sensations are already too much to take. One change in pace and I'm gonna blow all over the wall. One unintended twitch of my fingers in my ass and my cum is gonna rocket from my fist, which is barely gripping my cock anymore. Even my breath has to be paced.

My eyes are closed and all I see is Tanner Strong in that slinky might-as-well-be-naked loose red tank. In my mind, it's gotten even looser, so much so that I see a peek of his nipples when he moves. His pants are so tight suddenly that I see the outline of the beast between his legs. *And what about bathroom etiquette??* I want to accuse him. *You never go to the urinal right next to another dude, not when every other one is open!*

This is all his fault. I'm double-fucking because of him.

My cock squirms against my fist. My fingers slip in and out of me, knuckle to fingertip, fingertip to knuckle, over and over.

Tanner did that on purpose. That's the clear conclusion I come to. *It was some sort of power trip over me, taking the urinal right next to mine. It was a stake of dominance. Like jocks in a locker room, he was sizing me up while showing me his size at the same time.*

Message received, Tanner.

I squeeze my cock too tight. I jerk forward. I gasp.

Explosion. All over the shower wall. Shot after shot after shot. My breaths turn vocal as I empty myself. My fingers in my ass don't stop, pumping and pumping as I blow my load all over the wall. My eyes rock back. I see Tanner's victorious smile, so proud of himself, so proud of what he just made me do.

Him and his big arms.

All that sexy ink pooled on his shoulders.

His dominant smirk. His full lips. His dimples.

His bubble butt, abundant and perfect in its shape, the stuff of every gay boy's fantasies that's been slapped by a hundred grunting, masculine teammates, wrapped in shiny gym shorts, football pants, or torn jeans he knows shows it off in excruciating detail.

And those eyes that are so rich and brown, it's like he can see right into me. He knows what I really want and he knows how bad I want it. He knows I'd do anything. *What a cocky, arrogant fucker ...* But he's right. He's totally right and there's nothing I can do anymore to deny it.

I want you, Tanner Strong.

CHAPTER 4
TANNER

"Go long!"

The football zips through the air. My eye is on it every second.

I catch it with ease, then fly on across the field. The uneven divots and tufts of grass don't trip me as I blaze toward our designated end zone. Kirk tries to intercept me, but a branch intercepts him first, and he trips and eats mud. I slam the football into the ground when I make it and scream out a word of victory, fisting the air and doing half a moonwalk, taunting my buds.

"Fuck that shit!" cries Joel from across the field as Kirk rises off the ground, spitting grass from his mouth. "Ain't fuckin' fair!"

"C'mon," I encourage them as I pull off my shirt and pitch it aside, then swipe the football off the ground. "Up! Let's get goin'."

"Nah, I'm done," groans Joel, bracing himself with his hands on his knees, bent over and out of breath.

"No fuckin' way," I cry out at them with half a laugh. "We're just gettin' started, boys!"

Kirk grunts. "I'm not cut out for this no more! Look at that!" he shouts, pointing at my body. "I can't compete with all of that! You're the one who works out twenty times a week and looks like a goddamned Greek statue. I just can't. Shit, I shoulda slept in like Harrison did and said screw this."

"Fuckin' *aching*," mumbles Joel.

I stare at them, dumbfounded. They used to keep up with me even as recently as last summer. I guess just a year can do a number on a person. I'm tossing the football in the air and catching it over and over as I watch my two buddies slowly withering away like a pair of slugs in the afternoon sun. Except it's not even 10 a.m. yet.

"Alright," I finally concede. "We're gonna hit the gym and jog every morning, then."

"Like hell!" wheezes Joel.

"I'm gettin' you boys back in shape!"

Of course, an hour later finds me all alone back on the ranch—*without* my buddies—as I watch the sun slowly bake my morning into a crispy, sweat-inducing afternoon. I'm listening to my mama gossiping on the phone with Mrs. McPherson, talking sass about Mrs. Evans. Of course, just ten minutes ago, she was on the phone with Mrs. Evans doing the same dang thing about Mrs. McPherson. She is determined to come out on top in that imaginary competition they've been caught in since they were ten.

"Yep, that sounds just *darling*," my mama sings into the phone. "It's all for my son, don't you forget that. Yep. Oh, yep. You bet your bottom dollar, sugar. Tell little Tim and big Tim hi for me, and please shoot me that recipe. I don't care what Cassie said about your blackberry pie. It is just to *die* for. Mmm-hmm. That's right, that's what I said. Yep. Catch you later, Cissy! Mmm-bye!" The second my mama hangs up the phone, she's already dialing another number while muttering under her breath, "That bitch. She thinks she can just—Mmm ... No, she ain't. Oh, I'm gonna tell her. Yep. I'm gonna *tell* her." She brings the phone to her ear. Her voice changes instantly. "Hi! Becky! What a doll, you are! Listen, let me ask ya somethin' ..."

I wonder what's gonna happen when all of that fire between

those women comes to a head. They have so much common ground between them, I wish they'd see it and stop playing their lives like a daily race to outdo one another.

Then again, it's just too dang entertaining to put a stop to them. Besides, I have an agenda of my own today, and it involves a certain diner and a certain guy I went to school with.

I call out to my mama that I'm heading into town, but she just gives me a quick, dismissive wave of her hand while going on with her singsong voice into the phone.

The drive is a quick yet leisurely ride down the long country road that weaves through the farmlands. I go with my window down and my elbow propped halfway out the window, feeling the air blast across my skin. Even with the hot, sticky summer air, there's nothing quite like doing fifty-five down a country road with your windows down and nothing but fields of corn and grass in sight.

Of course, that glorious speed cuts to half when I reach downtown Spruce. I get three hellos and an excited wave as I drive slowly down Market Street, which I return with a tip of a hat I'm not wearing and a minute smile.

I have to come to a full stop for an old lady crossing the street, which might or might not be my Math teacher from junior year at Spruce High. She minds me not at all, either because she didn't take enough time to look my way, or she still figures my mathematic abilities to be just as much of a lost cause as it was back then.

If only she knew.

The truth is, no one here knows what it's really like out there. Spruce is a little place no one's heard of, and the world is unimaginably huge. When I strutted onto that campus, I found myself facing fifty other Tanner Strongs. After being seen as a star of the field my whole life, I was suddenly just another decent player with nothing special about me.

And to top it off, I learned some sobering facts about my academic abilities. Apparently, I have none. As I watch this old lady cross the street, I experience that same deep, sinking feeling I got when I had pulled up to my house just a couple weeks ago and sat there in the driveway for a solid ten minutes. I stared at my house and wondered what I'd tell my parents. Would I lie to them and say I'm doing well in college when I'm only barely skirting by? Would I keep inflating every good thing that happened to me? Would I continue to embellish so much, they think I'm rushing off to the NFL the second I graduate?

Then the woman is on the other side of the street and the way is cleared for me to go. I push away my fears of failure and drive on, perhaps with a touch more oomph than I intend.

I pull into the gritty parking lot for Biggie's Bites, and a rush of excitement fills me up to my eyeballs. With a squeal of the tired gears, I park the pickup and swing out, my boots crunching into the gravel when I land. Yeah, my ride's a bit of a bang-up, but that's how I like it, no matter how much of an eyesore my mama and papa say it is. I've had this pickup since my sixteenth birthday when I first got my driver's license and I don't intend to give it up anytime soon.

I push through the door and take a quick survey of the diner, brightly lit by the huge side and back windows and the beaming sun. There's just an old married couple in the back who might or might not be the Shannons, if I'm recalling their names correctly.

The rest of the place is empty, so I help myself to a seat at a booth by the back window, then throw my arm over the back of the seat, staring outside as the sun washes over my face.

I hear his feet shuffle near the table. A smile spreads across my face, then I turn.

Billy Tucker isn't the tallest guy, but what he's doing with the body he's got is damn nice on the eyes. He's got shoulders that have definitely been put to work over the years lifting a sack or two of flour, by the look of it. Just judging from his arms, I'd say he could probably throw one an impressive amount of distance.

But it isn't as much his body that draws me to him. He has a look in his eye all the time like he's trying to figure out the whole world in an instant. I can see all these tiny calculations speeding past his watery hazel eyes, even as he studies me with a part dubious, part excited look. He isn't smiling now, but I know how it lights up his face when he does, and it amuses me that he blushes so easily. His messy hair, which makes him look like he's always just come from wrestling a pig into submission in the kitchen, rests on his forehead in lazy, wavy strands.

One thing's for sure: the scrawny Billy I knew back in high school has changed. The Billy standing before me is someone who's held his own for years. He's someone who would stick up for himself. I'd bet he could even kick someone's ass if they crossed him the wrong way.

I also somehow feel like he wouldn't want to. Despite his eyes hiding a million thoughts a second, they also seem to crave peace. I swear I can see all of this with just a look. I might not be good at math and can't tell you X from Y, but I've always been an expert at reading people. College just sharpened my instinct.

"Well?" he prompts me.

I must've missed something he had said, too lost in observing how different he looks. "Sorry. My mind went someplace. What's good, Tucker?"

He lifts his eyebrows. "Tucker? Really?"

I chuckle. "Sorry. Football habit. Last names and shit. Tell me what's good, I'll eat it."

Billy purses his lips and crosses his arms. Wearing a fitted green plaid shirt and that little black server's apron, he looks so damned cute I could tackle him to the floor right now if the Shannons weren't sitting two tables over. Hell, I still might anyway.

Like hell you would, my mind retorts at me. *You know there ain't no one around here who knows about you. Not even your parents. Not even your closest buddies. You'd freeze just like the loser at the school dance who can't build up the courage to ask the pretty girl to the floor. Look who's the loser now.*

"Well," Billy begins, interrupting my thoughts, "if you want a little kick, I'd recommend the Tackle Burger."

"It's got a little kick, huh?"

"Yep. It was my idea. Got a special blend of spices. My pa took to it and *voila*: Tackle Burger."

I lift an eyebrow. "You do more than the desserts on Saturdays?"

"Oh, I do all sorts of things," Billy answers back, and I have a feeling those words of his are packed with about twenty other meanings.

I study him awhile. I really want to know more about him and what he's been up to. "Your ... apple pie thing was pretty good."

Billy tilts his head. "Why'd you come back?"

His question carries a hint of accusation. I don't know yet what exactly he's accusing me of. Why'd I come back to this diner? Or why'd I come back home at all? I bring my elbows to the table slowly, turning fully to face him. I decide that he means the latter. "Because it's summer."

"Yeah, but you're usually gone or all holed up at the ranch the whole time. You never come into town, seems like," he points out, his eyes narrowing. "So what brings you here? To *actual* Spruce?"

I bite my lip, staring at him quizzically and trying to reflect all the sudden sass he's throwing me. Damn, those eyes of his are striking. Why did I not notice those shiny hazel irises before? *Maybe because I was going from trophy girlfriend to trophy girlfriend, ignoring the nagging feeling that I wasn't getting what I really wanted and having no idea what that meant.* Everything in high school pushed me at the girls—my friends, my teammates, my parents. Everyone was more interested in what *they* thought I ought to be … and less interested in who I really was. Did it really take going to Oklahoma—where I knew no one and nothing—to figure all of that out?

I lift my chin. "I guess I'm just here for some tasty food and …" My eyes drift to the emblem on his chest, right where his crossed arms show off what he's got there for forearms. *He's definitely been working out these past few years.* "… and to see the sights," I finish.

"Tackle Burger, then? Anything to drink? We don't serve alcohol," Billy adds with a tired lift of his eyebrows.

Damn, this boy's fighting through some pretty dense preconceived notions of me. Was I a total asshole to him in high school and just don't remember? "Really?" I shoot back, feigning grave disappointment. "Man, if I don't get my beer fix by three in the afternoon, it's just a waste of a day to me."

Billy snorts, trying very hard not to smile. He's damn determined to keep a straight face no matter my cheesy jokes. "Alright. Spare me the sarcasm. With the eagerness your friends took to hittin' up the bar after they were here last time, I kinda ... assumed that ..." He sighs, his face flushing. *He's so damned adorable.* "I'm just givin' you a hard time. Fuck it. You want a Coke or not?"

"Is the Tackle Burger, like, really hot?"

"Big ol' athlete like you should be able to handle it," he quips, straight-faced. "Unless you want to try the kid menu alternative, the Wuss Burger. Made for wusses who can't handle heat."

Now it's my turn to try my damnedest not to smile. I bite the inside of my cheek as I stare up at the hazel eyes of Billy Tucker, who's throwing me more sass than I know what to do with. *He's had to fight off a hater or two in his time, that's for sure.*

"I can handle as much heat as you got, boy," I fire right back. "Oh, and I'll take a water."

Billy lifts a brow. He stares at me long and hard, as if expecting me to back down. I don't, smugly keeping my chin lifted with a victorious smirk. Then he gives a curt little nod, turns, and heads for the kitchen. I get a nice view of his ass—gripped by black slacks that sit on him perfectly to show off each cheek in round, perfect detail—as he saunters toward the swinging doors.

I lift my gaze to find Mrs. Shannon staring at me from her table quizzically. I clear my throat demonstratively, prickles of embarrassment rushing up my neck as I give her a little nod. Whatever expression she had, it vanishes in an instant as she smiles lightly and gives me a wave of recognition before turning back to her husband, who gives me a nod of his own.

I catch sight of Billy through the long window where you can see a sliver of kitchen. For a second, he seems to catch my eye, but then he looks away quickly, attending to whatever it is in front of him. *Is he cooking my burger?* I get a funny thrill out of the idea of him cooking for me. I wait to see if he'll catch my eye again. He doesn't.

Minutes later, the door swings open and he's coming my way with a plate carrying an enormous burger with fries piled by it like a stack of hay.

He sets it in front of me. "Enjoy," he mutters before turning away.

"Wait, wait, now," I call out, stopping him. "Aren't ya gonna keep me company?"

He lifts both his eyebrows. From the startled look in his eyes, it's like I might as well have just spanked him or something.

"I'm ..." He points somewhere, then changes his mind and points at the Shannons. "I'm, uh ... working."

But just at that moment, the Shannons rise from their table and head for the door. Mr. Shannon looks over his shoulder and says, "Thanks, Billy," before slipping out of the diner.

I cross my arms on the table. "There's literally no one else here," I point out. "Ain't ya due for a break?"

Billy chuckles dryly, then moves toward the Shannons table. "Sorry. I'm on the clock."

"Don't ya own the place by now?" I tease. "C'mon. Sit down and chat with me while I eat your totally wimpy not-hot-at-all Tackler."

"Tackle *Burger*," he states.

And then, appearing from nowhere, a thin woman with frizzy brown hair that looks twice the size of her face comes up to Billy's side. She gives him a nudge with her hip. "Skidoo, Junior. Go chat with your friend. I got this."

He leans into her and—in a voice I suspect he thinks I can't hear—whispers, "*He ain't my friend.*"

"You ain't even supposed to be here. You insisted on working today."

"*Ma!*" he hisses.

"Go! Get!" She pushes him out of the way to handle the plates and glasses on the table. In seconds, she has everything gathered and is carrying them to the kitchen, leaving Billy standing there with his back to me, likely swallowing his shame.

I wanna see that cute, beet-red face of his.

"Hey, Billy. Did I just witness you fight and lose a little battle with your mama?"

Billy's back straightens—*I could seriously reach out and pinch that tush of his*—and then he turns to me. He didn't give his face enough time to drain of blood; it's still red from chin to forehead. "Where are your buddies?" he asks brusquely.

"Doin' this and that, I suspect. Don't care. Sit down," I say, slapping the booth seat right next to me.

After a short bit of hesitation, he finally sits ... across from me. He crosses his arms and gives a nod at my plate. "Your burger's gettin' cold."

"Must mean it's not *hot* enough," I tease, then grab the burger with both hands—*it's a big motherfucker*—and I sink my teeth into it.

The taste is out of this world. Sure, I was expecting a decent burger, but the amount of flavor that coats my tongue the second I start chewing is beyond anything I have ever savored. The taste alone inspires salivation as I consume it, my tongue playing into every spice that Billy put into this masterpiece.

"That," I start, speaking with my mouth still half full, "is a fuckin' burger."

I swallow.

And then the heat hits me.

My eyes water, but I don't want to look like a wuss in front of Billy. It's clear that he's been hunting excuses to laugh me right out of those doors, and I sure as hell don't want to give him one. Sticking to my guns, I lift my brow, stare defiantly right into his hazel eyes, and take another hearty bite. The fire on my tongue multiplies. Already, I start to feel fluid in my nose. *Muscle through it, Tanner!* Before that bite's even done, I take another one, biting with such ferocity that I snarl. My eyes are so watery, the whole world's a blur as I chew, determined to keep my face straight and unaffected.

"Need me to hand you a little handkerchief there?" he asks lightly.

I literally can't see his face. "Nah," I croak, blinking rapidly. "Totally cool over here. You call this hot?" I chew and chew. The savory taste I was a moment ago enjoying has now betrayed me, biting me back inside my mouth. "Don't even need a sip of w—"

I swallow. My lips stay parted, breath after breath coming in.

"Water?" he finishes for me. "Y'know, if you wanna drop this whole act …"

"Fuck it." I set down the burger and grab my glass. Chugging the whole thing down, I breathe heavily and grab the napkin off the table, giving my whole face a thorough wiping. "Shit, man. I'm sweating!"

"So you're saying my Tackle Burger … tackled you?"

I draw the length of my arm across my eyes, wiping away the tears. Billy's superior face is the first thing I see. "Fuck that," I tease, smiling despite the agony that's only been mildly muted on my tongue. "Ain't nothin' you dish out can tackle Tan the Man!"

He finally lets on half a smile. "Shit, you're a mess. Let me get you some more water."

"Nah, nah, I'm good." I sniffle really loud. "Uh …"

Billy's already set a wad of napkins in front of me. I give him a short nod, then fist the napkins and bring them to my face, wiping away my sweat and tears with a vengeance. When I've finished, Billy's apparently gone and come back with my glass refilled. I grab it and chug right away, desperate for anything to ease the pain.

Now Billy laughs. Full-mouthed and guttural, he lets it out and kicks back in his seat, watching me with his arms folded and a toothy smile on his face.

"Y'know," I say when I'm at last recovered, "payback's a bitch."

"Hey, I'm innocent here. You said you liked it hot."

"Sure. Hot. Not *volcanic*."

Billy gives a light shrug. "Maybe I was a touch … *heavy* on the spice for your particular burger."

I lick my teeth, then lean forward with my elbows on the table. "Tell me what's been up with you since high school. You've been hangin' out in this place helpin' your parents? That's it?"

A flicker of hurt cuts through his eyes, his smile broken.

Shit. I probably said that wrong. "Nah, what I mean is—"

"You asking me if I've just been bumming around in my parents' diner?" he asks, his mouth tightened. "For the past three years?"

"That's not really what I meant. Came out wrong."

"Yeah? Is that it? Is all of this just ... wrong?"

"I was just tryin' to jump ahead. Try and guess what you've been up to, just judgin' from what I see."

"And that's all you see?" Billy lifts his chin at me. "So what've *you* been doing the past three years, huh?" He quirks an eyebrow. "Running around on a field every day? Throwing around balls wrapped up in dead animal skin? Tackling other boys to the ground? Three years of havin' your ass slapped on your way to the locker room? You sound like a real winner."

I laugh. Damn, this boy really plays a hard game. But I don't give up. *Tanner Strong never gives up.* "Hey, the ass slappin' is the best part!" I exclaim.

"I finished two years of online business courses," he says, his voice firm and his eyes narrowed. "I didn't just sit on my ass pickin' meat out of my teeth."

"Clearly not," I note with a glance at his arms.

The comment goes ignored. "And my pa really needed someone to step up, so I stepped up. I wasn't able to go off to college like *you* did right out of school, so I—"

"That's all great!" I exclaim encouragingly. "Real nice! Business courses! You've been ... wow, Billy. You've really been makin' a thing of it. Good." I drum the table with my fingers, trying to steer the conversation away from me and my stupid words earlier. "You gonna open up your own place, then? This whole thing just a practice round? You know," I go on, apparently incapable of shutting up, "my mama and papa, between them they own about ten different businesses, and one of them is a restaurant one town over. Nadine's, you heard of it? It's kinda upscale, I guess, but before they got a good grip on that, they had to sorta trial-and-error with some other restaurants. I heard a lot about it, but y'know, I was always at football practice so I didn't get too involved in the business aspect of it." I shove four fries into my mouth, then keep on talking as I chew. "Or are you thinkin' of taking over when your papa gives the place over to you? This gonna become yours? He afraid you'll mess it up? I swear, some papas should have more faith in—"

"Alright," he says suddenly. "I think I'm being called back to the kitchen."

I squint, two fries sticking out of my mouth. "What?" I swallow them. "I didn't hear anything."

"It was nice chattin' with you." He rises from his seat.

"Wait." He doesn't. The dude's totally just walking off. "Tucker! Did I say somethin' wrong? Come on."

"Oh, no biggie," he calls out to me. "I'm just gonna go back here now and piddle with my pa's business things I don't know nothin' about. Maybe if I try hard enough, I can figure out how the register works."

I'm up from the table and halfway across the diner already. "Billy, Billy, Billy. C'mon. Just forget all that crap I went on and on about. I don't even remember what I said. I'm tryin' to, like, chat with you. Y'know, like how two buds catchin' up after high school do. That's it."

Billy stops near the kitchen doors. "Why?"

Now he's got me caught staring into his eyes again and feeling like the loser at prom. "I ... I dunno. We never really got to know each other back then."

His eyes drift to my lips. "Why bother now?"

Damn, this boy is stubborn. I fucking love it. Watching the half-lidded look of his eyes and the firm way in which he stands there—defiant, poised, waiting—with arms crossed and mouth pursed in half a pout, I say, "I just kinda think you're ... a great guy, Billy. You seem to have all your shit together. You're gonna own this place someday. Or open your own. I don't know. You didn't quite give me a straight answer, but either way, you've got a direction in life. That's pretty damn cool."

The look in his face softens. He doesn't meet my eyes, still staring at my mouth as he listens.

"And if I'm being honest here, I ... don't really have that many friends here. It'd be kinda nice to have one."

"Me?" Billy meets my eyes at last. He looks baffled. "Of all the people here, of all your old football pals and fans who once filled your bleachers, you pick me?"

He's really testing me here. If I had more guts than I do, I'd reach down and make a well-needed adjustment in my jeans, which are growing tighter just by looking at his face and those damned eyes of his. "Yeah. You."

Billy licks his lips as he looks away. He takes his time in doing so, his tongue playing along the whole length of his bottom lip.

Okay, I don't want to be all crude and vulgar here because my mama raised a good boy, but Goddamn, I'm seriously seeing his face staring up at me while I push my big ol' stiffy past those wet lips of his. The scene hits me so hard, I catch my breath. *What's this boy doin' to me?*

I need to get him on my own turf. I wanna know more about what makes Billy Tucker tick. "Tell you what." I lean against the wall and fold my arms. "How about you come out to my ranch tomorrow?"

His eyes flash open. "Your ranch?"

"Yeah. You haven't been out there in a long while, huh? I'll show you around."

Billy seems unable to produce an answer for a second, his feet digging into the ground. Finally, he says, "I think I gotta work tomorrow, so I—"

"*Nope, you worked today,*" comes a voice through the door—his mama.

Billy gives a laser glare at the door. "Seriously, Ma?? You've been listenin' in there??"

"*You got all tomorrow off,*" she says through the door. "*Ain't got a lick of anythin' to do. Wide open. Whole dang day.*"

Billy scowls at the polished metal. "Ma ..."

Her face appears at the kitchen window as she half-leans out of it. "Hey there, Tanner, hon. Sorry that my son is a difficult stick in the mud sometimes. He gets that from his pa. Please, for the love of Pete, take him to your dang ranch. And tell Nadine I said hi." Then, just as fast, she disappears.

I suck in my lips, swallowing my laughter, then turn to face a very red-faced Billy, whose hands are jammed so far into his pockets that he might be reaching for his knees. His shoulders are all hunched up and pulling at the sleeves of his fitted plaid shirt, showing me more of his delicious shape.

Feeling a pinch of victory, I lift my eyebrows and ask, "You drive? Or want me to come pick ya up tomorrow mornin'? Ten, maybe? Eleven?"

"I drive," he says in the smallest voice known to man. His face is burning. "I know where your ranch is."

Now I'm grinning. "So tomorrow, then?"

He sighs, shuts his eyes, then gives me a short nod. "Oh," he says, his eyes flapping open, "and don't pay for your meal. It's covered."

I frown. "The hell you mean it's covered?"

Billy smirks. "That 'tip' you left me last time? That was way too dang much and I'm not acceptin' it. I'm using that money to cover your bill today."

"Like hell you are. That money's for you."

"Nope. I don't accept a tip that's more than the whole dang meal was."

"It was for you puttin' up with me and my buds."

"Your meal's covered today. End of story."

"Not happenin'. I'll just leave another fifty," I tell him.

I can't help but grin when I see the indignance that floods his still-red face. *He has to be so fucking hot in bed, this moody, tight-jawed Tucker boy who's set off by the tiniest of things.* There's something incredibly sexy about a person who's buttons I can press so easily.

He glares at me. "You're an ass, you know that?"

"Is this about that whole movie theater thing?" I ask, quite determined to press every last button of his so he's so hot and bothered that he *has* to spend the rest of the day thinking about me. "My buds? How they laughed and talked through the whole dang movie?"

"I wouldn't know if they talked through the rest of it, seeing as I didn't *stay* for the whole thing on account of—"

"Of wetting yourself?" I finish for him.

His lips press together. His ears nearly fold like a cat's as his eyes narrow.

"Go finish your dang Tackle Burger, Tanner Strong, before I regret ever makin' you an apple-*anything*," he says with a lazy drawl, then pushes through the swinging door to the kitchen.

When I finish the burger—*and damn it, I do finish the hotter-than-hell thing*—I leave him a folded fifty. Along its bottom, I write: *See you tomorrow, Tucker.*

CHAPTER 5
BILLY

That Tanner Strong thinks he can just bat his eyes and make the whole town fall to its knees in submission.

He thinks he can sweep into my diner and brave my hottest burger—*which I may or may not have had a hand in making three times as hot as intended*—and then make me come out to his big dumb ranch.

Well, here I am in my dad's rundown truck, heading down the country road to Tanner's big dumb ranch.

If I'm being honest with myself, I'm actually a nervous wreck. I tried my best not to let my guard down around him, but there's just something about Tanner that makes me want to tear off his clothes and go full-blown assault on him—or else curl up in the corner of my shower with the water raining over me as I shiver and cry. Maybe the truth is somewhere in between. All I know is that there is an inhuman amount of sweat in my palms and it's making steering this damn vehicle tricky.

We didn't quite decide on a time and I have no way to get ahold of Tanner, so I decided to give him a little time and head out at eleven.

Why am I driving to Tanner Strong's ranch? Why did I agree to this? This has to be some kind of prank.

I keep shaking my head the farther down the road I get, convinced more and more as I go that this is all just some elaborate scheme for Tanner to entertain himself. I start drumming my hands against the steering wheel with more vigor as the cornfields and the farmlands pass by.

Is there any air in this damn truck? I start rolling down the window, only to have it get stuck halfway down. Then, it won't come back up. *Shitty truck.*

There's a scent in the front seat that's bothered me since I left my house. Pa looked all nervous when I told him I needed to borrow the truck, since Ma's car was in the shop. Ma got on his case about letting me go off and do my thing today, so he gave me the keys, relenting.

It only now occurs to me, quite belatedly, that my pa's smoking again. That's the scent that's buried into every crack and fold of this truck. *He smokes when he's on his long solo trips to the next town over to pick up the produce we* don't *grow here. He smokes because he's alone and won't have me or Ma on his case.*

The realization puts me in quite a mood when I finally reach the long, winding driveway that leads to Tanner's ranch. The road becomes surprisingly smooth when the house finally comes into view. The driveway spreads out as it approaches the garage, where I see two other cars parked where the road ends at a fence. I take the only space available and shut off the engine, which protests with a loud mechanical cough.

I jump out of the truck. Tanner's house is one of those big and sprawling estates that seems to go on forever. It's an off-white color with tiny highlights of pale blue in the windows. The house has a wraparound porch decorated minimally with hanging plants, a swinging bench, and some chairs.

I go up the steps of the porch—which don't creak in the least compared to mine, where I also have to dodge stepping on the stray cat—and I stand before the front door. I fight a sudden fear I have that I'm too early, or that I'm too late, or that I imagined the whole Tanner-inviting-me-over thing.

I lift my knuckles to knock.

"Hey!"

I turn my head, startled, and find Tanner at the far end of the porch just before it wraps around.

And he is shirtless.

He is totally fucking shirtless and he's wearing a tight red bathing suit that does not, in any way, hide what he's got. And boy, does he *got*. Tanner's packing, and whatever he's packing is also packing.

Lord in Heaven help me.

"You made it!" he calls out as he saunters smoothly over to me. He's barefoot and wet. *Oh my God, he's wet.* The short strands of his hair is slapped to his forehead in tiny tangles and spikes. The beads of water dress his muscular, broad chest and his thick arms, showing off his ink. His bare feet slap the wood of the porch on his way toward me. The closer he gets, the broader he grins.

"Took a dip?" I ask his chest, hypnotized.

He stops in front of me. "Kinda. Come on, bud. The party's in the back."

"Party ..." I echo, at a total loss as I follow him.

I'm tempted for a second to slow my pace ... just to get a glimpse of what the two bounteous globes of his ass look like in those slick, wet, red swimming shorts. I literally feel a Merry-Go-Round of excitement in my belly and it won't stop or settle. The controls are broken and it's spinning out of control. All its occupants are gonna throw up and sue the operators.

When we round the corner, the wide L-shaped pool comes into view just off the back steps of the porch, where it's surrounded by a wide, smooth flagstone area adorned with lounging chairs and giant umbrellas. It looks like a lavish resort complete with four other guys in the pool playing water volleyball.

Wait a second. *Four other guys??* I stop at the top step, my eyes wide.

"My buds kinda crashed my morning," says Tanner suddenly. "You know Kirk, Joel, and Harrison. Did you know Robby back in school? He was on the wrestling team, but hung out with a lot of us. He also sang in Choir and was kinda known for being a man-whore. Every chick he sang a duet with, he banged."

"He sings at the church now," I recite in perfect monotone. I still can't believe my eyes. They're all in the pool, wet, playing, shirtless. Four athletes. About to be five. And ... "Wait, are we—?"

"I told you to bring a bathing suit, right?" he asks, his face wrinkled.

I stare at him. I don't think I've blinked once in the past minute that I've been standing here in front of the pool. "No, Tan. You didn't."

"Tan?"

"I meant Tanner."

"Nah, I like it." He grins. "Tan. Call me that."

"No."

"I'll call you Tuck."

"No, you won't."

"So you didn't bring a bathing suit?"

"No."

"What kinda underwear you got on under those shorts? These guys won't mind. Kirk's in his boxers."

No, Tanner Strong is not trying to get my clothes off. Me thinking that is not only absurd, but also just confirms that I'm desperate to have any tiny piece of my deepest, most private fantasies realized.

"I'm not strippin' down to my *briefs*," I mutter.

He lifts an eyebrow. "A tighty-whities guy, huh?"

My anxiety is so high right now that I literally feel my eyeballs shaking. I give one last glance at the pool, then shake my head. "Sorry. No. I don't think this is a party for me. I'm gonna go."

Just as I turn, Tanner touches my arm. "Don't go, man. We're odd."

I look back at him. "Odd?"

"Yeah. Five of us," he says, enlightening me. "I need you on my team. Three against three. Don't tell him I said this, but Kirk's a shitty teammate. Robby, Joel, and Harry are kickin' our asses, and for once I'd like—"

"I don't play sports."

"You know how to swim?"

I smirk. "Well, yeah, but—"

"Then you can play. Take off those shorts of yours! Off with that shirt, too. Or leave 'em on if you insist, but I'll get you out of them eventually. Let's do this! Three versus three! You're on my team." He slaps my chest, then heads over to the pool. "Come on, Tuck!"

I gape after him. Even with my mind still protesting, my hands go to the button of my shorts, slowly undoing them. *Is this really happening?* Then I stop, frozen in place. *I can't really do this, can I?* I do the button back up. Then I undo it. Then I redo it. *Does he really think I'm just gonna drop my shorts in front of a bunch of guys I barely know? Him, included?* I swallow hard and it does nothing to calm the anxiety that's building a beehive inside me. *I don't compare to a bunch of athletes. I don't even—*

"Hey, you!" one of the guys calls out. "Get over here!"

Is he calling to me? I come down the steps and find Kirk looking at me, the others busied bashing the ball back and forth at each other and arguing loudly about the rules while Tanner's standing by the pool listening to them.

"Oh, shit," blurts out Kirk, recognizing me with half a laugh. "It's William Tucker??"

"Yep." I feel so self-conscious and haven't even taken anything off yet.

"Dude, you joining our team or what?"

Tanner glances my way and our eyes connect. He gives me an odd sort of smirk before returning his focus back to the other guys and their heated debate.

Is that what this is? Some sort of challenge? Did he invite me out to his ranch to test me? Maybe this is payback for the Tackle Burger. Maybe it's all innocent and he really did invite me over to play water volleyball with his buds and hang out.

Whatever this is, I won't let him win.

"Yeah," I answer, pulling my t-shirt over my head and flinging it to the nearest chair. The summer air rushes over my exposed nipples and skin. I'm acting a lot braver than I'm feeling, for the record. "I'm joining your team." I confidently go for the button of my shorts one more time, then decide against it yet again. Instead, I yank my wallet, phone, and keys out of my pockets and set them on my shirt, then kick off my shoes and pull off my socks before coming to the edge of the pool.

"You ever play this before?" asks Kirk.

I have Tanner's attention again. He watches as I sit on the edge, slip my feet in, then hop into the pool. After one moment of letting my body acclimate, I face Kirk and say, "We're about to find out, aren't we?"

Tanner jumps in the other side of the pool, dips his head in the water, then shouts, "Serve!"

Harrison swims up to the net—recognizable mostly by his blunt, dark eyebrows—tosses the ball into the air, then pounds it. Kirks rushes forward to slap it. The ball rises high, for a moment appearing to be floating. Tanner's there to give the ball a spanking, sending it over the net.

But the choirboy Robby's quick, and he grunts in his effort to fist the ball right back into the air. As it comes down, he prepares to punch it over the net.

I realize with a start that he's aimed right at me. I push through the water, preparing myself.

He pounds the ball.

I'm there to slap it right back into the air. Then, after it floats and comes back for me, I give it all my muscle.

The ball slams like a torpedo over the net, and none of our rivals are quick enough to defend against it.

"Holy fuck!" shouts Kirk, his eyes wide. "SCORE!"

Tanner's face is a glorious expression of sheer shock. He looks over, jaw dropped, then shoots me a stunned thumbs-up.

I give him a nonchalant shrug. *Oh, y'know. Being this amazing is an everyday thing for me. No biggie.*

"Kid's got an arm on him," mumbles Zits—*sorry, I mean Joel.*

The ball's in the air again. They punch it over the net. Kirk slaps it into the air with a desperate huff, his body almost too slow to get to it, but he misjudged and the ball comes my way. I give it a smack and it's airborne above me. It falls and I swing my whole arm like a hammer, fist crunching into the ball and shooting it right over the net. Harrison rushes forward to get it, but the ball whacks him in the head and fumbles into the water.

"SCORE!!" screams Kirk again, throwing his hands and a spray of water into the air.

"Touchdown!" I cry out, mimicking him with my arms in the air. Everyone in the pool looks at me, silent. I bring down my hands. "Joke," I explain flatly. "It was a joke."

"TOUCHDOWN!!" shouts Kirk, inspired by my humor.

"TOUCHDOWN!" shouts Tanner with half a laugh. Joel, Harrison, and Robby seem less amused.

The game goes on for another twenty minutes, and after my little jest, every score earns a fanfare of the guys joyously shouting, "TOUCHDOWN!!" while throwing their hands in the air.

I must have a certain knack for riling up athletes, current and has-beens. I missed my calling. I should've been a cheerleader back in school.

"Fuck, I'm starved," moans Kirk as he dries off by the pool. He's put on a lot of weight since graduation, which I only now notice, seeing him with no shirt on and the belly he's grown. He was a big guy in high school, but his muscular form has since sagged and softened.

Harrison grunts his agreement. "Yeah, why don't you get out

the grill, Spruce juice?"

Oh, man. I haven't heard that term in years. At every game when Tanner took the field, everyone would chant the words. *"Spruce juice! Spruce juice! Spruce juice!"* It always made me think of about a hundred dirty things more than it ever did anything related to football.

"Oh! Oh! William!" Kirk spins, startling me. "Make us your Touchdown Burgers! Fuck, I want one so bad!"

"Dude! Yeah! Those were the bomb!" booms Harrison.

Suddenly four hungry wet-or-drying guys are staring at me in various states of undress with their hungry eyes and dropped jaws. I part my lips, unsure what to say.

"Nah, nope," says Tanner, appearing out of nowhere gripping a towel wrapped around the back of his neck with both his hands, his big biceps bulging in the effort. "Today is Billy's day off. He's not cookin' a damn thing. Leave that up to my mama or Jacky-Ann, if she's workin' today."

"I don't wanna bother your housekeeper," says Kirk after pulling on his shirt. "I'll grill up some dogs."

"There's beer inside," Tanner points out. "Harrison, Joel, you know where they're at. Go get some."

Blunt-Eyebrows and Zits take off. I'm dry enough to put on my shirt, but the second I reach for it, Tanner's got a grip on my arm. "What?" I say.

"Come on. I wanna show you around."

He takes me away from the pool while the guys circle the grill on the back porch. Kirk and Robby watch us while jabbering at each other, beers in their palms.

"You were pretty damn good in the water," remarks Tanner.

"I swear I've never played before."

"You must have really good eye-hand coordination. You jack off thirty times a day or something?"

I laugh. "Twenty, tops," I tease.

"Seriously, though. You have an arm on you. Kinda makes me wonder why you didn't do any sports back in school." He frowns suddenly, squinting at me. "You *didn't* do any sports, right?"

"Nope."

"You should have. We could've had some good times out there on the fields."

"I dunno if I have a winning play in me," I say back, my hands finding my pockets even though they're wet and hard to get into. I keep quickly sneaking glances at Tanner, who's body is just a ridiculous display of abs and pecs that are cut and defined beyond what I thought was possible outside the pages of a fitness magazine.

"Of course you do," he fires back, giving my shoulder a slap that's both too hard and also annoyingly erotic.

The sensation thunders down to my cock, just that little touch of his skin against mine.

His innocent slap turns into a grip he keeps on my shoulder. I feel a slight pulling sensation, and I can't tell if it's me trying to lean into his body as we walk, or if he's actually pulling me into him. The result is me staggering for a second, stumbling lightly over my foot, and then inspiring him to awkwardly let go as we keep walking.

Damn.

Before I know it, we're surrounded by trees that are spaced apart to give us room to weave between them. It's through all the brush that I see a lake.

"Shit. Is this *all* yours?"

"Well, I guess. My parents'. Mine. It's our land. You thinkin' of divin' into another body of water already?" he teases with a lift of an eyebrow.

"You're the one showin' me a lake after we just left a pool," I say right back.

He shrugs. "I just wanna show you around, Tuck. You haven't really been here before, have you?"

"I might've come to a fifth grade thing. Or maybe it was a junior high thing?"

"Oh! All the teachers were invited too, right? And we drank punch all evening and played games into the night? I think we even had some balloon artist making all these balloon poodles ..."

I gasp, stopping in my tracks. "Fuck, I remember that. It wasn't a clown?"

"Hell no. You kidding? Clowns are fuckin' freaky." Tanner shivers at the thought. "My brother is obsessed with them, though. They make him laugh even if they're just standing there. Creepy dudes."

"It's a serious profession," I point out. "Entertainment ain't easy."

Tanner scoffs at that. Before I know it, we've come to the bank of the lake, the ground at our feet turning soft. It's a small lake with a dock, the other side looking to be a few houses' widths away. I see a wooden fence tracing the bank on the opposite side and wrapping around, disappearing into the trees. I think I see cattle over there, but can't be sure. There's definitely some ducks floating at the far end. Or geese, maybe. I don't know.

We walk the perimeter of the lake, where the trees give way to a field of crops. He tells me what's growing there and how many farmhands they have regularly that tend to the fields, but a lot of the information kinda floats right past me, distracted as I am by Tanner's beefy ass, which I can't help but stare at when he walks ahead of me to lead the way. We also pass by a barn with cows, a shed that looks as clean as a damn house, and a long coop full of chickens that cluck when we stroll by. Apparently all the chickens have names, which he eagerly tells me. It's so weird, to watch Tanner get all excited after a lifetime of not knowing him at all. He even grabs a handful of feed and tosses it, showing me how the chickens get all crazy, flapping their wings and going to town.

"I love teasin' them and watchin' them go nuts," he says with a sly smile.

Yeah. You're an expert at teasing and driving me nuts.

By the time we make it back to the house, it feels like a whole damn day has gone by. The Strong Ranch is like a little city in and of itself, with so much land spread out for crops to grow and animals to roam. All these years, I seriously didn't realize how damn big it was.

And here we are, just two more animals roaming the paths toward the house.

The scent of the grill lures us to the large sliding glass doors off the back deck, by which the guys are all lounging in wooden chairs with empty plates all around them.

"The hell you two been?" blurts Kirk. Harrison slaps him on the arm and gives a quick shake of his head, to which Kirk wrinkles his face and says, "What?"

I'm not sure what all of that is about, but Zits gives me a lift of his chin and extends a bottle of beer my way. "Here you go. Kick back with us."

"Yeah, don't let Sprucy-Juicy pull you around the whole dang ranch showin' off all his animals he pretends to know everything about," teases Harrison.

I take the beer from Zits and give a nod of thanks. *I should really get out of the habit of calling him that before I slip and say it out loud.*

Tanner grabs one of his own, then picks up the tongs and pokes at the grill. "You guys ate already?"

"Y'all were gone for, like, ever!" says Kirk, his foot kicked up on the wooden banister. "We couldn't wait up, dude. My stomach was fuckin' eating itself."

"Alright, calm down, drama queen," teases Tanner, pulling some dogs from the package and tossing them on the grill. "Tuck, how many can you eat?"

It takes me a second of staring into nothingness to realize Tanner's talking to me. "T-Two, maybe."

"I'll make you three. Want more?" he asks his buds, to which they all decline in their various forms of grunts and head shaking. "Alright, screw you all. I'm eatin' five."

Kirk guffaws. "Tryin' to impress us? Shit, I ate seven."

"Five's just my first helping," Tanner fires back, then twists a bit to give me a smug smirk. Not gonna lie; just that little lift of his full lips is enough to make something erupt in my shorts.

When the dogs are grilled up, we kick back in the only available chair: the swinging bench. Either it isn't quite as wide as I'd expect a swinging bench to be, or Tanner's sitting closer to the middle than he is the side. Our elbows keep bumping as we eat. He makes no effort to give me more room, chatting away with his buds like he doesn't notice.

I don't mind that at all.

They talk about Kirk's girlfriend Bonnie a lot, who apparently worries she's pregnant every other month only to find out she's not. They've been together since high school and are pretty much ready to seal the deal, but Kirk can never find the right time to pop the question. Robby's not ready to settle at all, being content in taking his pick from all the girls who show up to church on Sundays to hear him sing, then later take off their pretty halos weeknights at the local bar.

When I'm starting my third unasked-for dog, I notice Kirk staring at me with a squinted, quizzical expression. After eye contact is made, he lifts his chin and, cutting off something Harrison was saying to Tanner, abruptly asks me, "Do you have, like, a boyfriend or whatever?"

Tanner half-chokes on his bite, dropping the rest of his dog onto his plate and staring at Kirk. "Fuckin' really, dude?" he asks, muffled through a full mouth of bread.

"I'm just curious, man," Kirk says defensively.

"*That* ... is his own private business," Tanner goes on, still muffled. He chews through his bite as Kirk lifts his hands up, backing off and leaning into his chair. After Tanner swallows, he tilts his head toward me. "So do you?"

Harrison snorts, amused. I feel my face starting to flush, as it always does, but I keep my voice even. "Nope," I state dully.

"Do you ever date?" Kirk blurts out, face wrinkled up.

Tanner's on him again. "Dude! What's with the whole interrogation?"

Kirk lifts his hands yet again. "I dunno! I've just never, like, gotten to know a gay guy before. You invited him over, so … like … I wanna get to know him."

"It's okay," I assure Tanner, who looks at me with two softened eyes. Despite my beet-red face, I address Kirk and his potbelly, upon which he's rested his emptied plate. "Not really."

"You don't date at all?"

"Nope."

"Why not?"

I give a short glance around me. "Well, what options do I got in a town like Spruce?"

"There's that one guy," Kirk points out. "Lance, was it? The dude with the, uh, hair?"

With the long flowing blond hair that curls at the base of his neck. He's sassier than any girl I've ever met and his eyelashes are glued on. I have nothing against him or his flair, but the two times I tried to make friends with him, he gave one sad look at my clothes and said, "No thanks," without even knowing what I was going to ask.

"You know," I say, "just because two guys are gay doesn't mean they're into each other. You wouldn't date just *any* girl in town, would you?"

"Robby would," says Kirk, to which Robby grins ear-to-ear and gives a slow, suggestive nod, grunting, "Yep. I most definitely would."

"But you have a type, right?" I push on.

Kirk shrugs. "Yeah, I guess so. Bonnie's my type. Even if she keeps havin' all these pregnancy scares. Fuck, we're just terrified of havin' a little one out of wedlock. Damn our strict-ass parents."

Immediately after saying that, he thinks better of it and quickly draws a cross over his chest. "Sorry, Jesus," he mutters quietly.

"What's *your* type?" pushes Robby, engaging suddenly and leaning forward.

In fact, all the dudes lean forward. I find the rest of my third hotdog completely forgotten on my plate as I take note of the sudden stage I'm standing on. All these guys are absurdly curious about me. I feel like the brand new exhibit at the zoo, and a whole classroom full of jocks has come up to the glass, faces pressed against it as they stare inside, fascinated.

"Well, uh ..." I swallow and stare at the floorboards of the porch, eyebrows lifted as I consider the question. "I guess I'm ... I guess I want someone who's smart, loyal ... can make me laugh. Maybe someone who knows what they want out of life, who's driven. Someone who—oh, this is a good one—someone with eyes I can just stare into for hours. That's really, really important to me," I emphasize with a nod at the floor. "Also, even though I know it's important to be able to keep a good conversation going with your lover, I kinda think it's just as important to be able to just ... do nothing. Lounge around. Stand the silence together and not get ... restless."

When I look up, I realize I still have all the guys' attention. It isn't lost on me how stiff Tanner's gotten at my side. I wonder if he was counting on me being all *gay* with his friends.

Maybe he was trying to ignore that part of me in his conquest to make me his new buddy.

"Dude, that totally sounds like *my* type," says Zits—*I mean Joel.* "Except, like, for a girl. I guess. Somethin' like that." He glances at his friends for support.

"Is it true that you got a 'gaydar' in your head and you can know someone's gay just by lookin' at them?" asks Kirk, the man of a thousand questions.

"Not really," I confess.

"I knew that wasn't true!" Kirk exclaims proudly, his eyes narrowed and his mouth tightened. "Oh, and for the record, I'm sorry about all the shit I said about you in high school. I was just young, dumb, and didn't know what to think about gay people."

I stare at him totally blank-eyed. Until now, I didn't know he'd said anything about me at all.

"But the good Reverend Arnold set me straight," he goes on with a self-assured nod. "He did. *'Everyone's born equal and good and deservin' of God's love. Even the homos.'* Or somethin' like that."

Robby snorts out with laughter at that, slapping his knee. "Shit, Kirk. When's the last damn time you've even stepped foot in that church?"

"Boy, I go every week! Whole Goddamned town's closed on Sundays. What the hell else you gonna do with your day except watch football? Shit." He draws another cross on his body. "Sorry, Jesus."

"Liar," says Robby. "I sing every Sunday. I haven't seen you in church since Christmas Eve service. What did Santa leave you under the tree that's gotten you so dang occupied for over six months? A blow-up doll and some lube?"

Kirk's out of his chair in an instant and so is Robby. Kirk chases the choirboy down the steps and halfway across the lawn, Robby cackling with laughter and shouting taunts at Kirk, who can't keep up, doubling over in the grass near the pool and breathing heavily, unable even to shout back at Robby's taunts.

"Don't mind them," says Tanner, poking me in the ribs with his elbow. "They haven't seen a lick of the world past the borders of this town. You're like a ... fuckin' exotic flamingo or some shit to them. But you're just another bud in my circle, Tuck. And I mean that in a good way," he adds quickly, furrowing his brow at me. "You're a bud I want around."

"A bud," I echo.

Just those two little words of mine cause a flicker of ... *something* ... to rush across Tanner's eyes. Why do I always get the nagging feeling around him that he's waiting for me to say something?

The back glass doors slide open and Tanner's ma steps out. The first thing you notice about his mom is her two perky boobs, which I imagine are about eighty percent bra and twenty percent nothing by the pencil-thin shape of her body and her twenty-inch waist. Her hair is spun upward in a tall, nest-like shape. Two hoop earrings bounce at her neck as she looks from the left to the right, her face wrinkled in a way that so reminds me of Tanner when he's trying to remember something.

"Did I just hear a scream out here, or have I done lost my mind?" she asks in her thick drawl.

"Kirk and Robby," says Tanner for an explanation.

"Ugh. Numbnuts one and numbnuts two." Her eyes come around and land on me. Her eyebrows pull together and her lips part five seconds before she says anything. "William Tucker? From the burger joint?"

"Biggie's Bites. Yes, ma'am," I say.

She stares at me for ten solid seconds with that brow-furrowed, questioning look. "What you doin' out here?"

Tanner answers his ma. "I invited him over, mama. He's hangin' out with us."

I clasp my hands together, feeling a sudden surge of nervousness. There's something somewhat intimidating about Tanner's mother's presence. "My ma says hello," I tell her with a tight smile.

She's still squinting at me. She bites the inside of her lip, then nods distractedly. "Uh-huh." She lifts her brows at last when she turns to Tanner. "You gonna send your friends away soon, son? We got some errands to run, as you recall."

Tanner sighs. "Can't those wait 'til tomorrow?"

"I might be dead tomorrow. We're doin' them today," she sasses him, then gives me one last look before retreating back into the house.

I bite my lip, wondering why Nadine Strong doesn't care for me or my ma. I suspect it has something to do with our family's diner being the only food business in Spruce that the Strongs *don't* have a hand in. We've gotten offers many times over the years to sell the place, but my pa's pride wins out every time. *The Bite's ours. Ain't no big flashy check gonna change that.*

"Sorry 'bout that," mutters Tanner quietly, then he lifts his voice to everyone else. "Hey, y'all heard her. Call it a day. I'll catch you around some other time, alright?"

Harrison's already out of his chair. "Sure thing."

Kirk's made it back to the porch, where Joel tells him they're being kicked out. "Well, shit," mumbles Kirk. "I thought we were gonna stay and binge some TV, dude?"

"Next time, next time. Get goin'," says Tanner. The moment I move, however, he puts a hand to my shoulder. "Not you, bud."

I lift my eyebrows at him expectantly, but he says nothing more.

Robby gives me a lift of his chin. "Hook me up with a discount or somethin' if I stop by Biggie's, will ya?" Then he and Joel are off, Kirk trailing behind.

Now it's just Tanner and I. With a little reluctance, I bring my gaze to meet his. I give half a shrug, as if to prod him into saying whatever it is he wants to say.

Tanner licks his lips—*damn his accidental sexiness*—and then he says, "We should hang out again, like, soon."

My heart flutters. I ignore it and try to act like a damn normal human being. "I have work the next two days."

"You guys close on Sunday like the rest of the town?"

"Uh, yeah."

"So Saturday night," he says, giving the meat of my arm a spank. "After you get off. Eleven, is it?"

I lift my eyebrows. "You know our hours?"

"It's pasted on your front glass door. I'm observant."

He's observant. Why do I find that fact so fucking hot? "Eleven ..." I murmur thoughtfully.

"These country roads out to the farmlands are scary as shit at night," he points out. "I'll come pick you up."

"That's okay," I assure him. "I don't need a ride."

"Yeah, ya do. It'll be pitch black out here by that hour. Eleven. I'm pickin' you up."

"Shit, you're stubborn."

"See ya then." He winks at me, slaps my arm again, then saunters off into the house, his beautiful, muscled backside the last sight I enjoy of him.

Staggering to the pool, I collect my shirt, keys, wallet, and phone from the chair. Clutching my things to myself, I feel the pinch of a smile trying to happen on my face. *You're an idiot to get excited about a straight boy gettin' all friendly with you,* I chide myself. *You're a damned idiot.*

But I smile anyway. I smile all the way home, driving shirtless with the wind slapping all around me through the rolled-down windows on the country road.

CHAPTER 6
TANNER

I'd never admit I'm nervous.

But I am.

I'm nervous as fuck.

I check what I have in the fridge seventeen times. *Seventeen times.* I don't know why, but I feel like Billy's gonna scrutinize it with those professional chef-in-training eyes of his and judge me for the contents piled up in there. Half of it's stuff I don't even eat, but I feel like he'll judge me just the same.

I give myself a look in the mirror. I didn't wanna dress up too much and didn't wanna dress down too much. I'm in a loose pair of blue jeans with a belt and have on a loose white sleeveless shirt half-tucked into just the front. I keep second-guessing myself, wondering if I should put on a button-up shirt or if that's too uptight. *Me? Uptight?* Fuck, I'm losing my mind. I mean, he's just coming over to my ranch on a Saturday night. No biggie, right?

"No biggie," I mumble at my reflection. "You're even startin' to sound like him."

Biggie's Bites. I tap my phone to check the time. *Shit.* I swipe my keys off the counter and thrust my wallet into a pocket before slipping out the door. With a hop, I'm in my pickup and rolling fast down the dark farm road toward Spruce.

When I come to a stop in front of Biggie's Bites, he's not waiting for me outside. I don't bother to pull into the parking lot, shutting off the truck. I swing out and come up to the door.

Through the windows, I don't see anyone inside, but all the lights are still on, so I gently pull open the door, careful not to let the door chime ring too loud.

Right when I'm about to call out his name, I hear voices from the kitchen. "You ain't got a thing to be nervous about, Junior."

"I'm not *nervous*," comes Billy's voice.

"You sure you wanna wear that?"

"*Stop.* Jesus."

"I mean, his family's all wealthy and Nadine sees your pa and I like a couple a' bugs in the corner of her big fancy kitchen, so really, if you're gonna start makin' friends with the Strongs—"

"She doesn't see us that way. And I'm just hangin' out with Tanner. That's it."

"I mean, did you tell her I said hi ... nicely? Or did you just blurt it like a clucking chicken? Maybe I should fix her a basket from the diner."

"No baskets. Please, Lord, no baskets."

"Well. She and I go way back. I know how Nadine was like in school and I know what she's like now, and it's two different people. Hey, Junior, maybe if you get all sweet with her son, then she'll get sweeter with you, and maybe with us. It's good for the business."

"Thanks for the tip, but this ain't a business meeting and I don't got any ulterior motives. I'm just hanging with a ... *friend*."

I'm standing so still that my legs start to tingle. I don't blink or breathe.

"Friend?" I hear his mama giggle. "He's pretty cute, ain't he?"

"Bye, Ma. Tell Pa I'm gonna need some more vanilla beans, since tonight's dessert orders used up my last."

"Don't change the subject, Junior. You got your heart all twisted up in that Tanner boy, don't ya?"

"*Goodbye, Ma.*"

"Be careful. Don't let a straight boy break it."

Quickly, I slip back out, carefully shutting the door so it doesn't chime. I thrust my hands into my pockets and play innocent as I wait, my heart hammering in my chest. I fight a smile that's trying to happen on my face.

A minute later, the door creaks open. I hear his soft footsteps as he shuffles. Pretending to be caught a bit by surprise, I look up quickly.

Then I *am* surprised. Billy's in a nice, fitted, baby blue polo over a loose pair of distressed jeans, bunched at the feet by a pair of chucks. He's got a black backpack slung over a shoulder. Also, he's taken time to fix his hair from the looks of it, as it's all pushed forward, ending in an attack of spikes and points at the front. I don't know if it's the fitted shirt or the size of those sleeves or the flex of his arm as he hangs onto the strap of his backpack, but his arms seem bigger than the last time I saw him. Has Billy been working out, or am I imagining it?

"Something wrong?" he asks, stopping.

I shake myself from the stunned expression that's probably on my face. "Nothin' at all. You ready, man?"

"Totally." He eyes my pickup.

I hop into the driver's seat as he lets himself into the passenger side. He clutches his backpack in his lap after doing his seatbelt while I just stare. Just when he looks up at me, I turn away quickly and start the engine.

Tonight's gonna be so much fun.

We break from the main roads of Spruce and into the countryside, where it's substantially darker and the only source of light is whatever reflects back into the pickup from my headlights. "So, Tuck, tell me ..."

"It's Billy. Please stop callin' me Tuck."

"Aww. Not a fan of nicknames, huh?"

"Well, unless you're down for me callin' you ... *Straw*."

"Straw?" I glance over at him, amused.

He shuts his eyes and shakes his head. "I was just ... thinking of whatever half of *Strong* would sound like."

I let out a laugh, which makes Billy smile just the tiniest bit. He's super wound up; I can tell. Maybe first thing we need to do when we get back to the ranch is kick back with some beer, or something stronger. I need to loosen this boy up. He works too damn hard all week and takes everything so seriously.

"You wanted me to tell ya somethin'?" Billy prompts with a lift of his eyebrows.

"Oh, yeah. Before you *rudely* interrupted me," I tease, "I was gonna ask whether you felt like my mama was rude to you. I don't wanna speak on her behalf, but I *do* wanna say that I'm sure she didn't mean to seem as cold as she did when she saw ya at the ranch earlier this week. She's just not used to me makin' new friends, that's all."

"New friends ... like *me*?"

I shake my head. "Nah, nothin' like that. I mean, she even acted weird the first time I invited Robby over, too. She was like, *'What's goin' on? You makin' friends with the whole church choir too, now? They didn't even place in regionals!'* She gets really obsessed with image, Tuck. I kinda blame the sour company she keeps, if you catch my meaning. Shit, I mean *Billy*." I chuckle. "I've made a habit I gotta break now."

"No problem, Straw," he teases back.

"Alright, alright. I get your point. No more tuckin' nothin'," I say with a wave of my hand and a laugh.

A few minutes later, we come up on the ranch. I pull into my spot and kill the engine, then watch as Billy hops out of the truck, catching a glimpse of his cute, jeaned ass. I grin, excited for whatever our night's about to bring. I shove open my door and hit the gravel. Coming around the truck, I find Billy staring up at my house with wonder in his eyes, the backpack hanging in his fist by his side.

It just now occurs to me that, after my whole grand tour of the ranch the other day, I didn't even bother to show him the inside of my house.

"I know," I say as I come up to his side. "It's, like, even bigger in the dark."

He looks at me and frowns. "Huh?"

Stop making stupid sex jokes. You're doing that because you're nervous. Be cool. He's just another bud. Treat him like another bud. "Nothin'. Come on in, Billy!" I slap him on the back as I rush up the steps of the porch to open the door. I hold it and let him in first.

Billy enters the house slowly with his eyebrows in a permanent lift. Distractedly, he kicks off his shoes, then shuts the door behind him. "House is big," he says, almost too quietly to hear.

"You don't need to take off your shoes if you don't want," I point out. "We're not that kind of—"

"Can I see your freezer? I gotta store somethin' in it."

I blink. "Freezer?"

"Mind if I ...?" he asks as he approaches the kitchen.

I kick off my shoes too. I don't have a dog anymore, so I guess there's no fear of him pissing in them, and I want Billy to feel as comfortable as possible. "Nah, go ahead."

"Thanks," he says, slinging the backpack off of his shoulder and setting it on the counter.

I come up to his side. "The hell you bring?"

"I couldn't show up empty-handed," he explains, his face lighting up adorably as he unzips the backpack. "I brought some of my homemade ice cream—two flavors—homemade hot fudge, and some other sweet surprises."

"Sweet surprises ...?" I echo, staring wide-eyed as he pulls out two sealed containers.

He gives a nod at my freezer. "Think you got room in there for these babies?"

I'm genuinely caught off-guard. I guess I should have expected he'd do something like this, being a sweets guru and all, but I'm surprised just the same. "Go right ahead. My place is ... your place," I finish distractedly.

"Awesome." He carries his—*Gift? Contribution?*—to the freezer, balancing them against his chest as he pulls open the door. He grunts a bit, underestimating how heavy the door is, and hunts for a spot to put his homemade sweets, for which I'm already salivating.

Of course, it's not the only thing I'm hungering for. I can't even begin to describe the amount of anxiety that's rattling down my arms and legs right now. I have never been within such close and personal proximity to a person who I could potentially ... *do* anything with. Even at college, I never got comfortable with any of the gay guys I knew of. I never confided my secret to anyone. I let all the girls flirt with me, but I never flirted back, not after I let myself believe what it was that I *really* craved.

And here he is, standing in front of my freezer as he awkwardly fumbles with his big containers of sweetness, pushing things out of the way on the shelves to make room. It does occur to me that I could help him, but he's just too dang adorable to watch. I'm hypnotized by his cute shape, the way his baby blue polo pulls across his back as he plays Tetris with whatever's in that freezer, still holding the containers against his chest. My eyes drift down to his jeans, the way they hug the backs of his thighs, and that sweet ass of his that I just wanna grab.

I've seen so many dude's asses in my life. I've slapped them. I've put my face in countless as I squatted behind them for the snap. I've hugged teammates after victories and screamed in their faces. I've thrust myself against big meaty bodies over and over again. I've grabbed men and tackled them to the grass. I've breathed their heat and shared their water bottles and sweated with them.

But Billy is the first one I feel completely allowed to be myself around. He's the first and only one I can grab ... and do *more* with. I can touch him. I can hold him. I can put my lips against his and feel what it's really like to kiss someone you *want* to kiss. Someone you enjoy kissing so much, you feel sick in the stomach. Someone who makes you weak in the knees and dumb in the head.

My heart thunders so hard, I could pass out just from staring at Billy and letting the millions of possibilities race through my frenzied mind.

In the next instant, he's finished and the freezer door slams shut, startling the fuck out of me. "That was a bit of a tight fit," says Billy, turning to face me.

The front of his shirt is wet from the containers he just held against it. The nipples on his cute, tight little pecs are poking through the baby blue material. My eyes go straight to them.

"Tight fit," I agree, my voice somewhat choked.

Billy crosses his arms suddenly, maybe becoming aware at once of what I'm staring at.

I shake off all of my thoughts and focus myself. *Don't fuck this up, Tanner.* "You wanna come chill on the couch and watch some TV?" I ask him. "Play some PlayStation? Xbox? Wii? I kinda got it all. Or ... well, shit, do you want a tour of the house first?"

Billy gives a small shrug and offers the tiniest smile in the world. "Whatever, man. I'm all yours tonight."

Fuck. Did he really have to say it that way? I think my cock just reacted to those words. I feel like a dumb, horny teenage boy.

"Cool, man. I'll show you around!" I exclaim a tad too excitedly.

The first floor is open-floor-plan style with the L-shaped counter and island of the kitchen opening to a big dining room on one side and the living room on the other. Two long, cushy white couches sit before the fireplace in the living room, upon which is mounted an enormous flat screen. There's an office area with a desk and computer that faces a big window overlooking the pool. A set of stairs near the fireplace leads to a balcony and game room that overlook the living room, plus four bedrooms, two and a half bathrooms, and an outside terrace complete with a table, six chairs, and a grill.

"You have quite the pad," says Billy in a small voice, staring out of the glass doors on the second floor at that terrace.

I can't help but feel a sting of worry. The more I show of my house, the stiffer and more closed-up he's seeming to get. *The whole point was to make him comfortable, to make him feel at home.* "Thanks. Are you ... alright?"

Billy lifts his eyes to me. "Um, yeah!" he says with a burst of energy. "Why wouldn't I be?"

"I don't know. You seemed a bit, um ..." I close my eyes and shake away whatever I was about to say. "Hey, why don't I get us somethin' to drink. You got a brand of beer you prefer?"

Billy shrugs and shakes his head. "Any one's fine with me."

"Cool!" I turn to head downstairs.

"Hey," he calls out as I go. "Where are your parents?"

I stop at the stairs and say, "Out of town. Business thing. Little brother went with them. They'll be back tomorrow afternoon."

His eyes glaze over. *I hope that's a good thing.*

"Something wrong?" I prompt him.

"N-Not at all," he says, his voice constricted.

I head down the stairs, hearing him following behind. Crossing the living room and kitchen, I pull open the big fridge and swipe a couple bottles. Cracking them open on the edge of the counter, I hand him one and immediately tip my own to my lips, kicking back. He does the same.

"Damn," he says, wiping his mouth. "This shit's good. Sorry, I don't usually drink, so ..."

"Oh? I didn't even bother to ask. I mean, I got other stuff too. I have tea, water, Coke. I think Jacky-Ann made up some lemonade yesterday."

"This is fine." Billy lifts his bottle. "To new friends."

The sudden impromptu toast catches me off-guard. I fumble for a second with my bottle, then lift it up to clink it against his. "New friends," I agree.

We both kick back again.

"Wanna sit down? Put on some TV?" I ask him.

"Sure."

I stumble over my feet on my way to the living room, and it has nothing to do with the alcohol. It's gonna take about five more bottles for me to feel anything. What I'm feeling right now is pure, untainted, unfiltered, undiluted terror. I'm the life of the party. I'm the guy who cracks all the jokes and puts his guests at ease. I have thrown some of the biggest, baddest parties throughout my whole high school career. And here I am now with literally *one* person to entertain, and I feel boring as fuck.

I plop onto the couch and swipe the remote off the coffee table. Billy makes his way toward the other couch. *Fuck no.* "Yo, Billy!" I say, catching his attention, and then I slap the cushion to my right. "Kick back, man."

"Okay," he says, his eyes blank as he relocates next to me.

He drops onto the cushion and lifts his eyebrows in surprise, perhaps underestimating how soft they are and how much he'd sink right into it. Once settled, he lets the bottle rest in his lap and starts tapping it anxiously.

Shit. Is he as nervous as I am?

I take a swig and flick on the TV.

Boobs and vaginas meet our eyes.

I choke on my beer, sputtering. I aim the remote to change the channel, but instead only succeed in raising the volume, filling the whole room with the desperate moans of horny women impaling themselves on foot-long black rubber dildos. I mash my finger into the remote again and the red light from the DVR flicks on, recording the scene in HD. I jam my thumb on the channel button and the remote makes a cracking sound. Now, no matter what button I press, nothing happens. I slap the remote ten furious times in my hand and keep aiming it at one of the women's wide-open mouths, tapping my finger into the button repeatedly. She keeps her mouth open like she's about to swallow the remote.

I look over at Billy apologetically and find him sitting there with his lips sucked in, the corners of his mouth pulled up, and his face completely flushed as he tries not to laugh.

I let the remote drop onto my lap as I stare at him. "Oh yeah? Amused, are ya?"

Billy runs a hand over his face, perhaps attempting to straighten it, then says, "Looks like someone left their porn on from last night."

I gape at him. "You think this is *my* porn? Boobs and dildos? You think that's my thing?"

"Actually," he says, takes a swig, then finishes, "that's *exactly* what I think your thing is. Get one of those girls to squat on a football, and you're all set."

I start to smile despite myself. "Well, shit. Am I really that transparent?"

Billy lets out a laugh. "You are now."

I'm not sure if he's still trying for humor, or if he's being serious and really thinks this is my porn. His humor is so dry that I can't tell, and it frustrates me a bit. *Why can't I just read him and know exactly what he's thinking?*

"This isn't my porn," I state, feeling like I have to. "I *do* have a younger brother. He's ... at that age. Maybe."

"So it's *his* extracurricular activity we're watchin'?"

"I don't know. I ain't pointin' any fingers, but ..."

Billy tilts his head and squints at the screen, then makes a random observation. "Hmm. She's flexible."

I look up at the women who are tirelessly going at it. Their moans still fill the room. *Wow*, I think to myself. *Porn in itself is a sport.* "Stamina," I remark. "Lots of it."

"Tanner. If you wanted me to come over and watch porn with you," teases Billy with a smirk, "you could've just told me so. But I'm pretty sure you'd know by now that ... *that's* not my flavor ..."

"Oh, this isn't doin' it for ya?" I nervously tease right back at the exact moment one of the women reaches her climax, screaming her pleasure over half my words. *Was there some totally innocent movie on this channel earlier, and now, at this hour, they have something less innocent on?* I can't begin to explain away the porn, shaking my head and taking another swig of my beer. "I swear, they probably had *Little Mermaid* on earlier, and—"

"Uh-huh."

"Listen. I could put on a Blu-ray. Fuck, I think I broke my remote."

"Tell me how college is goin'," he says abruptly.

I turn to him. Billy is facing me now with the beer resting in his lap. If I knew any better, I'd say he's trying to help salvage this and ignore what's happening on the screen in favor of us having a normal conversation. *He's trying*, I decide. Or maybe all of this is a rush of self-denial kicking in. *He's trying and I should, too.*

"Well ... it's goin' pretty ... good. I guess."

"You guess?"

He's definitely trying. Make conversation. Keep it going. "Yeah. I mean, I'm having fun. And—" One of the women howls and grabs her tits, pinching her nipples.

"Yep. She's having fun too," says Billy with a glance at the screen. Then he meets my eyes again, his hazel ones slightly glossed over—whether from the alcohol, humor, or anxiety, I can't tell. "Somethin' wrong at college?"

Staring into his eyes, I find a strange calmness enter me. Something about Billy—the way he is, the sweetness in his eyes, the calm way he holds himself all the time—makes me feel like he's not judging me.

His controlled nature centers me and really tunes out the whole world. Namely: the breathing and moaning of horny women on my big dumb TV.

"I guess ... you just come to learn a lot about yourself when you finally get away from home."

He lifts an eyebrow. "What do you mean?"

I feel the room spinning a bit. "I guess I sorta realized that ... Spruce is kind of a small pond. In a bigger pond, there's bigger fish. And there's *different* fish. And you find out that ... maybe you've been lying to yourself."

Billy studies me. I have his full attention.

"Have ... you been lying to yourself?" he asks quietly.

"Yep."

"What about?"

Fuck. Is he really gonna make me say it? "I ..." My heart is pounding so hard right now. "Billy, I ... I haven't even told this to my buddies. Or ... or my parents."

"It's okay. I'm your buddy, right?" He props an elbow up on the back of the couch. "You can tell me."

I take another swig of my beer. *Fuck, fuck, fuck.* My eyes are wet and glassy. Billy looks so fucking good. All of my insides are spinning like a windmill.

"I'm ..."

"Yeah?" he urges me.

"I ... I-I barely passed calculus," I state.

He stares at me. Something deflates in his eyes. "Oh?"

Now or never. "And I want to kiss you."

"What?"

I grip the back of his head and pull him to my face, crashing our lips together.

CHAPTER 7
BILLY

He presses his lips against mine.

It's exactly what I wanted to happen. Every fantasy that kept hope alive in me since my lonesome, horny teenage years are bursting to life.

I can't breathe and I love it.

My face is trapped against his, a prisoner to him as he holds my head in place, gripping me from behind. Just when I think the kiss can't get any stronger, he pulls me against him even more.

Goddamn, this boy's a hoover.

His tongue comes out, testing my lips. I part them to let him in, and our tongues meet for the first time. Sure, the taste of beer is there, but past that, it is all man and perfection in my mouth. Hell, maybe the beer is making this all the more hotter for me.

I never knew what I was missing.

I wish we were best friends back in school.

I wish I ran off to Oklahoma with him.

He's kissed people before. I know he has, but this feels too desperate and hungry to just be an experiment. He wants this, and he wants this badly.

It can't be just the alcohol talking. He's far from drunk, that much I know.

Suddenly, almost abruptly, the kiss slows. His lips stay pressed to mine, but he's stopped assaulting me. For just a nice, calm moment, our jagged breaths beat against our faces. The hand he's got at the back of my neck softens its grip, becoming something far more like a caress.

Then he pulls away at last and we're looking into each other's eyes. I can't even react, too afraid to shatter the moment we just had. Was that a moment? Is that what we just had?

"I'll put on a movie," he says suddenly.

I lift a brow. "What?"

Then he's off the couch and standing in front of the screen, pushing buttons at its side to manually change the input. The girls (and their howls of ecstasy) are gone in an instant, replaced by the expectant screen of the Blu-ray player with the logo bouncing around. He pops open some random case and tosses a Blu-ray into the player, which is housed next to all his gaming systems and cable box in a glass cabinet by the fireplace.

He's back on the couch as the digital surround sound swallows up the room. With a glance at me, he gives the remote a wiggle and says, "Blu-ray remote. Good to go. Get comfy, bud!"

I blink at him. Are we seriously about to ignore that insane, stuff-of-dreams kiss we just shared?

"Tanner ...?"

"I just popped in the first thing I found," he explains with a nervous edge in his voice. "I think it's *Avatar*. Do you like *Avatar*? I fuckin' love *Avatar*. Wish I had the 3D glasses and TV, though."

Okay. So we *are* going to ignore it. Alright. I sink a bit into the couch and stare up at the TV, gripping the beer bottle tightly in my hand.

The next instant, he's up from the couch again and doing a circle of the room, turning off all the lights. I watch him with wide eyes as he scurries around the room on feet so light, he might as well be floating. When he's finished and the whole living room is dark except for the light emitting from the flat screen, he plops right back onto the couch, causing me to jump from the rebounding cushions. He settles into place with just an inch of space between us.

I can't even focus on the movie. I mean, I've seen it at least two or three times years ago, but I have never had the experience of watching any movie sitting next to a guy—*a hot, beefy, sexualized, repressed, just-came-out-to-me, high-school-football-quarterback-crush sort of guy*—who just took all of my breath away.

And who could just as easily do it again.

Is he going to do it again?

Maybe it didn't happen. Maybe I imagined it. We've just been sitting here this whole time, the two of us.

The music and color of the movie wash over our faces. Nothing happens. I haven't even taken another sip of my beer, having forgotten I'm holding a bottle at all. If I can trust my peripheral view, neither has he.

Then, he shifts a bit, and the hairs of his arm graze my own.

My heart rate picks up instantly. Is it going to happen again? Is Tanner Strong going to suddenly become my hot jock-boy make-out fantasy, assaulting me when I least expect it?

Is this a sexual ambush? I kinda hope it is.

He shifts yet again. Our arms are touching now.

I don't move away. He doesn't move away.

Goddamn it, just kiss me again.

"You want some popcorn or somethin'?"

The question startles me. "Uh, no, I'm good," I insist with a tiny smile, my eyes lingering on him.

He gives me a short nod. "Cool!" he squeaks out, then faces the TV again, his eyes unblinking.

Oh, no. Was it a mistake? Did I kiss really badly or something? Maybe he's living a secret second gay life up there in college and he's kissed a hundred other lucky guys who are twelve hundred times hotter than me. He's disappointed with the kiss. I disappointed him gravely. The only reason he's been getting close to me is because I'm the one and only option he's got.

Oh, God. Is that it? Am I just a default to him? Am I the bottom of the barrel? *He regrets kissing me because I'm so awful. I taste weird. He used me.*

He used me.

"You wearin' somethin'?"

Yet again, I'm startled by the sudden question. "Say what?" I ask, turning my head his way.

"Cologne?" he asks, wrinkling up his forehead as he half-turns his face to me, his eyes glowing from the light of the TV. "Or your hair gel? I'm smellin' somethin' nice. Spicy. Woodsy."

I have no idea. "My deodorant, maybe?"

"Ah." He smiles broadly. "Smells great, man. I'm, uh ... always lookin' for ... uh ... new scents. I get bored of mine, y'know?" He chuckles dryly, and then his smile's gone in an instant.

Shit. Tanner Strong is one frazzled-ass nervous guy right now. I can see it all over his face. It's like we're on a date and he doesn't know where to put his hands. Maybe I have this all wrong. Maybe I'm the first guy he's ever kissed and that's why he—

Wait a second. *I'm the first guy Tanner Strong has ever kissed. I'm the first guy. Me. The first one.*

Now let's see if I can be the second one too.

"Um, hey, Tanner?"

"This is the good part," he whispers, pointing.

"Tanner," I say anyway.

"Sam Worthington! Look!"

"I *am* looking. At ... *you*." My eyes are burrowing into the side of his smooth, angular face and his bright eyes.

He pulls his gaze from the TV and connects them with me again.

A second ago, I had so much courage. Now I'm falling into the trap of his deep brown eyes once again, which render me speechless, breathless, and paralyzed.

"Yeah?" he prompts me, his voice small.

He looks so oddly vulnerable right now. I could bet a thousand dollars he'd never be caught dead acting like this in front of his buddies.

This whole evening, this whole side of Tanner ... it feels like it belongs to me. It's our secret. Somehow, without him even saying that, I already know that we're going to have to hide this. Either he's going to play the denial card, or he's going to grow some balls and ask me to keep quiet about it.

For some reason, I'm actually okay with that. I don't need my ma all over me about what happened here with Tanner. I don't need Mindy and her big mouth spreading the news to all her hundreds of friends. I don't need the constant interrogation of customers at the diner asking me how I succeeded in turning the town football star gay.

I suspect he's had these desires for quite some time. No one turned anyone into anything. This is who he is.

"Nothin'," I end up saying, the big ol' wuss I am.

"Oh." His eyes turn teasing. "Thought you changed your mind on the popcorn or somethin'." Then he elbows me in the ribs and returns his attention to the movie.

But I don't. I keep staring at him. My eyes drift to his inked-up arm, showing in that white sleeveless shirt he's chosen to wear. It isn't like the loose red workout one he wore to the movie theater. This one is fitted, tighter, like a regular white shirt with the sleeves removed. He's got it tucked in just the front, showing off the beauty that is the crotch of his jeans, bunched up and punctuated at the top with his belt buckle. The way his jeans are all nestled up between his legs, showing off his crotch, it's so inviting that I feel like I'm literally being drawn to it like a dog to a big meaty butt.

Or a dog to a bone, if Tanner's as hard as I am right now.

I let my right hand have the bottle, resting it on my right side. Then I let my other hand drop to my left, the knuckles of which are agonizingly close to his big jeaned thigh. *He wants to play the slow game? I'll play the slow game, and I'll make Tanner Strong squirm.*

After what might be a solid minute, I shift my left hand just a bit. It isn't enough. Then I shift a bit more.

My knuckles make contact. Knuckle to thigh.

He doesn't move.

I let my knuckles dance just a bit. Slowly. Softly.

I hear his breathing change. *I've got his attention.* My hand spreads slightly—slowly, *slowly*—as my fingers slip up the side of his thick, muscled thigh. He doesn't move an inch, keeping his body impressively still. I let my fingers rest there for a while to let him acclimate or make a move of his own.

He doesn't.

I guess it's my turn again.

My fingers slide more. After several long, crawling seconds, my whole palm is resting on his thigh. Just a few inches separates my hand from his junk.

Then, I feel a finger touching the side of my leg.

I stop breathing at once.

My cock goes rock hard.

His hand, just as slowly, slides onto my thigh. At first his fingers just rest there, but soon they start to grip, squeezing my leg.

I grip his thigh tighter, squeezing back.

I'm so fucking hard. I can't breathe.

Then his hand slides farther than mine even went. His fingers reach my inner thigh where it's most sensitive, and I fight an urge to close my legs from the sensation. I fight another urge to open them wider, for some reason feeling like I should pretend like all this business with our hands isn't even happening.

Is that the theme of tonight's hangout? Total denial?

He doesn't seem to move any farther, so I take it as my cue. I let my fingers slide some more, falling gently between his legs as I caress his inner thigh. I hear a short, abrupt breath come out of him. We're both staring at the screen pretending this isn't happening while our cocks throb in our jeans, which are quickly growing too tight for comfort.

My fingers crawl up his inner thigh, up, up, up. They reach his crotch.

Holy fucking hell he's huge. And he's hard as a rock. And he's filling those jeans so much that suddenly I'm the one who's frozen again, unable to comprehend the amount of *Tanner* that just ended up in my palm.

Then his hand's on the move too, and it's just a few seconds before it arrives on my crotch. I sigh with relief at the sensation of him touching my swollen cock, even if it's through the material of my jeans.

And that's how two horny boys from the small town of Spruce ended up on a couch with a hand planted in each other's crotches.

Then he starts massaging.

Oh, God, he starts massaging.

I make my hand move too, gently gripping, grinding, and exploring at first. *Sweet baby Jesus, he's huge.* Each time I squeeze, his massive cock flexes back at me. Then he gives *my* crotch a squeeze and I can't help but throb.

We're driving each other insane. The more fierce my movements get, the stronger his gets. It's like we're trying to outman one another. The whole thing's become a sort of challenge to see how much we can take.

And we're both determined to win.

He lets out a moan. That's all the encouragement I need. I start to move my hand up and down his meat, a jerking sensation.

This has to be new to him. No one's ever made him feel this way. And this is a first for me, too—in *so* many ways. He's gripping and squeezing me like he's never felt a cock other than his own before.

I feel so damn special.

With a stroke of bravery finding me, I slide my hand to the buckle of his jeans and start undoing it. The sound of clinking metal and slithering leather combats with the flair and drama of music from the movie. Or perhaps the music comically complements my triumphant action of undoing Tanner's belt and adventuring into his stiff and throbbing no man's land.

With the buckle undone, the button of his pants pops open quick and the zipper, quicker.

I can't get to his cock, which is more than frustrating me, so I shift my position on the couch and grip his jeans by either side. Tanner lifts his butt off the cushion just enough for me to slip his pants halfway down his legs.

His black boxer-briefs are tenting badly. After getting his pants off, I work just as fast to slip off mine. Me in my white briefs, him in his black boxer-briefs, our hands go right to where they were before.

The feel of his big hand on my cock—now with one less bit of material in the way—sends shivers of delight up my spine. He might as well be touching it directly. I could fondle him for hours and let him do the same to me. Both of us are breathing funny now. We are, without a doubt, no longer invested in the movie. His full focus is on gasping and restraining his own moans while I grope him.

Are we moving too fast? I can't get enough of him and I don't want this to end. I'm not sure who's seducing who. Is he a victim of my sexual cravings, or is he inviting me to do all of this to him?

Maybe he wants this as badly as I do.

Maybe we're moving too slow.

I grip the waistband of his boxer-briefs and pull them down. Yes, I have to pull extra hard for the waistband to stretch far enough to allow his huge, hard cock out. And even in the semidarkness with just the TV's light glowing on us, I see it in all its massive glory.

Eight inches, easily. Maybe nine. *Lord help me.*

When my fingers wrap around it, Tanner sighs, his head drooping back against the couch as his eyes flip up and he teleports somewhere far away.

Too far for my liking. *Let's bring him back, way up-close.*

I bring my lips to the base of his cock and plant a kiss. *He smells so clean.* I plant another kiss while I stare up at his leaned-back ripped body in that sleeveless white shirt. His chest lifts and falls with his increasing breath. I keep dropping kisses as I run up the length of his cock. *If this is his first time, I want him to remember it forever.*

Because I know *I'll* be remembering it forever, since it's sorta my first time, too.

My tongue teases past my lips, tasting the head of his cock where a bead of pre-cum lives. I flatten my tongue and drag it across the tip, licking up his gift for me.

Tanner snaps his head forward, his eyes wide and his mouth agape as he stares at what I'm doing.

Yeah, there's no denial game anymore. Pretending we aren't noticing how crazy we're driving one another is no longer an option.

I doubt it ever was.

I drag my tongue over his cockhead again, slowly and cruelly. Tanner sighs, his eyes squinting with disbelief at the pleasure I'm giving him. He's almost in tears with the joy erupting inside him.

Dude, I'm just gettin' started.

I grip his cock with one hand as my lips part to let in the slick, gleaming tip. I make sure to do it so slowly that by the time I'm ready to try engulfing this beast, his body is desperate for it. I only slide the tip into my mouth as I let my tongue dance and play all over it.

Tanner's expression is priceless. He looks in pain, in shock, and in awe. All three of those emotions are at war on his face, like he doesn't know how to feel.

And I'm about to give him something else to contend with. *You ready for this, big boy?*

I let in another inch. My jaw is already stretched wide to accept it. With my gaze still tracking his reactions, I watch as his eyes reel back and his hands grip the couch, practically clawing as his thighs tighten from what I'm doing. I'm in control here as I drive him crazy. I bet he's already ready to explode.

Not until I let you, Tanner.

Then I dive. My throat opening up, I let in as much of him as I can possibly take. I doubt it's more than half, to be honest, what with his ridiculous size—but boy do I try.

I let my tongue and lips massage his cock as I twist my mouth around it in the same way a wet, slippery hand would twist and jerk it, except warmer. I go up and down, rotating my head as I work him.

"I'm close," he warns in a voice that's about two octaves higher than the Tanner I've come to know.

I let his cock out of my mouth before he blows. His taste coats my tongue and his smell invades my nostrils, intoxicating me. "Don't last long, do you?" I taunt him.

His eyes grow double before a smile breaks across his face. "Well, shit, boy! Not with all that ... *stuff* you're doin' down there!"

"Think you can handle it if I go longer?"

"I can handle as long as you got, Tuck."

I squeeze his cock tight, inspiring a gasp from him, then lift a warning eyebrow. "What'd I tell you about callin' me that?"

His eyes turn defiant, despite me having his manhood in my fist. "Boy, I'll call you whatever I want," he teases.

I narrow my eyes. "Alright, Straw. You asked for it."

"You gonna suck it like a straw?"

I don't know if all these crude things he's saying is his way of normalizing all of this newness to him, or if he really is this comfortable suddenly with what we're doing. Either way, I let him egg me on and fill my inner hunger for his masculinity, for his overflowing testosterone, for his taste and smell and thickness.

Without answering him—or perhaps *to* answer him—I wrap my lips around his cockhead and slide down again, swallowing him inch by inch. It feels like forever before he hits the back of my throat. I almost gag, worried for a second that I've overestimated my abilities, which I've admittedly not had much practice with. I try to act on every instinct. I chase the mood as it comes. I say yes to every desire that enters my greedy mind.

I know how to do this, I coach myself. *I've watched my fair share of gay porn.*

But I never imagined it'd feel like this. There is an element of fear when you're doing this in real life, a fear that you might do the wrong thing, like nicking him with your teeth. All these thoughts race through my head, and it's all these thoughts that I have to push far away, letting my mind stay clear and my focus remain trained on him. I can't let myself get distracted. *Just feel your way through this. Feel what he wants and give it to him.*

Suddenly there's a hand on my head. With my mouth still full of Tanner, I glance upward, curious.

Tanner's fingers entangle in my hair. His eyes are zeroed in on me, smoldering and full of need.

The way his biceps bulge when he's reaching and grabbing hold of my hair, it's more than enough of what *I* need to erupt in my underwear without even touching myself. His biceps are already big, but from this angle, they are the stuff of gods.

"You want my juice?" he asks in a voice so low and deadly, I feel the vibrations of his words through his legs.

Any other situation, I'd laugh at those words. I might even be downright grossed out. But with a jock's cock halfway down my throat, kneeling between the thick and muscled legs of Tanner Strong, and with him gripping my hair tight with his burning brown eyes and his bulging inked biceps? Those words hit the spot.

And then he grins, as if knowing how hot he's making me. He repeats the words. "You want my ... Spruce Juice, Billy-boy?"

I moan my answer on his cock.

"Then get to work," he demands with a devilish smirk and a tug on my hair.

I descend on his cock, taking it in deeper. He doesn't let go of me. In fact, he starts to direct me, pushing and pulling my hair up and down his length. He keeps hitting the back of my throat and I keep suction, saliva drooling down his cock and making it more and more slippery with every pass. His pace increases as he uses my head like a toy, working me with such vigor that I start to slip on and off his cock. The popping noises my mouth makes starts to overpower the movie. *Huh? What movie? Were we even watching a movie?*

His cock grows tight in my fist. He's holding back. *I have him so* close, just one more lick can fling him over the edge.

Is he ready for this?

Am I?

The skin is so taut that it's evident he's not getting any harder. I feel the veins in his meat throbbing against my tongue with his impending orgasm. He's leaking so much pre-cum in my mouth. All I taste is him.

His hand drops from my hair as his eyes clench shut and he grips the couch. "Billy, Billy, Billy ..." he starts to moan urgently, a warning. His legs tighten as he struggles not to empty into my mouth, as if he has a choice.

So naturally, I pick up the pace.

I grip his wet, slick cock and I keep driving my mouth up and down it as far as I can go.

"Billy, Billy—*Oh, God*—Billy, Billy ..."

One of his legs kick up, smacking the coffee table. His hands slap the couch. His powerful body stretches back as he gives in, unable to hold off a second longer.

He erupts in my mouth. I don't stop moving my head, driving him even more crazy as I work his overly sensitive cock while he spills shot after shot.

And he's not quiet. Tanner Strong moans, loud and proud, his voice so deep that it booms all around me.

I have never tasted cum before. I didn't expect it to be so ... clean. *And good.* But if there's anyone I would have wanted my first taste to be from, it's Tanner.

He's breathing deep now, recovering. His eyes look drunken as he reels them onto me, his lips parted with an expression on his face that looks utterly awed, eyebrows lifted and mouth curled into an almost-smile.

"That ... was out of this world," he finally manages to say, then lets out a little laugh.

I'm still kneeling between his legs, by the way. And though my baby blue polo is still on, my pants are gone and I have a very stiff situation in my tenting briefs.

I rise a bit, leaning forward so my cock presses into the base of the couch. I have so many horny thoughts still racing through my mind. If I wasn't sure it'd ruin his couch, which his parents probably laid down a pretty penny for, I'd thrust my boner between the cushions at his legs and fuck the couch like a dog, my eyes on Tanner as his big muscled chest rises and falls with his every heavy breath. As it is right now, I'm probably humping the couch slowly, my cock desperate for some kind of relief after all of that.

I don't want this feeling to end. I'm enjoying it way too much. I want to be back on the couch with him fondling me again. I want to press my body against his and ... *do things to him.* And I want him to do things to me.

"Fuck, man," he breathes. "I'm just ... *fuck* ..."

A small part of me worries that I got him off too quickly. *Is he going to lose interest now? Is the night already over? Is he thinking of ways to politely tell me he's taking me home now?*

I sit back on my heels, trying to ignore the throbbing *issue* between my legs. My balls are pulled so tight against me, every tiny movement I make rubs the sensitive tip of my desperately hard cock against the material of my briefs, stimulating every nerve ending I'm trying to put to rest. It's just impossible to calm my excitement.

I wonder if I even *want* to calm it. Maybe ...

I look up at Tanner again, observing his thick build. I swallow in the sight of his big muscled arms, one inked more than the other. I admire the two muscular pecs that pull across his fitted white sleeveless top. He's basically my walking wet dream and he's all mine.

What do I want to do with him?

His stomach growls. He lifts his eyebrows in surprise, then meets my eyes. We both chuckle. "Ignore that," he says with a wave of his hand.

"Worked you up an appetite," I tease him, folding my arms and propping an elbow on each of his thighs. His cock, still slick with his cum, remains just an inch from my face, even as it's slowly softening.

His cock jumps at those words, and Tanner lifts an eyebrow. *Shit, did I just wake him up again?*

"You probably shouldn't be that close to my cock," he warns, "after what you just did."

"Why?"

"It's making me think things."

I try not to smile, but the evil right corner of my lips deceives me. "Oh yeah? Like ... round two?"

His monster cock jumps again, already growing back to full size. It's almost taunting me, how it inflates and sort of bobs in my face.

When I look up at him again, I see his eyes going half-lidded as he smiles lazily, his cute dimples showing. Quite suddenly, I realize I don't want to turn him (and this evening) into a cheapened night full of horniness and messes we have to clean up.

I don't know what it is about Tanner, but I suddenly find I respect him too damn much to objectify him.

I need him to know that I'm a person with a heart. He needs to know that, despite all the sass and snark I've thrown him, I care about him. I want to get to know him even better. I want us to become buddies ... and more. I didn't realize this before, but that's what I want above all else. Quite suddenly, Tanner's friendship is all I crave.

And I won't mind at all if that friendship develops into something far more.

"You want a snack?" I ask, tilting my head.

He looks surprised by my question. "Snack?" he asks, his voice cracking. Then, his eyes turn sinister. "Oh. You mean ... after the one I just gave you?"

His mind is still afloat in the gutters. He thinks you were making a sexual innuendo. "I meant ... a snack in the vein of something that's more ... sweet."

He tilts his head, confused.

I pat his thighs, then rise from the floor. "Come on."

I don't wait for him, strolling around the couch and toward the kitchen as I push on my cock, giving it a firm adjustment. I pull open the freezer side and wiggle my two containers of ice cream out, then shut the door with my hip as I turn to the counter, setting them down. By the time I pull open my backpack for the fudge and have it popped into the microwave, Tanner's finally approached. He's put his boxer-briefs back on.

And he's taken off his shirt. I have a blissful, slow-motion sort of moment where I get to experience my cock—which had *just* finally gone soft—slowly begin to stiffen once again in my small, white, leaves-little-to-the-imagination briefs.

Of course, Tanner sees every bit of what his presence has done to my unabashed cock in these tighty-whities of mine. Yes, my face is flushing.

"You lose your shirt on the way to the kitchen?" I try and sass, despite my fast reddening face.

"Used it to sorta, uh ... clean up," he says with a wince and a gesture toward his dick. "Hope you don't think that's gross. I didn't figure I'd need it, anyway. It's kinda warm in here, isn't it?"

Nope. Don't need it at all. Keep that and every other possible article of clothing far away from that gorgeous body of yours for as long as possible. "Yep," I agree with a squeak. "Let's have a treat to cool ourselves down. Strawberry or vanilla?"

He leans against the island, which makes a fantastic show of his biceps and thick shoulders. *Jesus, no matter how this man moves, he's a work of art.* I can see every individual fiber and ribbon of muscle in his shoulders and biceps and forearms flinch and flex as he leans. His chest is a whole other story with those two perfectly symmetrical mounds of muscle, each punctuated by a perfect, pink, lickable nipple. *What did I do to deserve this??*

I've forgotten what I even asked by the time he answers. "What?" he teases. "No chocolate?"

I flinch. I'm apparently unable to stop staring at him long enough to hold any form of reasonable dialogue. "Where do you keep your bowls?" I ask, turning away from him as I pull open his cabinets two at a time. "Ah. Found them. These ones okay?"

"Just as good as any other. Take your pick."

I pull out two glass bowls and set them on the kitchen island between us, ignoring the show of muscle just a countertop away from me. From my backpack, I remove a baggie in which I'd brought an ice cream scoop and a pair of silver spoons. I don't think my ice cream has had enough time to properly thicken, but it should still be tasty. It'll be like soft-serve, or a thicker pudding. *Maybe I should've rethought the hot fudge ...*

"Both," he decides.

I smile. "Mister indecisive." I pull open the strawberry container first and scoop a healthy ball of the light pink confection, setting it delicately into the bowl.

"More like I'm greedy and want it all," he corrects me leeringly, his eyes hungry and deep.

To his animal-like smolder, I laugh, shoving him off his pedestal. "Yeah, yeah. You act all bad-ass and tough, but I know you're just a big ol' softie deep down."

After scooping a perfect ball of strawberry into each bowl, I close the lid and move on to the vanilla, but the lid doesn't come off as easily. Three grunting attempts later, I hug the container to my chest and start pulling it harder, my fingertips going numb from the cold.

Tanner comes around the island, his big chest puffing up proudly. "I'll do it," he says with a superior smirk.

"*Like ... hell*," I grunt between big, strenuous efforts at opening the damned thing.

"C'mon," he insists, reaching.

Just as the microwave dings from the hot fudge being ready, the lid to my ice cream flies off and the container slips from my grasp. A thick white rope of my homemade vanilla ice cream slaps against Tanner's muscular chest. He gasps, flinching back with his hands in the air and shoulders lifted.

If he was truly warm a second ago, he just got a nice and sudden assault of cold all over him now.

He meets my eyes.

I stare at him with my mouth open and my hands up, frozen in place.

"Well?" he prompts me with a lift of an eyebrow. "Don't let it all go to waste."

I gape at him. Is he serious?

"C'mon," he coaxes me, sounding too much like he's beckoning a dog toward a bowl of food. "My nipples are hard now, thanks to you."

Seeing the look of superiority in his eyes, I find myself suddenly inspired. "Get down."

He lifts an eyebrow. "Huh?"

"On the ground," I order him.

Tanner takes a second to consider me, and then he lets out a laugh. "Yeah, alright. You spill your ice cream on my chest, and now you think you can just order me—"

I close the distance between us and slip a hand right into his boxer-briefs, gripping his cock with my ice cold hand. His body stiffens immediately and his eyebrows go halfway up his forehead. *That shut him up real quick.*

"Lie down on the floor," I tell him.

He looks so sexy when he's still trying to be big and tough, despite having his manhood grabbed. "Alright," he says, a curl in his lips.

He lies down on the floor. The ice cream has run down his body a bit, pooling in between each of his abs. I grab the hot fudge from the microwave and a spoon.

Tanner's smile wipes right away.

"You're my dessert now," I tell him with a grin.

"Uh ... Billy?"

"Don't worry. You'll get a taste, too."

"Is that hot fudge gonna burn me?"

"You scared of a little bit of ... heat?" I tease him as I lower myself, straddling his waist.

His lips part as if he wants to say something, but then he seems to freeze, his eyes on the container of hot fudge. I can see the war in Tanner's eyes. He's nervous about how the hot fudge will feel on his skin, but he's also still determined to put on this brave, alpha-male front for me. And better yet, there's a look of sheer curiosity that enters his eyes, almost like he's excited about how it'll feel, even if it hurts a bit.

Damn. Our first night together and we're already getting kinky as fuck.

I spoon out some hot fudge, then slowly lift it over his body. It sticks to the spoon at first, not yet dripping. We both watch with anticipation, just like awaiting the bead of liquid wax at the end of a candle to let go.

Then a string of hot fudge drips down. Tanner gasps, flinching underneath me. The hot fudge draws a line over his skin as I direct the spoon in little curlicues and spirals. Tanner seems to be in some sort of suspended state, like he can't tell if it burns or feels good.

Regardless, I'm about to make him feel *really* good. I set down the hot fudge on the floor next to us, the spoon inside, and then grip my baby blue polo shirt at the base and pull it up over my head. I fling it to the side.

Tanner's eyes drift to my chest. The hunger is still in his eyes. I know my body in no way compares to his, but there is something about the sexy way he stares at me that gives me a sense of unspeakable power.

Or maybe it's because I'm still straddling him and in full control of what he's about to feel.

"Dessert time," I murmur.

He meets my eyes, a flash of excitement in his own.

Then I lower my mouth to his chest. I lick the ice cream pooled between his pecs—and yes, it's a *lot* like a dog coming to his food bowl. I drag my tongue along his chest, following the trail of melted vanilla, and arrive at his nipple. He gasps when I lap the flat of my tongue across it. *He's got sensitive nipples*, I discover. *I'll make note of that.* But I don't go soft on him. I lick his nipple slowly like a lollipop, making sure to take my time and stimulate him as much as humanly possible. I can already tell that it's working by the way his muscles tense, his body squirms, and his face contorts with pleasure. I finally suck the nipple into my mouth, earning me a deep-seated moan from Tanner.

God, I love this.

After spending too long on that nipple, I slowly work my tongue back across his chest, catching a trail of fudge along the way. When I arrive at his other nipple, I can tell he's already expecting it by the way his body squirms, almost like my tongue's journey is tickle torturing him. He's so overly stimulated that I feel his cock stiffening under me, already rock hard again. I flatten my tongue and work his nipple while the fingers of my other hand, cruel as they are, slide up his body to flick and pull and squeeze the nipple I'd just left.

He's a fidgeting, moaning, stiffened mess by the time I'm finished torturing him. I just can't get enough of what I'm apparently capable of doing to Tanner. By the time I've licked the majority of ice cream off his body, I regret not having spilled more on him.

I hover over his face when I'm done. I'm sure there's a speck of chocolate on my nose, a smear of vanilla on my cheek, and maybe a drop or two on my chin. But the only place Tanner looks is straight into my eyes.

"I think you just invented a brand new dessert," he murmurs almost gently as he stares up at me. "What'll you call it, Billy?"

I give it a second's thought, then say the first thing that comes to mind. "Football Sundae."

"But it's Saturday," he complains with a little smile, his dimples appearing.

"Not anymore. It's past midnight."

"I kinda wish this night could last a lot longer."

"It can," I tell him. "I got nowhere to be. I'm all—"

"Yeah, you're all mine. You said that already."

"I did?"

"And that's exactly what I intend for you to be." His face is serious again. "Kiss me, Billy Tucker."

I don't need to be told twice. I lower my lips onto his, fudge and vanilla and all. His lips are surprisingly soft, full and plump in the best way possible. He seems to chase every instinct I do when we kiss. It's so perfect, how our mouths join, that I don't know whether it's him leading me, or me leading him. He gives me the perfect amount of lip and just a tease of his tongue, and I do the same.

When I feel my cock flexing between our bodies, I feel a sudden panic invade me. *So much for innocent ice cream,* a voice taunts me in my head. *You've gone and turned your sweet gesture into a big sex fest, too. Does your hunger know no end, Billy?*

I end the kiss and hover over him again. "Is this too fast? Should I stop?"

He looks startled by the question, his eyes shining in the cool kitchen lighting. He hesitates, apparently unsure what to say.

I decide to voice a few of my private concerns from earlier. "I just don't want to take advantage of you or nothin'. Don't get me wrong. I want this. I'm having a good time. I just ... I don't want to ruin it, either."

He nods suddenly. "Yeah. I don't wanna ruin it. I'm having ..." He swallows, then finishes. "I'm ... having a real great time. Best time ever. You're not ruinin' nothing, Billy. Except my underwear, maybe."

I frown. "Your underwear?"

"I'm leaking all inside it, dude. I'm a fuckin' mess for you."

That might be the hottest thing I've ever heard come from Tanner's mouth. And I've heard him moan while I had his cock halfway down my esophagus.

"Let's shower," he says suddenly.

"Yeah, good idea. I got the ice cream all over me now, too," I note, glancing down at our bodies. "You wanna go first? Or ..."

"We can both go. Like, together."

My eyes snap to him. "Really?"

"Yeah. You know. Save water. I mean, really, I'm just being environmentally conscious here." He shrugs innocently. "Just two dudes. In a shower. Together."

"Gettin' all *sudsy*," I quip. Then I bite my lip. "Isn't it gettin' kinda late, though? I could shower at home."

"Don't be dumb," he says back, bringing his hands around the small of my back as I continue hovering over his body. "You don't work on Sundays. My family won't be back 'til this afternoon. Just crash here."

Crash here.

He's inviting me to stay the night.

Is this really happening??

"Alright," I agree in a choked, excited voice.

We get up off the kitchen floor. As he goes upstairs to prepare the shower, I put away the ice cream, figuring we can have it later. Or tomorrow.

Tomorrow.

Holy shit, this is really happening.

I leave the hot fudge on the counter with the spoon in it as I go to the living room. I pull my phone out of the pocket of my pants—bunched up on the ground in front of the couch where I'd left them, still half-entwined with Tanner's pants. I shoot my mom a text, letting her know I'll be back in the morning. I hesitate before pressing the send button, unsure what can of worms I might be ripping right open in sending this text. *It could be innocent*, I tell myself. *She won't automatically assume I'm getting naughty with Tanner. I've crashed at a friend's house before.*

You know, when I was eight.

"You comin', dude?" calls out Tanner, peering down at me from over the upstairs banister.

I stare up at him. "Hopefully," I say, my hard cock still filling my briefs to the max.

His shower is like an enormous, tiled, walk-in closet, and yet we can't seem to give each other any room. I'm all over him, insisting on washing every inch of his muscular body, sticky from the ice cream. I press myself into his back as I lather him up. When the soap reaches his ass crack, I let it slide between his cheeks, teasing his hole for as long as I can get away with. Finally he turns his head and says, "The hell you doin' back there?" to which I only grin, bite my lip, and say, "Makin' sure you're all nice and clean, that's what. Now stand still."

Then it's his turn to be all over me. It's like Tanner's determined to revenge-soap me after the fun I just had with him, judging by the vigorous (and pleasantly thorough) way he washes every fold and crease and curve of my body. I feel so invaded and I love every second of it.

He takes the most time on my cock, but not with the soap. "What's that?" I ask, my voice echoing everywhere as I watch him pull a bottle of something off the metal shelf on the wall. "Heaven in a bottle," he answers as he carelessly squirts a happy helping into his palm. "Hope you're ready for what I'm about to do to you."

His fingers caress my sensitive, desperate cock, which has been rock hard throughout this entire soapy, sudsy showering experience. The lotion in his big hands makes everything so slippery and perfect as he rubs my cock and massages it everywhere. He works my balls and even reaches behind to work his fingers between my butt cheeks. I can't help but lean against him, short of breath, and moan as he rubs and grinds into all my most sensitive spots. His hands are incredibly skillful and know exactly what to do with me.

Then he focuses all his attention on my cock. I think he's just cleaning it for a bit, but when his speed and strength doesn't let up in the least, I realize I'm in it for the long haul.

He stares at me hard in the face as he works my cock below, twisting and pulling and massaging in all the right ways. He has me close in seconds.

"*Oh, God ...*" I moan, my eyes rocking back.

"Better not blow on my hands," he warns me. "Not after we just got all clean."

"*Fuck ... Please ...*" I'm already so close. He's working me relentlessly and won't stop to give me even a second's worth of reprieve.

And after all the build-up and horniness tonight ...

"Not until I say," Tanner demands.

I'm squirming, helpless to get away from him, unable to stop his endless, ruthless tormenting of my slippery, rock hard, edge-of-orgasm cock. I press against him, gripping the thick, firm meat of his shoulders as the slippery sound of his hand working my meat fills the shower.

I clench my eyes, desperate for permission.

"Look at me."

I flip my eyes open. His rich brown smolder is on me, hypnotizing me, owning me.

"I want you looking at me when you blow," he says.

"Tanner ..."

"Not yet."

I'm struggling with every muscle I have. My cock and body is no competition to the expert, tireless, muscular work of his big bicep as he jerks me off without end. I am completely at his whim, naked and slick and desperate for Tanner. I'm clawing into his muscles, my toes clenched, my arms tensed, my teeth gnashed together, and my eyes locked onto his with the desperation of someone at the very end of a long, long path toward ecstasy.

Then, in stark contrast to the relentless pull and jerk of his hand below, he softly brings his lips to mine. It's a caress of mouths. I feel his jaw working as he twists his lips on mine, kissing and nibbling on me.

In a tuft of hot breath to my face, he says, "*Now,*" just before pressing his lips to mine once again.

And with our mouths attached in the most tender kiss I've ever known, I shoot my load. It's endless. Just when I think I've finished, I shoot some more. He doesn't stop jerking me, even after I feel empty.

And then I shoot even more.

I collapse against his body, electric shocks ringing through every nerve and muscle in me. I'm deflated in an instant and soaring through a cloud of otherworldly pleasure. My first instinct is to laugh, tickled by the joy that's rocketing through me. My next instinct is to cry, because I've never felt anything more pleasurable in my whole life.

Then I lift my lips back to Tanner without opening my eyes, knowing exactly where they are. It's like returning home when our mouths lock, and everything is perfectly, simply, exactly where and how it ought to be.

The shower continues to drum on our backs and sides, and it's in that position that we remain for half an eternity, cradled in each other's slippery arms.

Bliss.

Twenty minutes later after we've dried off, we slip into his bed side-by-side, spent. The sound of *Avatar* still playing in the living room echoes up to us, likely somewhere at the end of the movie. His sheets are silky smooth—or maybe it's just his skin and mine—and I let him cuddle up to me, being the big spoon.

His arm goes around my waist, and he pulls me in tightly to his body. I've never felt more at peace.

I've never felt safer.

"Good night, bro," he says in my ear, and I feel the smile of his lips against it.

"Night, Tan," I whisper back.

I want this feeling to last forever.

CHAPTER 8

TANNER

When I open my eyes, Billy isn't there.

I sit up in the bed, alarmed. Then, the faint smell of bacon reaches my nostrils. I inhale deeply, a big, sleepy smile finding my face.

I put on a fresh pair of red boxer-briefs that have big white hearts and black kissy-lips all over them, then head out of the room. From over the banister, I hear a spatula scraping metal in the kitchen. I pad down the stairs.

Billy is facing the stove wearing only his jeans, which are sagging slightly and showing off his cute butt, a pinch of his crack visible. He's humming to himself as he uses tongs to pull bacon off of a large pan and put it on a spread of paper towels. I see containers on the counter, including my mama's brown sugar, maple syrup, and a few other spices that I can't identify.

For a while, I just lean against the counter opposite of him and watch Billy work. This is where he belongs. This is where Billy feels the most comfortable, turning what would have otherwise been a totally boring breakfast into something memorable and savory.

Deciding I've had enough, I waltz right up behind him and spank his ass so hard, he nearly hops a foot in the air.

"The fuck!" he shouts out, nearly dropping the pan of eggs he's got in his hand.

The incredulous look on his face makes me bend over in

laughter. "Sorry!" I finally manage to get out as I calm down from the hilarity. "It was totally worth it. You got a sweet ass, Billy."

He shakes his head, then says, "Yeah, and you got a sweet-ass kitchen. I figured I'd ..." He lifts the pan of eggs and nods at the flat pan of bacon. "It's the least I can do."

"No one's ever made me breakfast before," I remark lightly.

I snort. "Like hell anyone hasn't. Your sweet ma. Your paid housekeeper. Maybe a granny or two."

"But no dudes ever have."

He presses his lips together, considering that as he continues to scramble up the eggs. Then he tilts his head and quirks an eyebrow. "You ... ever had any?"

I lean on the counter and cross my arms. "Any what?"

"Boyfriends?"

I feel my chest tighten at his question. I was kinda hoping we wouldn't go there yet, for fear that he'll freak out when he learns how much of a *virgin* I am to all of this. I'm desperate to ensure that nothing at all ruins the good thing we had going on last night.

But I have to be honest. It's the only way he's going to trust me. "No."

His pan-scraping stops. "No?" he asks the pan.

"Nope," I confirm. "None at all. No boyfriends." My eyes linger on his face expectantly.

"Not even at college?"

"No." *Honesty, Tanner. Honesty.* "I mean, there *were* gay guys there, but I was too chicken shit to approach any."

"Hmm."

I can't stop staring at the side of his face. Suddenly, there's worry snaking its way through my body. My toes and fingers prickle with anticipation. *Does he not believe me? I'm telling the truth, but does he doubt it?*

"I hope that doesn't freak you out," I decide to say, giving him more. "I've never ... done anything with a guy before. I'm sorry, Billy. This is all new to me."

He sets the pan down gently and turns to face me. His eyes are soft, yet wary.

I go on. "Truth is, I couldn't even bear to admit the truth to myself until I left this town. It took getting away from my family and bein' on my own at college to ... find myself, I guess."

"How'd you find yourself?" he asks.

I sigh, staring at the floor. "Well, I guess it ... kinda started with the dreams."

"Dreams ...?"

"I even had them in high school. I dreamed of one of my teammates in the locker room. We didn't even do anything sexual in the dreams I had. It was, like, we were just getting geared up together, but it was only us. Me and him. And I couldn't stop looking at his body. I think I was always ... looking. I just didn't know what it meant."

"Nothing sexual at all?" he asks, almost disbelieving. "You had dreams of staring at your buddies in the locker room, and—"

"Yeah," I say, cutting him off with a dry chuckle. "I told you, it ain't gonna make much sense, but it's the truth. I played the role that everyone thought I was. I had the girlfriends and I won the football games and I slapped my buddies on the ass. Then I marched my own ass off to Oklahoma and ... I didn't know anyone. That role I'd been playin' for years, I didn't need it no more. Everyone's so dang different in college, Billy. It's like a whole other world. I felt, like ... *compelled* to be someone else. I didn't realize that that someone else was ... *me*."

Billy's arms are crossed too as he listens, hanging on my every word. I appreciate his attention to my story so much, it stirs me up inside. I haven't been able to talk to anyone about this. These thoughts have never left the safe, private confines of my own head, which has been so damn cluttered since I went off to college.

"Anyway, you're the first guy I've ever gotten to ... *express* myself with," I finish. "I hope I didn't do anything last night to overstep. I really care about you, Billy."

"No," he says right away, his voice light. "You didn't do nothin' wrong, Tanner. I ... I actually worried the same thing, if I'm being honest," he admits with a shrug. "I was worried *I'd* overstepped and ... took advantage of you or somethin'."

Now it's my turn to laugh, feeling the weight on my shoulders lighten at once. "I don't think invitin' you to my bed after all that happened is an indication of me feeling 'taken advantage of' at all. Dude, I loved every second of it. What we did. What you did to me. What I did to you."

Billy uncrosses his arms and returns his attention to the pan for a short moment, thoughts clearly brewing in his mind. "Well," he finally says, "I guess that makes two of us, don't it?"

I come up to his side, chasing an impulse. He stops fussing with the pan and looks up at me. It's on those soft, sweet lips of his that I plant a kiss. This time, neither of us are chugging bottles of lame-ass beer. Neither of us are feeling the lightning bolt of horniness in our guts.

And I kissed a dude on the lips in the broad daylight of morning.

It isn't a fantasy. It isn't some made-up scene I've stored in my spank bank. This is real. He is real.

And I fuckin' kissed him.

"What about you?" I prompt him, standing so close that I feel the warmth of his body.

He lifts his gaze. "Me?"

"Yeah, you. Have you been ..." I'm not sure how to ask it. "Have you been, like, datin' anyone?"

Billy lets out a tuft of breath through his nose. "With my busy-ass six-day-a-week schedule I got? Seven, if you count the produce drives I take sometimes on Sundays? I don't got time for any *datin'*."

"Really? All these years?"

"Haven't dated a single person," he confirms. "Not in high school. Not after, either. So ..." He bites the inside of his cheek as he squints at me. "So what I'm sayin' is, this is all a bit ... new for me, too."

It's amazing, how one piece of information can quite suddenly put you completely at ease.

We're both in this together, I realize with overwhelming relief. *It's new for him, too. He's scared and nervous, just like I am. We're walking the tightrope blind, the both of us.*

"Makin' breakfast sure ain't new for ya," I note, trying to lighten the mood.

He chuckles. "Well, hope you're hungry, because it's about ready."

"Starved."

Five minutes later, we're seated at the formal dining table by the kitchen eating plates of bacon and eggs. This isn't just any old bacon, though. Billy oven-baked it with maple syrup and brown sugar, sweetening it to nearly dessert-caliber succulence. The eggs are spiced with garlic and herbs, so full of flavor that I literally wonder if I've ever truly tasted an egg before. I'm in awe with the sheer quality of this unassumingly simple breakfast.

"Goddamn, Tucker," I blurt out after my fourth bite. "You need to take over *Biggie's* breakfast menu, too! Shit!"

He smiles, obviously proud of his work, then passes a plate of buttered toast my way. "I'd have made pancakes, but I couldn't find the flour and I didn't want to be diggin' through your ma's cabinets more than I already had to ... to do all of this."

"Nah, man. This is perfect. All of it. Perfect."

Judging from the pink that creeps up his cheeks, he's obviously a bit shy about his amazing talent. *He shouldn't be. This is true talent, to be able to work ingredients like this and make miracles in my mouth.*

"So," he asks suddenly, "have you had sex with girls?"

I stop chewing, my eyes wide. *That's quite a segue.* "You serious?"

"Just curious." He shoves another bite of egg past his lips, chewing innocently as he awaits my answer.

I guess I could be amused by his bluntness. I mean, we did get pretty damn intimate last night, and I really do want to get to know him better. It's important to put it all out there.

"Yep," I answer, my one little word so dang clipped it hardly exists.

"Was that a yes?" he prods.

I smirk. "*Yes.* I have had sex with women."

"In college?"

"A few in my freshman year. First time was when I was sixteen. After I went off to college and ... discovered myself after a few drunken mindless encounters ... I just couldn't keep up the charade anymore. Kept to myself. Haven't had a lick of sex since last fall." A mischievous smile finds my face. "Well, until last night, that is."

Billy's face goes red again, except this time the flush takes him over completely. *God, I love when I make him all red in the cheeks. He's so damn adorable.*

"Does that answer all your questions?" I ask. "Or you got another for me, Billy?"

"How was I?"

I can't fight the smile on my face now. "You? Like ... what we did last night? You're asking me how you were?"

"Never mind." He chuckles once, then chews his food as he stares out the big dining room window.

I watch him for a moment before answering. "I don't know how to say this without sounding ... really fuckin' cheesy. But what we did just filled me up with all these happy thoughts and feelings. It felt better than every girl I ever banged combined. Sorry to put it so bluntly."

"I like the bluntness," he says, his eyes still gazing out the window, but with a hint of a smile on his lips now.

"Also, I still haven't tried your ice cream," I note, "and I'm not lettin' you leave until I do."

Now Billy grins, blushing all over again. He turns back my way finally. "I woke up to two bowls on the counter with melted strawberry scoops inside them," he tells me, then shrugs lightly. "I guess we found a better use for my homemade *cream*."

I snort. I love how we can make each other laugh at the dumbest things. "Bro, after seein' what you can do with breakfast, I wanna taste your sundae for myself. But y'know, maybe in a *bowl.*"

"Sorry, Tanner. It just so happens that my award-winning Football Sundae is a very delicate and precise dish that absolutely *must* be plated on the body of a hot, muscled jock," Billy explains with mock prestige, "and seeing as I don't fit that description ..."

"I'm tasting your *cream* whether it's 'plated' right or not," I shoot back, "and besides, you've already tasted mine, haven't you?"

"Oh, I tasted your cream alright."

"Would you call it a delicacy?" I ask, straight-faced.

Billy's trying not to laugh. "To be clear, we *are* talking about the fact that I ate your cum last night, and we're talking about this over bacon and eggs."

"And toast," I add, wiggling my slice and gnawing a huge bite off of it.

He grins and shakes his head, stabbing a slice of bacon with his fork. He brings it to his sexy mouth, then chews while the grease keeps his lips slick and wet and inviting. It takes everything in me not to brush all this delicious food off the table and tackle him right on top of it. I don't know what in hell I'd do to him, but it'd be something between a kiss and damn near everything else.

Deciding to relax, we get cozy on the couch and turn back on that dang movie we didn't even watch more than ten minutes of before our hands found a different lap other than our own to rest in. We cuddle up right next to each other, my arm thrown around Billy's shoulders as he nestles into my chest, half-sitting in my lap with his legs folded back. Every now and then, he'll give me a sudden kiss. It makes me hard instantly, but I'm able to control myself and ignore the throbbing in my underwear. When he gives me one kiss too many, though, he pays the price of awakening the beast in me, and a good twenty minutes of *Avatar* is ignored completely as I tackle him into the couch with a growl.

My cock hard as bone in my boxer-briefs, I assault his face and push my weight into him, rendering him breathless. The making out between us is feverish and animal. He moans, knowing he's asked for it with all that teasing and kissing and driving me insane.

When the movie's over, we're back in the kitchen and he's fixing us both a Football Sundae, which is what he's decided to officially call it. I feel a certain stroke of pride as I watch him deftly prepare the bowls with meticulous attention to detail, feeling responsible for the name. It's like I'm the muse of his special dessert. My chest puffs up as I cross my arms and lean back on the kitchen island, watching him.

I have to take my time when I eat the sundae. Every bite of his homemade strawberry ice cream is a fucking party in my mouth. I've never truly tasted the essence of a strawberry before. Not like this. Then I have the same experience with the scoop of vanilla, which reminds me of the *apple-dessert-thing* I had that first night I went to his diner, since it did have a scoop of this with it. The hot fudge seals the deal. The richness of his homemade chocolate outdoes any brand name chocolate bar or snack I've ever had. His dessert is not something you can just scarf down. Its taste forces you to enjoy it slowly, eyes closed, savoring every little sensation and prickle of flavor that ignites on your tongue.

"Damn, Billy," I say after I set my spoon into the empty bowl. "You've spoiled me for life. Every sundae I eat from here on out's gonna be boring and tasteless, bro. You've fuckin' ruined me." He smiles brightly, proud of his work, then reaches to take my bowl to the sink. "Hell no," I blurt, startling him. "I want another."

And another's exactly what I get.

When the clock's pushing past noon, we decide to call it a day, since my family's going to be coming home at any minute. "Your mama know you stayed the night with the big bad wolf of Spruce?" I ask when he's dressed and has all his things.

"Ain't nothin' big or bad about you," he says.

"You sure about that?" I ask, grabbing my junk tightly and giving him a tongue-out, open-mouthed grin.

To that, he slings his backpack over his shoulder and comes right up to me, pushing a kiss onto my lips. All the humor drops away and suddenly I have him pinned to the front door, making out with him in a whole new assault of desperate yearning and not knowing where to grab him. I want my hands everywhere on that sexy body of his.

I just can't behave myself around Billy Tucker.

After putting on an old heather grey high school t-shirt and some gym shorts, I take him to my pickup and hop right in. The afternoon sun's beaming down on us as we drive down the country road to town, the warm summer air flapping through the rolled-down windows.

He directs me to his house, which I'm surprised to see is just down the road and around the corner from the diner. When he hops out of the truck, I get one last look at his cute butt in those jeans.

He shuts my door and leans into the window. "Thanks for last night, Tanner," he says, his voice a little sunken.

I lift an eyebrow. "We're gonna do it again, yeah?"

His face brightens up a bit. "We are?"

Billy, you damned adorable fool. You think I'm through with you? "If you're willin' to put up with me again, I want us to hang out as much as possible."

His face flushes so furiously pink that his eyes water. He bites his lip and looks away, fighting a smile.

"You got my number," I remind him, since we traded phones at one point this morning and put our numbers in each other's contact lists. "I ain't lettin' you go easily, Billy Tucker."

"I'll text you," he says evenly, meeting my eyes.

Then with a slap to the side of my truck, he heads to his door and slips inside. With one hand hanging off the top of the steering wheel and the other on the stick shift, I watch him every step of the way.

My heart swells with something warm, something light as helium, something that almost tickles. I'm pretty sure I've never felt this before with anyone. It's scary. It's exciting. It makes me feel sick and makes me feel happy at the same time. It's a taste I'll never find in any kitchen. It's a specific kind of thrill that no amount of touchdowns can grant me.

And I can't get enough of it.

CHAPTER 9
BILLY

If there's a single spare minute in my day, it's spent with Tanner.

When I get a two hour break from the diner midday Monday, since it's slow, I sneak off to catch a movie. Of course, he's waiting for me at the front, leaned against the wall with his ankles crossed and his hands thrust into his pockets. He looks up at me from under a ball cap, then gives me a sly grin. Given the time of day, there's almost no one at the movies to witness us, but we buy our tickets separately anyway, then slip into the theater. I don't even know or care what movie it is we watch, but we sit in the back, sneak kisses, and lean against one another. There's never a moment when one of us isn't touching the other, even if it's just our shoes or shoulders.

Of course we agree on the phone that same night that discretion is key for both of us.

"Are you feelin' like I'm feelin'?" Tanner asks me through the phone. "About ... other people knowing?"

"I think so." I'm lying back on my bed and picking at something on my finger, the phone wedged into my neck as I consider his question. "Honestly, the idea of everyone in town talkin' about us and ... sayin' things ... sorta freaks me out. I mean, the gossips that come through the diner alone ..."

"Exactly, man. We'd never hear the end of it."

"Shit. Mindy would be a nightmare."

"Did she ever hook up with Steven? You told me how she was supposed to see him at the movies ..."

"Dude. Steven's basically whorin' around with all the girls he can. I keep tellin' Mindy to find someone else but she won't listen."

"Can't control our hearts, huh?" he asks rhetorically.

His words carry so much more weight, thinking about how he must have felt all those years dating girls and not knowing what the emptiness in his heart was trying to tell him all along.

Every night that I'm not with Tanner in person is like this: we're on the phone talking about everything and nothing at all.

When I'm at work, I can't stop texting him.

I'm not particularly proud of feeling like the "bad employee" when I sneak to the kitchen between serving customers to read and respond to whatever text Tanner just sent me. I picture him hanging out at the ranch wearing nothing but one of his signature crotch-and-ass-and-thigh-hugging boxer-briefs as well as sunglasses, looking cocky as fuck, while texting me throughout his day. Somehow, I love that image of him.

The excitement within me at work makes me feel like my heart's racing all day. I'm running even while I calmly stroll through the diner filling glasses of sweet tea and water. My insides are galloping as I serve baskets of burgers and fried chicken as well as plates of my pa's spicy meatloaf special. Even Mindy gives me an annoyed look or two when she catches me hiding in the office texting. Now and then, Tanner will send me a silly selfie of himself as he's in his pool, or kicking back on the deck with a dot of suntan lotion on his nose, or tangled up in his sheets with a bad case of bedhead.

One Friday, my pa tells me not to come in until the night shift, so I take the chance to drive out to Tanner's ranch in my ma's car where I join him and his buddies for another round of water volleyball. After knowing how unexpectedly good I was last time, everyone is fighting for me to be on their team. It's a good feeling.

The whole time we play, Tanner sneaks a wink at me here and there. Once when we're on the same team and the ball comes between us, we both go for it and bump shoulders in trying to hit it. We stare into each other's eyes a second too long and I feel my heart drum with desire, causing me to instantly hate the presence of all the other guys. I want to be alone with Tanner and I want to do things to him *now*.

The hunger is real. *And it never dissipates.*

The magic night is Saturday. The magic day is Sunday. When I get off every Saturday night, my stomach turns and thunders with desire. I can't get out of the diner fast enough. His parents make a habit of taking off every weekend to check on their various businesses in the next town over, and they stay at a hotel they apparently own. Tanner's little brother Jimmy either goes with them or spends the night at a friend's house. That leaves us a long, beautiful night and a long and glorious morning to ourselves.

Football Sundaes become our delicacy of choice, so I always bring a container of my homemade ice cream each time I come, plus some new cookie or pastry I've been working on. But we always end up saving the desserts for Sunday morning, since we're much too busy all Saturday night doing ... *other far more important things.*

Things like exploring one another's bodies, sprawled out on his bed in various states of undress.

Things like taking our time with washing one another's backs in the shower—and then washing one another's *fronts*.

Things like seeing how far we can edge each other's pent-up, horned-up, bone-hard cocks until we can't take it anymore and have to explode all over one another.

Late Saturday night, things take a turn for the tender. When both of us have gotten our due relief, we turn into noodles in each other's arms and cuddle up on the couch. Remarkably, we actually *do* get through a whole movie without distracting ourselves with too many kisses.

And the safe, warm, tight sensation of falling asleep in his big strong arms doesn't compare fairly to anything in the world. I'd daresay it's even a more fulfilling sensation than an orgasm itself, the way a tight embrace against his muscled body feels. I know, that's a very bold statement to make after a night with Tanner, but I don't know how else to describe the level of joy in my mind. My heart is set on the notion that I'm the only one he wants. No one else in the world could turn his eye the way I do. I trust him completely.

Sometimes when I lie there at night, I wonder if he thinks the same things about me. Does he trust me? Does he feel as safe and as cherished as I do? I sure hope he does. Tanner deserves someone to make him feel special. I don't really know what this is we have going on. I don't know if we can call ourselves boyfriends, or if it's too soon, or if I'm in too deep and setting myself up for a major heartbreak. We're both so new to this.

It's a tightrope we're both choosing to walk. Let's cross our fingers that if one of us loses our balance, the other will be there to lend a quick and timely hand.

Sundays are a warm hug and a splash of sunshine after our dark Saturday nights of desire. I cook us up some tasty breakfast, and then we sit out by the pool and share a Football Sundae from the same bowl. We do annoying things that I've, for years, made fun of couples doing in the movies. I feed him with my spoon. He feeds me with his, then deliberately misses and gets some fudge on my nose. Then he'll lick it off. Then he'll kiss me, our cold lips touching to seal the cute moment. I'm pretty sure if I was watching this in a movie, I'd roll my eyes hard and take a little bathroom break to let the scene play out. But now I'm in this scene. *This is really happening.*

Now I get it.

I want to star in a hundred lovey-dovey scenes. I want Tanner and I to try out every single one of them. I want to ride in the little lover's boat at the amusement park that takes us through a darkened tunnel of romance. I want to go to the fair with him and share cotton candy. I want to throw the perfect ball, knock over a bottle, and win him a big stuffed Pikachu. I want to raid a playground at three in the morning with him and swing side-by-side, giggling when we go too high and then daring one another to leap off and land in the sand before making out under the pale moonlight.

Tanner is the one I want to do these things with, at long last. After years and years of coldness, I want Tanner to be the one who makes me *thaw*.

Throughout the week between our Saturdays, it's all about the stolen moments, the sneaky visits to the movies or the ranch, the hundreds of back-and-forth texts, and the endless hours at night on the phone. He tells me via text and phone call about the classes he took this past semester and how dumb he felt his freshman year, like everyone was three years more advanced than he was in every damn subject. He mentions a guy who fell asleep and snored through half his Algebra classes, which was as amusing as it was distracting, since no one had the heart to wake him up until the professor slapped a rolled-up newspaper on his desk, which happened at least once a week. He tells me about a Chemistry professor he had who was kinda young and hot, but totally straight, as he would constantly make corny chemistry-related jokes involving his wife and daughters.

I also learn about some of his friends from college, including the two different roommates he's had in the dormitory there. One roomie was named Joe and he kept completely to himself all the time—*and creepily so.* The other, coincidentally, was also named Joe, but he was far more lively. They'd eat lunches together almost daily. He was straight, but he was still hanging on to his girlfriend from high school who went to a different college halfway across the country. All year, Joe suspected his girlfriend was seeing other guys, but he never confirmed it, and the year ended before Tanner learned the truth. The next year, Tanner got his own room, and he and Joe lost touch.

"You think you'd ever tell your ma?" I ask him one evening when we're in the back of a movie theater that only has three other people sitting way in the front—an old couple with a little girl, maybe a granddaughter.

"Shit no," he whispers in reply. "Appearance is everything to her. I bet if I told her, she'd give me the whole you-just-haven't-met-the-right-girl speech. Then she'd proceed to set me up with every damn woman from here to Kansas until one of them stuck."

"Would any of them stick?" I tease him.

"Sure. If one of them's you," he whispers, then laughs. As if second-guessing his joke, his face straightens at once. "Uh, sorry. Was that too much?"

It wasn't. I love how much he's into me. I've never had this level of elation present in my life, ever. "Not at all," I tell his face, illuminated blue by the dim light from the dark scene reflecting off the silver screen. "I'm still tryin' to figure out how you made it work in the bedroom with all those lucky women before. I mean, did you dream of your sweaty, geared-up teammates or what?"

"Sometimes a hole's just a hole."

I gag. "Damn, Tanner. You gotta be so gross about it?"

"Is it hot when I talk like that?"

"No!" I say, laughing despite myself.

The old couple in the front turn around, frowns on their faces. Or at least I *think* they're frowning; it's hard to tell, even if we're just seven or eight rows apart.

I scrunch down in my seat, sucking in my lips. Then, after a sigh, I say, "Saturday can't come soon enough."

"Tell me about it," he mumbles.

After that movie theater tryst, Tanner surprises me by strutting right into the diner on Friday with Kirk and Joel flanking him. He wears shorts and a dark green t-shirt, which has a duck in a jersey on the front carrying a football under its wing. I greet them all like my own friends. They sorta feel like my friends too by now, since we've made a midweek thing of playing water volleyball and chomping down some hotdogs. I even gave a couple of his friends a lesson, showing them the best way to grill dogs. During the whole lunch experience, Tanner keeps shooting me these knowing looks, smugly smirking when his friends aren't looking. I just play coy, despite the excitement bubbling up from inside me.

When I go to the kitchen to help with their orders, Tanner texts me from the table.

TANNER

U look cute today, Tuck.

I smile from ear to ear, then look up through the kitchen window to find Tanner grinning stupidly at me from the table, flashing his teeth and cocking his head, looking all superior and proud of himself. I try to mask my obvious smile with a roll of my eyes. He looks down at his phone and types some more. Then my phone vibrates with another text. I glance down at it.

TANNER

Wanna taste my cream 2morrow nite?

When I look up again, Tanner's pressed two fingers against his lips and he's wiggling his tongue between them. I snort and look away with a shake of my head, then tend to their burgers.

Yeah, Tanner's sort of a big kid at heart, but that face of his drives me nuts. The whole time I'm making their orders, my body decides it's a convenient time to remind me of what Tanner's hands feel like when they're running up and down my slick, sudsy body in the shower. *Great. Just what I need: a boner while I'm trying to make three bacon cheeseburgers with garlic fries.*

When the guys leave, Tanner lingers behind. Since no one's looking, he leans into me and whispers, "Is it tomorrow yet?"

His words send sparks of longing down my body. I hand him a bakery box and whisper back, "I stole away a few new pastries I'm serving on tomorrow's menu. Tell me what you think."

On Saturday morning, I'm at the diner two hours early. My feet move faster than my mind can keep up with for some reason. I randomly giggle when I'm talking to customers, like a psychotic happiness keeps hijacking my brain. I hum to myself while I'm making orders and even find some time to calculate some weekly totals in the office. Mindy asks me twice what the hell new meds I'm on, which makes me laugh rather than sneer. My pa seems to be infected with my mood, as he's taken to whistling to himself in the back as he flips burgers with one hand and reads the paper with the other.

When the diner's closing, I'm almost short of breath, the excitement of heading to Tanner's taking me over so potently. Before I escape, my ma's voice catches me at the door. "Junior?"

I'm clutching the door handle, a second from pulling it open. *So close!* "Yeah, Ma?"

"Before you hop off to Tanner's, can you help me with somethin' on the computer?" she calls from the office.

Mindy's mopping near the booths, and she looks up at me with a quizzical expression, having heard my ma.

"Sure," I call back to her, then ignore a question that Mindy whispers to me as I head to the office.

Ma's gnawing on her lip as she glares at the screen, clicking the mouse irately. "The hell is goin' on with this thing? Is it a virus? Did I piss off Bill Gates?"

I smirk and take over. After a quick visit to the task manager and a few forced-closed windows, the computer is unfrozen. "Just try not to look at so much porn while you're on the clock," I advise her.

She cackles and slaps me on the arm. "Thanks, Junior. Hey, sit down and chat with me."

"Ma, I gotta go."

"Tanner can wait. C'mon. You've been like a fruit fly the past couple weeks, the way you're all buzzin' around." She slaps the chair next to her, a squeaky one from the 70s with a big rip in the cushion. "Talk to me."

"Ain't nothin' much to talk about," I say tiredly. "I've had a long day, Ma. I just wanna kick back."

"With your new best friend Tanner, right?"

"Ma ..."

"Are you two ... seein' each other?"

I was about to say something, but now all the words are bottlenecked in my throat by her question. My face flushes instantly from the base of my neck to the top of my forehead. I'm paralyzed.

"I'm not meanin' to pry," she goes on, oblivious, "but please do tell me everything."

"We're ... just f-friends," I finally manage to get out, despite the annoying stutter. "Can't a guy just hang out with another guy and it not be gay?"

"Y'know, I always had a sneaking suspicion about that boy ..."

"*Ma*," I hiss at her, praying that Mindy is back to being busy with her mopping and isn't hearing any of this. "There ain't a dang thing happenin' between Tanner and I besides two dudes chillin' with each other."

And kissing. And fondling. And cock-gargling. And cream-licking.

And shower-taking.

And bed-sheet-wrestling.

"Aaalright," she sings in her *totally-don't-believe-you* voice. "Tell Nadine I said hi again, will ya?"

"She's out of town."

Why did I say that?? My ma looks up at me, her eyes growing double. "You ain't goin' out to that ranch to smoke crack, are you?"

I sigh and stare at her with half-lidded eyes. "Really, Ma? You know me better. Besides, back in the 70s, you and Pa probably smoked more weed combined than the whole populace of Spruce."

"So you two are just hangin' out then? Really?"

"Really."

"And if somethin' *interesting* was goin' on between the pair a' you, you'd let me know?—if for any other reason than to just let me have something delicious and juicy to hold over Nadine Strong's head?"

"You're a piece of work, Ma," I say, then give her a kiss on the cheek and head for the door, determined to hop out while the getting's good.

"I'm keepin' my phone on all night!" she calls out after me. "You text me if you hit trouble, Junior! Or if you're stayin' over again!"

Of course she'd shout out that last part as I cross back through the diner. Mindy's leaning on her mop with an eyebrow quirked. "Stayin' over at the Strong Ranch?" she asks, her face flat.

For some reason, I can handle Mindy a hundred times easier than my ma. "His sound system is killer," I tell her, rationalizing my hanging out with Tanner in one easy, spontaneous instant.

"We watched *Avatar* a few weekends ago. It was the best cinematic experience I've ever had."

Yeah. Complete with a blowjob and muscled-jock-groping to boot. You can say that again, self.

She studies me dubiously for a minute. "Y'know what the benefit of bein' a girl in this town is?"

I blink. Here I am, once again caught with my palm on the door handle and being prevented from heading off to Tanner Strong's ranch by yet another damned question. "What's that?"

"Other girls trust you with their secrets."

"Well, just so happens, I ain't much interested in your secrets."

"Yeah? Not even the one about how Tanner couldn't get it up for Lindsay Randall on prom night? Or how he complained about a headache the next three times she tried to get in bed with him just before he dumped her?"

Despite the tension building in my stomach—which is now confused with the excitement that was already living there—I give Mindy a blasé shrug. "So? Maybe he wasn't interested in her no more and didn't know how to tell her. Sounds like the classic 'relationship's over but only one of us knows' situation."

"Or maybe he just wasn't interested in havin' a girl at all," she says with a smug smirk and a tilt of her head. "Your ma ain't the only one with her suspicions."

"Thanks for the advice, Mindy, if that's what you'd even call it. I'm late. See you Monday."

"It ain't advice," she replies, crossing her arms with her mop hugged within them. "It's a warning. Hopefully he don't go through boys the same way he went through girls."

Mindy and my ma both are just determined to throw a big ol' dark cloud over my Saturday night.

But nothing's gonna touch the feeling of elation I'll experience when I bust through the door of Tanner's house. Instead of playing the denial card all the time, I figure it might be more believable for me to play with her, being my sorta-friend and all.

"Well, shit," I say to her in a singsong, teasing voice. "Wouldn't I be the luckiest damn guy in town if someone like Tanner Strong had it in for me?"

Mindy finally breaks a smile and shakes her head, returning her attention to mopping the floor.

Success!

At long last, I push through the door of the diner—then realize I forgot the ice cream. With a huff, I swing back into the kitchen, grab my backpack and fill it, then hop out the door and make the quick walk home to get cleaned up and change. After the first couple of Saturday nights, I decided to not make Tanner come and pick me up, opting to borrow my ma's car and take myself.

When I make it down the long, dark country roads—*Tanner wasn't kidding; it's scary as shit driving alone out here in the pitch black*—I pull to a stop in front of his house and hop out of my car, the gravel crunching beneath my shoes as I position myself in front of the driver's side mirror and give my hair and face one last check. When I'm absolutely sure that I'm at least halfway (let's be realistic, here) up to par with the totally gorgeous, sexy, ripped, college-jock-wet-dream that's beyond those doors, I spin on my heels and head for the house.

Tanner opens the door before I even get to knock, grabs me in a tight and bodily hold, then plants his lips all over my face. He greets me like a dang dog and I love every slobbering second of it.

"Boy, am I seriously starved for some grade-A Billy Tucker meat," he growls.

I laugh into his lips, then reach between his thighs to grab some grade-A meat of my own—encased in his tight, crotch-hugging jeans—and give him a full-fisted squeeze. "You're tellin' me," I grunt, earning a gravelly moan from Tanner before the door slams shut at my back.

CHAPTER 10
TANNER

Kicking back on the deck sipping a lemonade, I tap my phone and find Billy's latest message: a cute selfie of him pointing at a customer who's fallen asleep at one of his tables, mouth agape and a string of drool to his chest.

I snort and shake my head, grinning. As I start to type my response, there's a tap at the back glass door. I look up to find my mama standing inside with an inch-long red fingernail on the glass, her pencil-thin eyebrows raised expectantly. She beckons me inside with a finger, then disappears.

I pocket my phone into my gym shorts, then swipe my sweaty tank from off the arm of the deck chair and sling it over a shoulder. My legs almost give when I rise from the chair, thanks to my aggressive-ass workout from this morning. *Leg day sucks.*

I slip through the sliding glass door and find my mama at the dining room table in front of a spread of books and folders and a laptop. She's in the same chair where Billy likes to sit when we have breakfast.

"Your friends out there?" she asks without looking, poking her fingernails into a calculator on the table.

"Nope. Just me today," I answer.

"Mmm-hmm." She's wearing her glasses, rested right at the tip of her nose. "Hon, I got a couple a' questions for you. First is, vanilla or strawberry?"

The question freezes my insides. Those are the flavors of

Billy's ice cream that he always brings over. *Were we not careful? I ask myself. Did he leave the ice cream in the freezer from last time he was here? How does she know?*

"Or chocolate. Or pecan. Sorry, hon, but those are the only flavors the Cold Spoon offers in big quantities that would go with the theme for your party," she explains with a slow shake of her head. "C'mon. Suck it up, wipe that scared look off your face, and pick one."

I feel a small sigh of relief inside, but show nothing on my face. "How about we do all of 'em, mama? Make all the guests happy."

"All of 'em. Just like your daddy, you're no dang help," she teases with half a smile. "Weren't you gonna help him organize that shed out by the coop this summer? It's all full of your high school stuff."

"Yeah, of course. Tell me again why we're havin' this party?" I ask, coming up to lean against the back of a dining chair. "Didn't realize it was this weekend already."

"It's not. Your daddy and I have to go out of town this weekend one more time. The party's *next* weekend. Cassie Evans will be there. So will Cissy McPherson *and* Marcy Whitman. The whole tri-*infecta*," she says with a bite.

"I don't think that's the saying."

"I was bein' clever, hon. Get your friends to come, but make sure they bring their girlfriends, too. It makes them behave."

"Kirk's the only one. Joel just had that bad breakup a couple months ago, Harrison's single, and Robby's bangin' every lady in Spruce with a pulse. Shit, he might have run out of them and moved on to the ones without."

"Hon. That's just wrong. Listen, I got another question for ya." She props her elbows up on the table, her hands clasped lazily together with all her fingernails showing. "Your grandma's comin' in, too."

This is my papa's mama we're talking about. I don't know if it's just a mother-in-law's duty to scrutinize and criticize her daughter-in-law's every move, or if it's personal. Either way, the two smile to each other's faces while wielding knives behind their backs. It ain't pretty.

"That's not a question," I remark. "Papa invited her?"

"Yes. But he, like you, has no concept of time. And he didn't know what dang weekend he'd invited her on. And no, of course she refuses to change her plans on visiting." She sighs and slaps her pile of folders. "Not to mention all the work your daddy and I still gotta do for the restaurant in town. Anyway, she's gonna stay in your room, hon."

I gape. "Mama ..."

"Don't complain," she snaps. "I don't wanna hear it."

"But why not Jimmy's room, then?? Also, the guest room is perfectly—"

"*Drafty*," she cuts me off, "and Jimmy's has that weird smell. Remember last time she was here? Oh, we didn't hear the end of it. Besides, your room has that beautiful view of the farm, and we wanna show off how much your daddy's improved everything."

"I guess that makes sense." Truth is, I know that her efforts at impressing grandma are a lot more about *her* than they are about grandma. *Appearances are everything to my mama.*

"By next Thursday, I want you to straighten up your room," she says with a short nod. "Jacky-Ann will change the sheets and clean up your bathroom. It's just for that weekend, hon. You can take the guest room or the couch or the dang chicken coop, I don't care."

Billy and I are really gonna have to make the most of this coming weekend, if it's the last one we're gonna have for a while. I'm already sinking inside, frustrated with all of this business getting in the way of us spending more time together. Of course, I could invite him to the party, no matter what my mama thinks of him or his family, but how would we behave around everyone else? Can we keep ourselves under control the whole time? We'll be insane.

A thought explodes in my mind. My jaw drops and my eyes flash wide. "Mama. Who's caterin'?"

"Cold Spoon for the desserts, I already told you. Of course Nadine's will be doing the food. Plus, I'm gettin'—"

"Cancel it. Cancel all of it. I got just the right place to cater my party. It *is* my party, so you gotta give me what I want, right?"

The look of absolute indignance that crosses her face is both riotously entertaining as well as downright scary. She tilts her head, her whole beehive hairdo moving with it. "Pray tell. What's this place you got in mind?"

My heart gives a jerk of misgiving. I ignore it, pushing myself to be brave. "B-Biggie's," I get out.

She blinks, her forehead wrinkling. "Huh?"

Did she really not hear me? Or is she pretending not to know what I'm talking about? "Biggie's Bites, mama. You know the place."

Her lips part for five seconds before she says anything at all. "You want the *Tucker* family to cater this party?"

I don't want to say she sounds disgusted or repulsed by my choice, but her voice borders too close to either adjective for my liking.

"Yes," I state, standing my ground. "My buddies and I happen to go there pretty often. They serve some killer burgers—"

"*Burgers? For the party??*"

"Pizzas, four kinds of fries, meatloaf, chicken-fried steak with garlic mashed potatoes, veggie fritters, you name it. They're all made from scratch, too. It's all so good, I'm just salivating standin' here talkin' about it."

Her eyes detach as she digests this information, her lips still parted as she slowly shakes her head. I visibly can see her mind trying to work out how Biggie's Bites can possibly fit in to her whole theme and design of my party.

"And," I add, leaning against the table and drawing my mama's mystified gaze back up to me, "they also have a secret weapon beyond their lunch menu. It's probably somethin' even the Evanses and Whitmans don't know about, or wouldn't care to acknowledge."

"Enlighten me," she says as blunt as a hammer.

"Billy makes these desserts that are to *die* for, mama. I can't even begin to describe how high-quality, top-shelf his inventions are."

"Inventions? Hon, you got your head all twisted."

"His creations. His pieces a' heaven. His works of art. You just call it whatever you want. But I think Biggie's should cater my party. I know my friends would love the hell outta that. And I'm sure the Tuckers could use the extra business."

She crosses her thin arms and leans back in her chair. I can't tell if she's scowling or thinking. When she's got her mind set on planning an event, all her expressions look the same.

"He's your friend, huh."

The statement is uttered so blandly, it doesn't sound like a question. Plus, her gaze is averted, staring at the window as she gnaws on the inside of her cheek.

"Yeah," I say. "Billy and I have been ... spendin' time together, sure. But it ain't just a bias. The food speaks for itself, I swear it."

She sighs and shakes herself out of the dark trance she was just in. "I'm gonna have to rethink this whole dang thing now. Burgers? Pizza? Are we doin' a daytime thing, then? Picnic? Deck party? Do I gotta rent awnings and tents now?"

"You're the event-plannin' genius," I say, smiling.

She purses her lips, fighting a smile as she looks up at me. "Oh, you. I'd do damn well anythin' for you, Tanner, and you know it. You and your brother are the most important things in the world to me."

"Bring it in," I tease her, opening my arms and giving her a warm hug.

During that hug, she whispers in my ear. "Your ass is gonna owe me for messin' up all my plans, boy."

"Noted," I mutter back, inspiring her to smile.

CHAPTER 11
BILLY

This Saturday feels different. We don't assault each other with our usual tackle-to-the-floor routine when I first show up; we just hug tight and kiss on the lips. When we're on the couch watching something on Netflix, neither of us make a move to grope or get rough with one another; we just cuddle with his arm around me, holding me close. Everything is twenty times more tender. Every little act of affection is slow and sweet. We are both *way* too aware that we don't have next weekend to spend together, and that's a problem.

"I wish we didn't have to sneak off on just Saturdays," I murmur, playing with a loose thread coming from the trim of the tank he's wearing. "Would be nice to—"

"I know," he cuts me off, then sighs. "I wish it wasn't such a big deal, y'know? Like, can't we just be ourselves and do our thing and no one gives a shit either way what we're doin'? No one cares what Kirk's doin' with Bonnie. You realize we'd be movie of the week if people found out about us, right?"

"Movie of the month, more like."

And though I agree on principle with him, it still bugs me that this is even an issue. If I'm being perfectly honest, I think I could put up with the limelight if it meant that I didn't have to run around hiding all the time with Tanner. Maybe I'd even enjoy it in some sick way.

"But the gossips would get over it eventually no matter how

much they talk about it," I point out, "Right?"

Tanner's jaw tightens up as he stares at the TV. He doesn't answer. I feel his body getting all tense from the subject.

His silence makes my thoughts board a different train. Is he embarrassed of me? I might not question whether or not he's into me, since that much is obvious by our clear and mutual behavior behind closed doors, but is a part of him ashamed about us? Does it compromise his carefully crafted, lifelong reputation? Will his buddies not get it?

Or is it that the thrill of this arrangement is the main attraction to him? Is it only hot *because* we have to sneak around? Maybe the idea of "coming out" and doing this in the open is boring to him. Maybe it'll sterilize all the heat and crackling sparks between us.

Maybe it's why neither of us are saying the L word.

Or the "boyfriend" word.

I'm such an idiot.

"Somethin' wrong?"

I flinch and turn to him. "No. Nothing," I blurt out too quickly.

He frowns. "You pulled away from me."

I glance at the few inches that have come between us. God forbid there's a few inches between us on the couch. "Oh. I was thinking ... I was thinking we could have a little snack or somethin'."

His frown doesn't go away as he studies me. "Dude, somethin' is up with you."

I sigh and push myself off of the couch. "Alright. I'll make *myself* a sundae, then."

Before I make it to the kitchen, he's on his feet and his voice is raised. "Billy, c'mon. What the hell's up with ya?"

I stop at the counter, my back to him since I don't like the tense, fight-picking look on his face. "Tanner, what're we doin' all this for?"

"All *what* for?"

"Playin' house every Saturday. Actin' like we have any business bein' a real couple when all of this is just ... fuckin' pretend."

"There ain't nothin' *pretend* about this," he spits back.

Chills rush down my arms, standing all the little hairs up. It turns my stomach to hear Tanner's angry voice for the first time, especially after weeks of nothing but bliss and sweetness. I feel sick in an instant, desperate to rush out of the door and race home where everything is safe and comfortable and back to normal.

"The second I leave tomorrow," I tell him, still facing away, "I'm back to bein' just the dude from the diner."

"C'mon. My friends ain't idiots. They see me invitin' you over all the time. They see me pushin' them to go to the diner with me. Hell, I got my mama to boot her fancy caterer because I wanted the deliciously talented Billy Tucker at my party next weekend. I don't hide it. Every damn person in my life's gotta know you're more than just 'that dude from the diner' to me."

"But do they know how *much* more? And really," I say, finally turning to face him, "how much more *am* I? Is this just ... two guys havin' booty calls?"

His face, I'm both relieved and frustrated to say, is just as gorgeous and hot when he's upset as it is when he's perfectly calm. He even looks *more* sexy, which is annoying to admit, considering I'm trying to keep myself focused. I've had these thoughts for a while, but never felt struck enough by any situation to voice them. I guess the time has found me.

"You know the answer to that damn question without me givin' it," he answers tersely, his eyes half-lidded and his posture stiff as steel.

"Then say it."

He crosses his arms, takes a deep breath in, then lets it all out as he shakes his head.

"Billy. You and I know what we are. We feel it in our bodies. We think about each other all the time. Why do we gotta go and state whatever it is that ... *this* is?"

"Maybe for the same reason that you can't seem to call yourself *gay*."

His face wrinkles right up. "When the hell did I ever imply that? You think this is some kinda self-hatin' gay thing or somethin'? I know what I am. I ain't afraid of it."

"Then ... *say* ... it."

Tanner's jaw tightens again. I'm learning a whole lot really quickly about how Tanner's face changes when he's angry or bothered.

He uncrosses his arms and comes up to the counter, a foot or so between us. He breathes heavily, each breath cascading down my front.

"I'll tell you some things, Billy Tucker."

"Go right ahead."

"These are facts. *Facts.* Not just little words I'm puttin' together to untie your dang panty-wad and *appease* you. Got it?"

I narrow my eyes. "Got it."

"Billy. I'm fuckin' crazy for you."

The words knock the wind right out of me. I only just a minute ago told myself that I knew how he felt about me, but to hear it in words—*and to hear it in his voice*—is not something I was at all prepared for. My lips part, suddenly unable to close.

"That's fact number one," he adds in a quieter voice. "Fact number two is: I'm dead sure that if the hottest girl in Spruce knocked on that door and wanted my nuts, I'd turn her away on account of yours."

"On account of ... *my* nuts?" I ask quietly, quirking an eyebrow.

"Yep."

"Just makin' sure I heard that right."

"Billy, you gotta be blunt with me. Is it all the secrecy and hiding that's been botherin' you? Or is it somethin' between us? Because I know like hell that these Saturday nights are the damned best nights I've ever had my whole life. And I've scored game-winnin' touchdowns and was voted Prom King twice."

"I remember that," I say, staring at his chest while he speaks, feeling a pinch of pride from his words. "The Prom King thing."

"So what is it? What's got you actin' like this?"

I cross my arms and lean my back into the counter, biting the inside of my cheek for a bit before I answer. "Maybe I'm just ... feelin' insecure. Like sure, you'd turn down a girl. But what if I'm just your gateway to really livin' a life? What if you're only into me ... because I'm convenient? Because I'm *here*? What'll happen when you go back to college and—"

"Whoa, slow down there, boy," he says, putting up a hand. "I got about one month before I head up there. A shit lot can happen in a month."

"I know." I slap a hand to my face and wipe it over my eyes, nose, and mouth. *I'm being unfair. I'm manipulating him into saying what I want to hear.* "I'm bein' dumb about this," I finally get out. "Shit. I don't need you to tell me you're gay. Fuck. It's just a word. It don't change what you're into either way."

"But it bothers you 'cause we hide it?" he fishes.

"Maybe not even that." I sigh. All of my anger falls to pieces in seconds. I don't even know what I was so pissed about anymore. "Hell. Maybe it's better we keep everyone in Spruce the heck outta this. It really ain't none of their business. I don't need others to know about us ... to make this real. It *is* real. You said it yourself. Maybe it's better for us to ... stay in the closet."

"Shit, is that what we're doin'?" Tanner grimaces and gives a big, demonstrative shiver. "Never saw it that way, to be honest. Sounds horrible, sayin' it out loud like that."

"I just ... I just needed to hear that you're not ashamed of me or nothin'," I finally admit, my eyes closing and my face beginning to burn.

I hear him sputter a few times incredulously. "Really, Billy? You think I'd be ashamed of you?"

My eyes are still closed. I shake my head, unable to answer him.

He comes closer to me. Then I feel his warmth against my arms.

I open my eyes and look up. He's standing right in front of me, leaning into me with his big hands braced against the counter on either side of my body, trapping me in place.

"Billy, I want you to be mine," he says, "because damn it, my heart's all yours, and there ain't a thing I can do about it."

That rush of exhilaration I felt when he first kissed me on the couch, weeks ago.

That stroke of electricity that coursed through my body at his first touch.

That fire that was set the day he looked into my eyes.

It's back. It's what I'm feeling right now. It's exploding within me and I'm helpless to calm it.

"So tell me," he says, his voice low and gravelly. "Do you wanna be my boyfriend, Billy Tucker?"

CHAPTER 12

TANNER

My heart is slamming all over the place inside my ribcage. I'm putting on this big show of being the strong guy—*pun intended*—and trying to sort out Billy's feelings and make him know how much I want him, but inside, I'm terrified that I'm laying my neck out too far, that he's gonna decide all of this is too much to handle, and head out the door. He could break my heart with a word.

Instead, he kisses me.

And kisses me.

And then he's pushing against me so hard, the two of us back away from the counter, his hands clinging to my body and my arms wrapping around him.

His breath beats against my face.

I tumble to the floor.

He's on top of me and he's pulling off my clothes. My tank slips off so fast, it's like I was never wearing it. As he tugs on my shorts, I'm unbuttoning his shirt blindly, our mouths attached by our wet, wrestling lips.

We break apart for one moment. "I take that as a yes," I manage to say, out of breath.

"Can we make it official?" he asks, one of his hands sliding down my body and coming to a firm, almost-too-hard grip of my balls. I gasp in response. "I wanna fuck you so bad, Tanner."

My eyes flash. I never considered going all the way. We've had so much fun doing every other thing there is to do in the bedroom. "Are you serious?"

"So, so bad." The look on his face is desperate. His lips hang open, gleaming and wet in the dim lighting. His eyebrows are pulled together slightly, as if he's in pain. *Longing is a kind of pain.* "I even brought condoms."

I gape. "Damn, boy. You're prepared."

"And strawberry-flavored lube."

I break half a smile. "Ain't no one gonna be tastin' it if it's goin' where I think it's goin'."

He squeezes my balls, shutting me right up, and then his hand slides further down, slipping right between my legs and my ass cheeks. A finger of his teases the outside of my hole, which he finds right away.

I can't move. I don't know whether to be scared or to be excited. My heart's drumming so fast, I feel like I'm racing toward the end zone. I know that's kind of a corny comparison, but it's the first thing I see: an end zone toward which I'm racing with a football in my grip.

And a naked Billy awaits me, sauce pan in one hand, a tube of strawberry lube in the other.

I'm gonna have to shelve that bizarrely hot dream for another time. "I ain't never—"

"Neither have I," he murmurs. "We're gonna have to coach each other."

One look in his cute hazel eyes, and my mind is set. "Go get your lube, boy."

He's off me in seconds. I get up from the floor to watch Billy's cute bare butt bounce as he hops to the couch and pulls open his backpack with such force, I hear a thread or two pop. After a quick rummaging, he's back with condoms and an unassuming white triangular tube with a bright red strawberry on it.

"Get your butt up to my room," I order him.

He lifts an eyebrow, amused. "Yeah? Toppin' from the bottom, are we?"

I give his ass a big, full-handed swat, causing him to yelp out and get moving. I grin, ready to try this. I never even fantasize about doing this, but now it's all I want to do, and he's the only person in the whole damn world I want to do it with.

And we're about to.

All I hear is my own damn pulse.

In my bedroom, Billy turns on the lamp by the bed. I hear the pop of a lid, and then a snapping shut of it. He looks over his shoulder, catching me looking at his ass. "On the bed, face down," he tells me. "Legs apart."

Damn, he's hot when he orders me around. "Yes, sir," I say with an amused smirk and a touch of sarcasm.

I crawl onto the bed. I keep myself facing away with my ass towards him, on all fours, knees and palms digging into the soft sheets. My legs are apart, my cock and balls dangling between them.

After a time of me just chilling here, I finally look over my shoulder, face wrinkled. "Uh, now what?"

"I ... want to look at you," he says, his voice suddenly quiet. "Every ... inch ... of you. Naked. At my ... *whim.*"

He seems almost out of breath with excitement. The way he's losing his composure—just by seeing me in this exposed, naked, leg-spread position on my bed—turns me on so much. I feel my cock getting hard, pointing upward to my abs.

"You ready to saddle up, boy?" I ask with a little grin, egging him on.

After one last second of hesitation, he must find his courage, because he climbs onto the bed behind me. I feel his hand slowly glide over my ass. Just the sensation of his skin against mine sends shivers of desire down my body.

I have no idea what he plans to do. The anticipation of getting to experience whatever he has in mind is almost too much to take. My nerves and senses are stimulated to their maximum.

Nope. No, they weren't. I was dead wrong. A lubed-up finger finds my hole. It's cold, but I don't flinch; I close my eyes and focus on every little slick movement of Billy's finger. He lets it run in tiny circles around my hole, activating every possible nerve ending there is to wake up down there. I'm excruciatingly sensitive in seconds.

If I'm feeling so much pleasure already without him even touching my cock yet, how am I gonna last when he puts something bigger inside me?

Bigger. *Fuck.* I just pictured him behind me with his cock at my hole, pumping it in and out of me. I feel my heart catch in my throat, instantly overly excited.

Calm, boy. Don't anticipate it. Live in the now. Experience every moment as he gives it to you. And for fuck's sake, Tanner, tell him what he's doing to you. "Billy ..."

"You have the most perfect ass."

"I'm, like ... really trustin' you here," I tell him.

"How's it feel?"

I let out a moan. "I'm fuckin' high as the stars, man. Don't stop whatever it is you're doin'."

"You ... are *so* hard," he observes.

"I haven't blown a load in days," I confess.

I hear him chuckle lightly. It almost sounds evil. "Oh? Been savin' all that up for me, huh?"

His words make me shiver with anticipation. I wasn't expecting this dynamic to happen between us tonight, but I'm so horny, and he's hitting just the right spot with his words—*and that evil finger*. "All for you."

"Boy, this is gonna be torture for you," he teases.

I turn my head slightly, trying to catch his gaze over my shoulder. "What do you mean?"

"The second I enter you," he says, "you're gonna want to explode. Hell, you might even spill all over the sheets just from my finger entering you."

"You're ... *driving me nuts*, Billy."

"I want to try something," he says suddenly.

I'm about to ask him what, but his finger moves away from my hole. I swallow hard, my chest tightened up with anticipation.

Then something else takes the place of his finger.

It's his tongue.

Oh my God.

I feel his face press into my ass. My cock jumps, the tip of it going wet in an instant. *I'm already leaking.* I can't even breathe, my eyes rocked back as I feel his tongue gently, slowly, cruelly licking over my hole. *Holy shit.* I've never felt so tickled and so turned on and so horny all at once.

And then he pushes his face deeper.

His tongue pushes in.

Oh. My. God.

"B-B-Billy ..." I hiss out, short of breath. *What is this boy doing to me??* "Oh my fuckin' Lord ..."

His hands grip my ass, one at each cheek, and I feel him massaging them as he continues to lap at my ass and push himself as deeply into it as possible. My cheeks must be engulfing his whole face. I wish my whole room was made of mirrors so I could see what he looks like back there, his face stuffed in my big jock ass.

Yeah, I'll call it my big jock ass. Don't judge me. I'm feeling electrical surges crackling everywhere in my body, my stomach is trying to teach itself how to do double back handsprings, and I'm literally living out a fantasy I've only seen in porn.

Suddenly, he starts to turn more aggressive. This is not good news for my cock, which only grows harder in response. I feel like I could blow at any second, yet I'm always held at bay somehow. It's like the sensation of his tongue in my ass is just enough to press me against the edge of imminent orgasm, yet not enough to get me *over* that edge. I'm suspended in a state of utter bliss and sexual torture. I desperately crave relief equally as much as I crave for this feeling to never, ever end.

The more he works me, the crazier I get. I start to make sounds. *I'm making sounds like they do in porn.* His hands start to do this thing where they squeeze my ass, then slide down my thighs, almost massaging them along the way, then racing back up to my cheeks.

My hole is so wet that I feel the slickness each time he pulls away for half a second of breath. He's suffocating himself with my ass, drunk on it. *He's in heaven back there.*

When he pulls away, I can still feel his tongue.

"How'd ... that ... feel?" he asks, breathing hard between each word.

But I don't get a chance to answer. His finger is back at my hole, and this time, the tip of it slips inside.

My body tenses, first with my thighs, and then with my ass cheeks themselves. It's so sensitive that it's damn near ticklish. There's so much swimming of emotions in my belly right now, I feel like an aquarium.

"Relax," he coaxes me, his free hand gently running up and down my side. "Relax, babe."

Babe? "Did you just call me babe?" I ask, my body relaxing a bit as I fight a laugh.

His finger slips in more.

I gasp. My eyes stretch open wide. I can't believe what I'm feeling right now. I never knew sex could be like this. I guess I just never quite dreamed this deeply. No special experience with my right hand in the privacy of my room can replicate the amount of head-spinning ecstasy I find myself caught in right now.

"I can't wait to get inside you," he whispers.

"I don't know if ... if I can handle you," I finally say, my eyes rocking back as his finger gently pulls halfway out, then sliding back in deeper—in, out, in, out, in. "This is too much. I'm going crazy. Oh, God."

I already feel my cock dripping on the sheets.

"Tanner ..."

If he touches my cock at all, I'll blow. I should warn him. I might even blow with his fingers in my ass.

"Tanner ..."

"Yeah?" I moan.

"In case you were wondering," he says, "your ass ... tastes like strawberries."

I grin. Billy has such a way with putting me at ease. *He has to know you're as scared as you are excited. Fuck, this boy really cares about me.* "That's the lube ... *babe.*"

"Were you serious about wanting to be boyfriends?"

His fingers twist in my ass, sending a wave of pleasure through me. I suck in air, holding my breath as my cock bobs desperately. I hold back from letting go, not letting myself have another breath until I'm in control again.

"*Fuck, that was close,*" I whisper. "Billy, you better get to the next step before I—"

"Your pre-cum is dripping like *crazy,*" he says. "Am I turning you on or somethin'?" he asks innocently. "You want me to do somethin' about it, babe?"

Now he's using the "babe" word deliberately to egg me on. "Yeah, I do."

"And what's that, babe?" He leans in a bit, his body pressing against me as his mouth gets closer to my ear. "What do you want me to do to you ... babe?"

I bare my teeth and peer back at him. "Fuck me."

He lifts an eyebrow superiorly. "Do what now? You gotta be really ..." He twists his fingers. "... *really* ..." He twists them again. "... *specific.*"

This boy is gonna make a grown man cry. "I want you to pull those fingers out and put your cock inside me. I want you to fuck me. *Fuck me, Billy Tucker.*"

He grins, his whole face flushed with excitement, and then I feel his fingers slip out of me. The absence of all the stimulation makes me crave him worse.

I'm afraid. Is the real thing going to hurt? I'm so turned on. Is he going to feel so tight in my ass that I spill all over the sheets the second he's inside me?

I need him in my ass right now.

I hear the crinkle of a condom wrapper, then the unmistakable pinch and smacking of rubber. Feeling smart, I decide to sass him a bit. "Did you get strawberry-flavored condoms, too?"

"Nah. Spermicide. Supposed to be safe or somethin'."

I frown. "That's, like, to prevent pregnancies."

"I didn't realize what I was grabbin'. I've never bought condoms before."

"Oh, but you pick top-of-the-line strawberry-flavored lube in a pinch, huh?"

"Keep sassin' me," he warns, "but you better remind yourself that *you're* the one who's about to get his beefy ass reamed by his boyfriend."

I'm thrust back into our tender moment downstairs with that one word. *Boyfriend.* My heart drums excitedly and my mouth parts in half a smile.

I hear the pop of the tube of lube, and then the snap of it closing. Soon, the tip of his cock touches my hole. I feel a tiny bit of pressure as he pushes forward ever slightly. It doesn't go in.

"You're mine," he whispers from behind me as his hands gently grip my hips.

I don't respond, my eyes closed and my lips parted as I remain frozen in anticipation. My cock is rock hard and bobbing with its excitement. My mind and body are fast flooded with crackling energy that makes me feel like I'm floating.

He applies a tiny bit more pressure.

I feel my hole give.

His tip slides inside.

"Oh my *God*, Billy," I groan out, mouth agape.

He fits me perfectly *and* tightly. Not a second goes by that I don't feel completely aware of where he is and what he's got inside me and how incredible it feels. I want to cry, the joy is so much. I want to laugh, every nerve in my body awakened to the point of tiny tremors and little raised hairs. I fight a shiver.

Gently, I feel him rocking his own hips, making his cock slip a little further in, then partway back. A little more in. A little bit back. Then even deeper. Then a tiny bit back. Deeper. Back.

I trust him completely. My body was tense at first, but every instinct now is telling me to relax and to let him fill me up completely. I want him so deeply inside me that I feel it in my teary eyes, in my raging heartbeat, in the pulse of my own desperate cock.

I have never been this close without even touching myself.

"This feels ... *so* good," Billy says.

"You're tellin' me!" I groan out.

He pushes in deeper. I almost fight it, then let myself give in. My breath is so shallow, both in an attempt to make my cock behave as well as to keep my ass and body open and receptive to him—and his big, penetrating meat.

Soon, he starts rocking my hips, his cock so slippery now that it almost seems to glide in and out on its own. I'm already there, an orgasm growing more imminent by the second.

"Billy ..." I warn.

"I'm already close," he informs me. "Fuck, Tanner. Oh, God, *fuck ...*"

He's starting to slam into my ass, jostling my body with every skin-to-skin slap. The motion makes it all the more difficult to hold back. I feel myself skirt the edge of orgasm twice, a pained expression crossing my face as I squirm delightedly against Billy's strong-armed pumping to hold back. I'm hypnotized by what he's doing to me.

"I'm all yours, babe," I hear myself saying. "I'm all yours. *God*, I'm all yours."

And then he grabs my hair, yanking my head up. I feel my cock flex harder by his aggressive action, my heart pounding with desire. I'm so turned on by Billy's sudden manhandling of me that I feel myself drop over the edge.

"*BILLY!*" I howl out.

The streams of cum that rocket out of me are endless. I groan and growl like an animal as I empty all of my pent-up frustration and horniness out of my cock, spilling all over my sheets. Ropes of cum stick to my abs. There's even a drop that hits me in the chin when I droop my head down, unable to hold it up as I convulse in my relief.

"Fuuuuck," I breathe as Billy keeps pumping me, making my orgasm—even after it's ended—feel like it's still going and going and going. I'm losing my mind.

"I'm coming," he hisses, letting go of my hair to grab my hips again.

And I feel him pulsing within me as he empties his load. His moans fill my room. I swear the walls bend outward with the volume of his roars of release. It seems to go forever until his hip-rocking slows and he collapses on my back, half-hugging me as I fall to my side, and then the pair of us just lie there, spent for a minute.

We lie there on our sides forever. I just listen to him breathe in my ear and he listens to me breathe. It's the most intimate I've ever felt with a person. The lazy way in which he caresses me right now touches my heart, his arm thrown over me limply as we lie on this bed like a pair of noodles.

I could lie here for days and days.

"Oh, Tanner ..." he whispers in my ear, his breathing even again.

"I made a mess all over the bed," I murmur, sounding like I give approximately zero shits about it.

"The answer's yes, by the way."

I slowly roll onto my back, ignoring all the wetness on my cock and the sheets, which have already grown cold. I crane my neck to face him, our noses touching. "Yes to what?" I ask.

"Your boyfriend," he says softly. He gives me a little, soft kiss on the lips. Then he finishes, "I want to be your boyfriend."

I grin, then grab his body and pull him tightly against mine, embracing him on the bed. All our sweat and fluids and *sex* between us, we don't give a care in the world.

CHAPTER 13
BILLY

I love and hate Sundays. But so does my boyfriend Tanner.

My boyfriend Tanner. Fuck, I love the sound of that.

After making us our usual breakfast, we lounge out by the pool in just our shorts chilling on the deck chairs and chatting about the most random stuff. He tells me about girlfriends from high school. I tell him about awkward situations in gym class. Digging up memories starts to make me see my whole childhood differently, now with Tanner and I having "found" each other.

"Did you ever look at me that way?" I ask.

He smirks. "I wondered the same thing. I mean, even back in school when I was still convinced that girls were doin' it for me, I was curious. I heard the rumors. I knew you were probably gay."

"Did you ever ... catch me checkin' you out in gym?"

"You checked me out in gym class?" He laughs when he sees the wince on my face. "I was such a cocky bastard back then. Or I think I was. I probably assumed everyone was checking me out."

"I never saw you that way."

"Really? You didn't see me as a cocky bastard?"

"Nope. I saw you as ... confident. You knew what you wanted. You were going to go far. I could see it in your eyes. And I knew you had a sweet side, too."

He frowns at me. "Sweet?"

"Yes. Remember scrawny Elliot? That freshman who tried out for football and got laughed off the field?"

"Oh yeah. What's he up to? I haven't seen him."

"Dude. He's still in high school. Senior now. And he's on the football team. He's not nearly as good as you were, but shit, he's come a long way."

"No way!" breathes Tanner.

"Yep. Anyway, I knew he didn't have a lot of friends back then, and he always seemed to sit alone or with, like, one other person at lunch all the time. And ..." I smile, thinking of it. "I saw you go right up to his table one day and sit with him. All your buddies kept looking over their shoulders from your usual spot in the cafeteria, looking confused, but you just sat there confidently and chatted with him. I never saw Elliot smile 'til that day."

"He came to all of my games," Tanner says with half a smile, "even after all that tryout fiasco. I saw him in the stands. He was always cheering us on. I think we had just won a game the past weekend, so I was walkin' by with my lunch tray that day, saw him, and wanted to share the excitement and give him some encouragement."

"Well. He must've taken the encouragement to heart because rumor has it he hit the gym that whole spring and summer, and showed up to tryouts his sophomore year and blew the coaches away."

Tanner's eyes are wide and sparkling. "Wow."

"That's the effect you have on people." I laugh, the memories rushing to me. "You were the kind of guy who would help someone pick up all their things when their backpack split open in the hallway," I go on. "Hell, most people just move on or stop and laugh."

"Would you stop and laugh?"

"Well, no."

He grins at me, as if proud of the point he's making. "I guess that makes both of us nice guys, then. You know ..." His eyebrows lift up, wrinkling his forehead. "You have some seriously good talent with those desserts of yours. Why haven't you run off to culinary school yet and turned it into a thing?"

"Over the past three years, I've gotten an associate's degree in business. Online courses," I amend. "And I *am* going to culinary school this fall. In Florida. I'm going to stay with my Uncle Aaron who lives out there."

"Why now?" he pushes. "Why not after high school?"

He's really intuitive. I've always liked that about him.

"My pa ... had a heart attack after I graduated," I tell him. "I had to kinda stay to help with the diner."

"Oh." His face pulls back, tightening. "I didn't know about that."

"And medical bills kinda ate up the money that was going to go toward my tuition. I took over so many things with the diner in his absence. The chaos of it all inspired me to start taking online business courses and working toward getting my associate's, since I wouldn't be going to culinary school yet, and I wanted to learn how to run the business better. It was a tough time in all our lives."

"Shit, Billy. You must've had so much weight on your shoulders."

His words strike me. No one's actually ever said that out loud to me: *"You must've had so much weight on your shoulders."* Even my own parents. I knew they appreciated how much I'd taken on, but I guess they never voiced it. Not the way Tanner just did.

"My pa couldn't even get out of bed for weeks, slowly recuperating since the heart attack was pretty bad and ... almost took him from us," I go on. "He takes everything easy now. I took over every aspect of the business for a while ... all at the age of eighteen. And every year, I told myself, 'I'll go to school in the fall.' But each year came and I was ... still here."

"I see. So ... Florida, huh?"

I lift my chin. "Yep. That's the plan. Hope my uncle's ready for me. Uncle Aaron's my father's brother."

A flicker of emotion passes through his eyes. He claps me on the shoulder. "I'm really proud of you. I didn't stop to think about all of that. How you got so ... driven. So focused. Shit." He shakes his head. "I envy you, Billy."

I shrug. "I've envied *you*, Tanner. You got to go off and do your thing right after high school."

"It isn't all it's cracked up to be. Besides, you will too."

I catch myself smiling, then I lift my gaze to him just as he rises from his seat and comes over to straddle my lap. His muscle weight is a lot for my legs, but I'd be a fool to complain.

Besides, my cock isn't complaining. With those sexy, firm ass cheeks of his pressing down into my lap, I already feel myself stiffening up.

"Confession," I murmur. "I ... thought you were hot in high school. Not gonna lie."

"You were checkin' me out even back then, huh?" He grins superiorly, then hooks his hands around the back of my neck. My view is swallowed in muscle and Tanner, and that's plenty alright with me. "I kinda wondered about that. I, uh ... don't remember if I was a dick to you ever or, like, if I seemed to ignore you ..."

"I kept to myself," I assure him. "We never really had friends in the same clique. I did an English group project with Robby once, but—"

"Oh, right. He was in all the Honors classes, huh?"

"Yep. And he was in half the Honors girls, too," I add with a smirk. To that, Tanner snorts. "But he does have a great voice. I kinda wish he'd pursue that, like, as a career. Don't your parents own a recording studio by now?"

He chuckles. "They own a lot of different businesses, but a recording studio ain't one of them."

I hook my own hands around him, feeling the ridge where his back muscles dip in the center. "I'm gettin' kinda hard again," I warn him, my voice low.

"Ready for another round? Last night didn't wear ya out?" he teases.

"Nor this mornin'," I shoot right back, the devil in my eyes. Suddenly, my face softens. "I didn't hurt you, did I?"

He shakes his head at first, then quickly reconsiders, squinting down at me. "Well, I mean, I felt my body resist a bit at first. But with all the stimulation you were doin' back there with your ... tongue ..."

A wave of pleasure *and* pride rushes through me. With his ass in my lap, I already can't wait to dig back into it. My cock flexes just at the thought.

He feels it. "Damn, boy. You already reliving the time you spent with your face between my ass cheeks?"

"Every waking second."

"Bet it was like heaven, huh?" he teases, fighting a grin that's trying to happen on his face. It's so adorable when he tries not to smile; his dimples pop out more and one of his eyebrows does this cute, twitchy thing.

My hands smoothly run up and down the small of his back. "I just want to make sure you enjoyed it and that I did alright. I mean, you kinda took it like a pro."

"I *am* a pro."

"And my cock ain't the biggest in the world," I note.

"It's damn well enough for me. Perfect, in fact."

I feel my face heating up a bit. I've never had anyone talk about my dick like that before. "To be honest, I was kinda expectin' to finish you off."

"Dude, I was shocked that I came hands-free. I didn't even think that shit was possible. But you had me all worked up, and you were fillin' me up back there, and your hands were all over my ass and my hips ..."

All of his talking makes my cock flex again, twice as bad this time. And again, he notices, cutting himself off and staring down at me.

"Shit. You just can't wait for a dang second, can ya? Like a puppy dog."

I buck my hips tauntingly, humping him as best as I can despite his weight. "You gotta admit, I pretty much turned you into my bitch for the night."

His jaw drops. I grin smartly. He coughs out a laugh and brings a hand to my hair, running his fingers through it. "Is that what you think happened, boy?" he asks with sass. "You turned me into your bitch?"

"Pretty much," I say, enjoying his fingers as they gently tease and tickle through my hair.

He leans his torso forward a bit, bringing the beauty that are his pecs and abs close—and his face even closer. "Billy, you didn't hurt me. You couldn't. I'm a strong guy, y'know that? Says so in my last name."

"What does that imply about *my* last name?" I sass back. "Do I *tuck* things away? Keep 'em safe?"

He reaches down between his own legs—and mine—and grabs my hard cock through the material of my shorts. Given the flimsy fabric, he might as well have just grabbed my cock bare. I gape, then groan my pleasure.

"Seems pretty *tucked* away to me," he confirms. "But we could remedy that pretty quickly."

"Yeah?"

"Oh yeah."

And then he shifts downward, rising off of me just enough to yank my gym shorts right down. The fabric is so loose and mesh-like that they fly off like nothing along with my underwear. He descends on my cock, taking half of it in with one quick wrapping of his wet lips. His warm mouth engulfs it, trapping half the inches I got in there.

"Holy fuck," I can't help but exclaim, gripping the armrests of my chair and throwing my head back.

In a matter of seconds, he's transported me, mind and body. It's a bit of an experiment at first as he twists his head and works my cock with just his mouth, his lips wrapped tight and maintaining an impressive amount of suction. *Strong, he is. Really, really strong.*

It isn't long before I'm already squirming, my legs trapped under his weight as he starts to pick up pace in sucking me off.

I reel my head forward, staring at the top of his fast-bobbing head with urgency.

"I'm too close," I whimper.

He lifts off of my cock and gives me a wicked grin. "Who's the bitch now?"

My eyes narrow. "We're going to your room. Now."

He nods. "That's my boy."

The next instant, he grabs me and, with a soft grunt, slings me over his shoulder.

I yelp out, surprised by his move.

My hard, wet cock presses against his chest as he carries me through the glass doors, across the living room, up the stairs—*with my slickened cock sliding up and down his chest, like his body is jerking me off with every step he takes*—and into his bedroom, where he throws me down onto the bed.

"You're all mine," he growls before he pounces on me once again, his mouth engulfing all my inches.

"Fuuuuck," I moan, slamming my head back against the sheets, out of breath in an instant. The sensation is almost too much.

He pops off of my cock, then swipes the condoms I brought off of his nightstand where I'd left them. He tears one open. "I ... am gonna sit on Billy Junior," he murmurs lightly.

"Say what?"

"*I'm* gonna ride *you*," he clarifies, straight-faced, as he rolls the condom onto my wet cock. "You heard me right. You took the reins last night. It's my turn now, bud. I'm gonna turn *you* into *my* bitch."

My eyebrows lift, impressed.

Tanner takes the tube of lube from the nightstand and pops it open. He gives it a sniff. "Strawberry, huh?" Then, with a sly smirk, he squirts a big glob of it onto his palm.

The next second, there's banging at the door.

He turns his head, alarmed. I sit up straight, ignoring my rubber-wrapped cock—which is also very much sitting up straight.

The two of us listen, holding our breaths.

There's a muffled shout. Then more banging.

Someone's at the front door.

Tanner and I stare at each other, wide-eyed. "Your family's back early??" I hiss. "I thought they don't come in until after three in the afternoon?"

He gives it a second of thought, then shakes his head. "No, they'd let themselves in." Still balancing the glob of lube in his hand, he rushes to the window and cranes his neck. "Fuck. *Fuck, fuck, fuck ...*"

I look around the room. I left my clothes by the pool. I'm naked and have nothing to wear. "Dude ..."

"It's Kirk and Joel," he announces.

"Just pretend we're not here," I blurt, pulling off my unused condom and tossing it at the nightstand. "You could be in the shower or—"

Then we hear the sliding of a glass door downstairs and a shout from within the house. "Dude! Tan! Where you at, bro??"

Tanner experiences a second of not knowing what to do with the gooey strawberry substance in his hand. He grabs a tissue and feverishly wipes off all the stuff, then races to his closet. After I shake out of my panicked stupor, I follow suit, hurrying to his dresser and tearing open a drawer. I grab the first pair of his shorts that I can find and start pulling them on one leg at a time, hopping halfway across the room in my clumsy effort. The shouts that continue to come from downstairs do not help ease our joint panic at all. Tanner nearly thwacks me in the face with his arm when he pulls on a shirt. Neither of us bother with underwear. We collide into each other as we trade places, him fetching a pair of shorts while I snatch and slip into the first shirt I can manage to pull off a hanger in his closet.

"Tan!" calls Kirk from downstairs, seeming closer.

Tanner's eyes grow double when he sees the lube and condoms on the nightstand. He grabs them and shoves them into the drawer of his nightstand, then rushes to his door. He stops when his hand touches the doorknob, then turns his head to me, his eyes imploring me to have an idea of what the hell to do.

I come quickly to his side. *"They know we're friends,"* I whisper. *"Just tell them you wanted to show me something in your room."*

"What? Like my dick?" he hisses back.

"TAN!"

Tanner slips through the door and starts down the stairs. "Hey, man!" he calls out, his voice totally normal, yet sounding an octave higher. "The hell you doin' here? Joel. You two got nothin' better to do today, huh?"

"Bored as fuck!" comes Kirk's voice. I listen from the door, debating whether I should sneak out the window and climb down the side of the house, or boldly make an entrance and justify being upstairs somehow. They never use the game room up here, so I gotta think of something believable. "Bonnie's drivin' me nuts. Where's Billy?"

"Who?"

"Billy. His car's out front."

Shit. I swing out of the room and hop down the stairs. "Hey, Kirk!" I call out. "Thought I heard ya."

Kirk and Joel are standing by the couch. Tanner is a few feet away from them with his arms crossed tightly and his face looking stern. He is so uncharacteristically uncomfortable that it's obvious something's off. *You are horrible at playing it cool, Tanner.*

"What's up," grunts Kirk, squinting as he watches me come down the stairs.

His gears are already turning. Distract him. "Not much. Chattin' with Tanner about the party next weekend."

Kirk's eyes narrow even more. "Interesting shirt."

I don't even know what I grabbed. I glance down at my chest. I'm wearing a green shirt with what appears to be a cat licking its own paw. There's words underneath that I apparently can't read upside-down. "Uh, thanks," I grunt, still staring down at them confusedly.

Kirk helps me. "It says 'Professional Pussy Licker'."

I freeze. A snort of laughter comes from Joel across the room. I guess there are worse shirts I could have pulled out of Tanner's closet.

I meet Kirk's eyes and give him a grin. "You know me. Lickin' all that pussy."

Joel bursts into full-blown laughter now. Kirk smirks and shakes his head, biting the inside of his cheek. A glint of suspicion still lives in his eyes, which I would like to quickly put an end to.

I glance over at Tanner. He's just staring ahead with his eyes unblinking, as if he didn't even hear all of this exchange. He looks like he wants to piss himself. One of his legs has started bouncing and fidgeting in place. *Oh my God, Tanner, calm the hell down. We're going to be fine.*

When Joel recovers from his fit of laughter, he says, "Aww, shit. I'm so stoked for this party. My summer's been dead as fuck without a good ol' Strong Ranch party! You throw the best fuckin' parties ever!" he says, slapping Tanner on the back so hard that he jumps and his eyes fly wide open.

"I'm catering," I explain to them, still trying to pull Kirk away from whatever damned train of thought he's determinedly riding. "Well, Biggie's Bites is. We're doing it all. Just here to, uh ... discuss the details."

"No shit!" cries out Joel. "Fuckin' awesome! Burgers?" He looks at Tanner. "Your mom's alright with that?"

Tanner chuckles. The chuckle is too tight-throated to sound natural. "Yep. She's excited to see what he, uh ..." He swallows, interrupting himself. "What he comes up with for the desserts. He's doin' desserts, too."

"Dude." Joel comes up to me and slaps a hand on either of my shoulders. "We're gonna have to taste-test all that shit. Bring it over here, day before the party. We will eat everything you make, and we'll—"

"Like hell you are," grunts Kirk, pulling Joel away from me with a throaty laugh. "Get off of Billy. Give him some dang space."

"I'm just excited, man!"

From the look on Kirk's face, it seems like his mind has moved on. *Maybe we really dodged the coming-out bullet for now.*

"Well," I say, "you guys *can* try out some of my stuff right now, if you really want."

Joel's eyes flash. "Dude."

"Yep. I brought some over for Tanner to try." I give Tanner a lift of an eyebrow, hoping he'll snap out of his stiff demeanor and loosen up a bit.

He does. "Y-Yeah. I already had some earlier, but shit, I'll have ten more. Desserts Billy makes are *that* good."

We relocate to the kitchen as Joel and Kirk start to tell Tanner about something to do with Joel's pa's auto shop. Then Kirk starts complaining about Bonnie and how she's on his ass every minute of the day.

Meanwhile, I've pulled out the different flavors of ice cream from the freezer as well as some other pastries I brought, since I apparently can't show up here without bringing a selection of goodies for us to sample. I pull down four bowls from the cabinet and pop a perfect ball of strawberry ice cream and a perfect ball of vanilla ice cream into each one. After my homemade hot fudge is all warmed up, I glaze it over each bowl in my signature pattern: a football shape complete with the stitching across the middle. Then, I stab a spoon into each bowl and place my flaky butter cookies along the side.

I set a bowl in front of each of the boys at the counter, keeping one for myself. "Is this your—?" Joel starts to ask.

"Yep. My homemade *cream*," I tease with a smirk.

Tanner snorts and shakes his head. *Yeah, I'll never live it down; let me make fun of myself.*

Kirk's already spooned up a mouthful. His eyes turn glassy after he tastes it. "Holy fuckin' Jesus Lord." He quickly draws a cross over his chest. "Shit. Your dessert made me cuss on a Sunday."

"Appropriately so. It's called a Football Sundae," I say.

Joel, his mouth full, quirks an eyebrow. "It's not just called 'ice cream'?" he asks, muffled.

"Well, the ice cream is homemade, and so's the hot fudge. I put a secret ingredient or two in them to give them my own spicy twist," I explain. "So it ain't just your normal ice-cream-in-a-bowl. The taste should speak for itself."

"Even your strawberry ice cream is like ... *fuck*," says Kirk, then draws another cross. "This is so good, dude. Damn. Thanks for this, really," he adds, pointing at his bowl with the spoon. "I know you'd prolly charge us at your diner for this. I recognize we're eatin' some serious delicacy for free right here. So thanks for this."

That was pretty thoughtful of Kirk to say that. "Well thanks right back," I say, smiling.

My eyes meet Tanner's. He wears a mixture of worry and happiness. I see both of those emotions warring in his rich brown eyes as he eats his sundae and steals nervous glances at his friends. I wish there was a way I could calm him down, but nothing comes to mind. I lean my back against the kitchen island and watch as the three guys eat and start to chat about whatever it was they were talking about before—the auto shop, Kirk's girlfriend Bonnie, the party next weekend. I try to let their conversation drift me away to a mental space that's more peaceful, but I can't stop peeking at Tanner and noting the apprehensive look on his face.

To be honest, it's starting to bother me. I know he's scared his friends might be suspecting that something's going on between us, but is it really *that* big of a deal? Sure, I don't want the town talking about us either, but is it worth sulking over?

I can't even finish half my sundae. When everyone's done and the conversation has moved on to a neighbor of Harrison's named Whitney who's dog ran away, I collect the bowls, give them a rinse in the sink, then deposit them in the dishwasher. Returning to their conversation, I feel a bit like an outsider suddenly, with Tanner across the counter from me and focusing on Joel trying to explain why Harrison and Whitney are the perfect match.

Tanner won't even look at me.

I know he's not mad at me. I know he's just nervous. I know that feeling all too well; I used to get it all the time in high school when I felt like someone was trying to dance their way toward the question of whether or not I was gay. I felt it coming like a storm, every time.

That's really the worst part about coming out. You don't do it just once; you have to do it again and again, your whole life.

Tanner has zero experience with coming out. Zero. He has never been questioned. He has never had someone give him the quizzical eyes that Kirk just gave him. Unless Tanner has some experience that he's never told me about, this is all very new—and very scary—for him.

I should be sympathetic. I should feel for him and not take this personally.

So why am I standing over here getting more angry by the second? Why is the ice cream turning over in my stomach? Either I'm really far more bothered by Tanner's behavior than I'm letting myself admit, or I'm discovering after all these years that I'm lactose intolerant. Somehow, I doubt it's the latter.

"I think I'm gonna head out," I say suddenly, cutting off something Joel's saying.

"Oh, alright," he says. "Hey, thanks for the sundaes. I can't fuckin' wait for the party. It's all about puttin' them in my mouth!"

Kirk chuckles dryly and says, "Fa—" He cuts himself off. His eyes turn serious after almost uttering a certain three-letter word. He brings his anxious gaze up to meet mine. "Uh, sorry. Didn't mean it."

I'm in a shitty mood, but none of these guys will know because I'm an expert at keeping an even face. Blame the years of customer service. Blame my demeanor through all of high school. Blame my calm-tempered pa or my quirky ma. Doesn't matter.

"Sorry," Kirk repeats. "Really. Uh … I should've …"

Joel jumps in. "Shit. That word doesn't sound right at all now. I mean, like, before I knew you … before I *knew-you* knew you, it didn't really mean much. The word. You get me? But, like …"

"Now that you know a fag, you're thinking twice?" I ask, determined to keep my temper despite the acid bite in my tone.

The word has never, ever bothered me. I don't give a shit who uses it. Why is it bothering me so much right now? Why do I want to go on some angry gay tirade on these guys, Tanner included?

Joel shakes his head. "Look, I'm sorry. Fuck it. I'm not gonna say fag again. Except for right now when I just said it." His face wrinkles up. "And yeah, I guess you're right. Sorta different when you got a—uh—homosexual that you can call a friend."

I could cringe at that word—*homosexual*—and how agonizingly clinical and sterile that word sounds, but I know he means well, so I just give him a tight-lipped smile and a little nod. "Well, for what it's worth, I'm probably *not* the first gay guy you ever met. We're all hiding in plain sight. Not all of us … advertise," I finish.

Tanner stares at me with sudden intensity, his eyes glazed over, stunned.

I don't even realize what I said until the words are already out and Joel and Kirk are digesting them. I meant them innocently. I was referring to anyone and everyone that Joel or Kirk could have interacted with at any point in their lives—teachers they've had, the local dentist, a shop owner, someone who passes by them on the street, a relative ...

A teammate.

I didn't mean Tanner at all. He didn't even cross my mind. Yet there he sits, in plain sight, and the look in his eyes has changed. Is it anger I'm seeing? Is it betrayal?

Now I have to leave. "Anyway, I'll see you later," I get out finally, my heart racing with emotion as I head for the door, swiping my backpack off the couch on the way.

"Hey, Billy," calls out Kirk.

I stop at the door and turn to him, lifting an eyebrow expectantly.

"You forgot somethin'." He nods his head subtly at the glass doors ... where my clothes are sitting in plain sight by the pool.

I stare at the door for a solid five seconds. "I ... jumped in the pool earlier and ... didn't want to, um ..." I clear my throat. "We got so caught up talking about the party—"

"Yeah, I get it," Kirk adds, cutting me off, his eyes still dubious.

Fuck. Can I just get out of this house already? "Thanks."

"No prob."

I hurry past them toward the glass doors. For some reason, I want to burst out into tears. I don't even know anymore what emotions are sparring within me. Anger? Sadness? Hurt? Indignance? *I wasn't talking about you when I said what I said, Tanner. I hope you trust me and know me enough to realize that.*

"Billy."

I stop at the sound of Tanner's voice. My hand against the glass door, I turn to face him. My eyes are heavy with emotion. Tanner's are glassy and faraway. I have no idea what's going on in his mind or heart right now. It scares me, not knowing.

"Yeah?" I say, my voice tiny, a squeak.

He gives a nod at my chest. "You can keep the shirt, bro. It doesn't fit me anymore."

I stare at him long and hard. For a second, I thought he was going to ask me to stay. His comment does nothing to comfort me. I feel ice gather in my belly.

"See you around, man," he adds.

Bro.

Man.

Is he serious? Is there a second meaning he's wanting me to grasp? Or is he furious with me? Will he deny that the whole thing happened, and it really *will* be like this thing between us was just a fantasy all along?

Is it over?

"See ya," I say back, then let myself out.

CHAPTER 14

TANNER

Well, don't I feel like the world's biggest shit.

I don't call any of my buddies to hang out on Monday. I don't want to. All I do is stare at my phone and wonder whether I should call him, or if he's going to be the bold one and call me first. I must have typed out fifty texts to him and deleted them all before hitting send. I stare out my window as if his car is going to just show up around the bend and appear in my driveway.

I'm such an asshole.

I deserve this.

Damn it.

The worst part is that he's not calling me. The ball *is* sort of in his court, after he said the words he said and then just abruptly up and left my house on Sunday.

Kirk and Joel didn't ask me a damn thing about it, but I could see it in their eyes. They're trying to put the pieces together. Or maybe I'm full of shit and they already know. Maybe they've always known. I'm an idiot to think I can keep up any sort of mask around them.

And really, what's my problem? What the hell am I so afraid of? He was right. We hide in plain sight. *Don't hate him for those words. He's so fucking right.*

After a hellish, emotionally awful Monday, I get into my pickup and drive into town Tuesday. I take a full ten minutes of deep breathing before I work up the courage to enter the diner, only to find out he's not working. "He's taken the day off," Mindy explains as she smacks on the biggest chunk of pink gum I've ever seen. "Gettin' ready for your party thing. Y'know after tomorrow, the diner's gonna be closed the rest of the week, right?"

I park in front of his house next and just sit there for the longest while, feeling like a creep. I don't know which window is his, since I've never been inside, but I stare at all of them. I picture him inside there, hard at work designing and thinking and baking.

I'm such an idiot.

I pick up my phone off the passenger seat where it's sitting and text him.

TANNER
Hey man. I'm outside. Can we talk?

I stare at the text I just sent, then sigh, wishing I had worded it better or said more. I suck on my teeth and continue to scowl at my phone like it's done something wrong to me.

There's a tap on my passenger side window. I look up, startled.

It isn't Billy standing here. It's his mama.

I fumble with the switch on my door—as if I suddenly don't know how it works—then finally manage to get the damned window rolled down. "Hello there, Mrs. Tucker," I say politely, giving her a smile.

She leans into my window. "You lookin' for my son?"

I blink. "Yep," I squeak out. "Is he ... busy?"

"And not here at all," she confirms. "He took my car to Fairview for some supplies we need for your party. Hey, do you like sautéed mushrooms on your burgers?"

"I'll take just about anythin', ma'am."

She squints. "Noted. Anyhow, he'll be back in three hours or so, I'd reckon. It's an hour drive each way and he just left half an hour ago."

Just missed him. Damn. "I appreciate it, Mrs. Tucker."

"Hey." She leans into my window more, then lowers her voice. "Is everythin' alright with him?"

I lick my lips. They're so dry suddenly. "I'm not sure. What'd he say?"

"Not a damned word," she blurts, her eyes going wide. "That's why I'm askin' you, silly."

I break a smile despite myself. I've never really gotten to know his mama, but I can already tell she's someone I could spend an afternoon or two chatting with. "I think he might be ... a little pissed with me."

"You been a fool with my son, huh?"

I'm not sure what she means by that. "I might've said the wrong thing. Or, uh ... not said somethin' I should've. I'm a bit confused, to be honest."

Her voice turns soft. "My son likes you."

I meet her eyes at once. For some reason, I don't feel the need to keep anything from this woman. She invites a deep sense of trust and care the second you start speaking to her. I've never had this sort of instant connection with someone else's mama before.

It must be that sudden trust in me that makes me say my next words. "I like your son too. A lot."

My heart's in my throat after the words tumble out of me. I do realize I could be talking platonically. I would've said the same thing about Kirk or Joel or any of my other buds at some point; I *do* like them all. But I don't like them in the way I like Billy. They don't drive me crazy the way he does. They don't stir up my heart and twist my brain to the point where I can't think of anything but him.

But I doubt the meaning is lost on Billy's mama, who lights up her face with the subtlest of smiles. "He'll be home later if you wanna drop by," she finally says. "I'm gonna be at the diner with my husband settin' up some stuff. You two will have time here all by yourselves."

My eyes detach. I feel my heart beating way too fast in my chest. Despite the comfort I feel around her, I can't reveal what's really going on in my head.

She seems to sense it because she gives the side of my door a slap of her hand and takes a step back. "I'll see you later. You and Nadine and Paul and little Jimmy are gonna be mighty happy with what my son's come up with."

I grasp at the little rope of comfort she's thrown me. "He ain't so little anymore," I say with a breathy chuckle. "Jimmy's damn near my height now."

"He'll always be 'little Jimmy' to me," she teases, "as you'll always be that sweet boy from the Strong Ranch who always knew how to steal someone's heart and then some. Keep treatin' people nice and good, y'hear?" Then she gives me a wink and strolls down the road, I presume making her way to the diner around the corner.

I stare at my phone again, noting that Billy hasn't responded. I don't know if he's still driving, hasn't checked his phone, or already read my text and just isn't bothering to answer back.

I turn up the ringer on my phone and set it on the other seat, then lazily drive back home. I want to take his mama's words to heart and assure myself that everything is going to be alright, but I won't know for certain until I talk to Billy. I don't know how much he's told her, but if I take into account our conversations of how much gossip passes through his diner, I doubt he's mentioned much to her, if anything at all.

Our secret. It feels less like that now more than ever.

When I pull up to my house, I see a beige car already parked in my usual spot. I don't recognize it at all. I pull in behind it and kill the engine, hopping out and heading for the door.

The elderly woman stands in the kitchen with a dark purple shirt stretched over her big belly and a green cap. She literally looks like a plum. Her legs are like twigs in brown leggings and her face is caked in so much makeup, I don't even recognize her for a full minute while she's rambling on to my papa about how shitty her drive was.

Her big eyes find mine and she stops speaking at once. "Tanner!" she shouts out, deep and raspy. It sounds like a scolding.

"Grandma," I say, grinning as I cross the room and give her a big hug.

"Ouch, ouch, careful, shit," she grunts, smacking me as we release from the hug. "I'm a hundred years old. You can't be snappin' all my bones like that. Hey, look at you," she says suddenly, her voice changing and her mouth wrinkling into half a smile. "You're all big and strapping now. Shit, you've grown."

She always acts like the last time she saw me was when I was three and couldn't even see over the kitchen counter to wash my hands. "I probably just had a big ol' growing spurt in college or somethin'," I tease.

"Growing spurt," snorts my papa, shaking his head.

"I'll say," my grandma murmurs, giving me her eyes from my head to my toes. "You got a girlfriend?"

I laugh. "Ain't no girls at that college I wanna date."

Or girls anywhere else, I'd say if I had the balls.

Which I apparently don't.

My mama's in total heaven standing near the counter with her arms crossed, a glass of wine dangling in one of her hands and her eyes rolling at the exchange me and my grandma are having. Looks like there still isn't any good blood between them. I was really hoping that would change by now.

"Anyway, should be obvious, but I'm here early," she says, her voice as blunt as a fist to the gut. "Just came in half an hour ago and I haven't even been shown to my dang room."

Papa laughs and gives me a nod. "Show her to your room, son."

"Oh, good," Grandma grunts. "Don't set me up in that drafty box you call a guest room. Really should look at that, Paul."

My papa gives her a snort and a smile. "I'll put it on the list right under about sixty other things."

"You better do," she says.

I lead Grandma to my room where our housekeeper Jacky-Ann seems to still be dusting. She gives the two of us a quick, tired nod as all one hundred pounds of her continues to wipe away between all the things on top of my dresser.

"Is your luggage still in the car?" I ask my grandma.

"Shoot. I ain't carryin' that up here. You kiddin'?"

I laugh. Really, she hasn't changed a day. I can't wait to see how long it'll take before my mama loses her shit this visit. "I'll go get your things."

"Better do," she agrees, walking up to my window and taking in the view with squinted eyes. Just as I turn to go, her voice stops me. "Tanner, hon. I heard you've got a party happenin' this weekend."

I face her, then lean against the doorframe with my arms crossed. "Yep. You heard right."

She scowls. "That mama of yours just don't know when to say enough's enough, huh?"

I grin. "It's just a party," I assure her. "Nothin' big."

"There ain't nothin' that happens on this ranch that's organized by your mama that ain't *big*. That woman's about as subtle as a shotgun."

"A shotgun *can* be subtle if it ain't bein' fired," I point out.

She narrows her eyes. I think she's about to quip back with something super sassy, but then a smile wrinkles up her face. "You sayin' I'm better off to keep the shotgun from firin'?"

"I'm sayin' quit playin' with the trigger, Grandma."

She snorts and flicks her hand dismissively at me. "I'll behave. Oh, and Tanner." She lowers her chin and lifts her eyebrows. "Thanks for givin' me your room. Awful kind of you and you didn't have to do it."

"Yes, I did," I sass back, earning a smile from her, then I leave her to get settled while I hop down the stairs and out to her car to get her things.

When the evening has settled in and I've moved my computer, clothes, and other essentials I need to the guest room, I

stare out the window at the chicken coop with my phone in hand
when Billy finally texts me back.

BILLY
Hey. I heard you came by earlier.

I feel a rush of excitement. Leaning against the glass, I text
him back, punching the letters so fast that I have to retype and
correct half the damn text.

TANNER
Just wanted to talk. I hate how Sunday
ended. Can we meet?

I stare at my phone and wait for his response. I swear, it feels
like hours go by between each of our texts. I just want everything
to be back to normal. I don't want to feel like everything's come
crashing down to the ground because my buddies showed up
unannounced and drew out all these paralyzing fears in me about
people knowing and what they'd think or say.

My phone dings at me. My heart jumps.

BILLY
I'm home. My parents are at the diner.

I can't respond fast enough.

TANNER
I'll be over in ten.

I'm dressed so fast, I don't even remember putting on pants. I hop down the stairs and grab the keys off the counter.

"The hell you think you're goin'?" calls out my mama from the living room.

I stare into their nightmare. Mama, Papa, my little brother Jimmy, and Grandma are occupying both of the couches. A big bag of tortilla chips and two bowls of salsa, red and green—completely untouched—are sitting on the coffee table between them. They're stiffly watching a movie on the flat screen.

I fight the cold chill that grabs hold of my stomach. "T-To Billy's," I finally get out.

My mother's eyes are indignant. "You're runnin' off to hang with *him*? You ain't gonna spend some time with your sweet and *loving* grandma?"

The way she says "loving"—you know, *with* the "g"—makes me want to fight a laugh. She might as well have just asked me if I intend to let her drown in that river of tension and frustration between those couches all alone.

And yes. When Billy's involved, I *do* intend to let my mama drown.

Grandma saves me the trouble. "Nadine, there ain't been anything sweet *or* lovin' about me since the 50s. And even then I was one tough ball-bustin' cookie. Go and see your friend," she tells me. "We'll have plenty of time to spend together over the next several days."

My mama looks about as pleased as if grandma had just taken a piss in her glass of wine, but I grab hold of my grandma's lifeline and give them all a polite nod. "Thanks. Love you guys. Enjoy the, uh …" I give another nod at the TV. "Movie."

"Can I come with?" blurts my brother suddenly.

He's also drowning in the tedium. He's scrunched into the corner of the farthest couch clutching his phone like an oxygen mask.

"Take your brother," says my mama.

Fuck. "Nah, sorry, Jimmy. I g-gotta ... We're gonna ..."

The lie I need doesn't come to me quick enough. I'm just sputtering like an idiot. I wish I was as creative and fast-thinking as Billy is in these situations.

"This movie sucks," grumbles Jimmy, staring at me with that sad, imploring look in his eyes.

"Sorry, man," I try again. "Billy and I just want to go over some things for the party this weekend. He wants to show me this new dessert he was thinkin' of, and ... and it's gonna be really boring. Just business stuff. Then I'm comin' back."

"It's really boring *here*," Jimmy keeps on persistently.

"Tanner." Grandma's voice is firm as a whip. "Take your damn brother. He's literally dyin' over here."

Jimmy's already on his feet and crossing the living room, thrusting his phone into a pocket.

A hundred different things I could say race around my head. *Fuck, fuck, fuck. Come on. Fuck.*

"We ready?" asks Jimmy when he's at my side.

I clench my jaw. "See y'all later," I say with a touch less enthusiasm, then slip through door, leaving it open for Jimmy to follow.

I slam the door to my pickup with more force than I intended. Or maybe I slam it with exactly as much force as intended. As my brother swings into his side of the cab, I take a deep breath and let it all out on the steering wheel before kicking on the engine and pulling out onto the road, chasing the sun that's quickly trying to set.

"Why don't you ever wanna hang with me?"

The sound of my brother's whimpering voice is not what I need right now. I sigh. "Sorry, Jimmy. I didn't mean for you to feel that way. Just ... I kinda had somethin' I wanted to do on my own tonight."

"Oh. So the Billy thing was a lie?"

"Well ..." I sigh again. "Not exactly. I'm meeting him."

"Oh, were you two gonna do somethin' bad? Are you going over to his house to smoke weed?"

I laugh halfheartedly. "Nah. I don't smoke and neither should you."

"I *don't* smoke," he fires back defensively. "So, like, what were you gonna do with Billy, then? You got girls meeting you at his house or somethin'?"

My brother is the most persistent damn person in the world. He should enlist in the military and become an interrogator. "No girls."

"What, then?"

I wonder if I can get away with being half honest. Is there such a thing as that? "Billy and I kinda had a fight," I tell him, though I'd hardly call what *actually* happened a fight. "I wanted to go over to his house and just ... talk." I peer over at him for a second. "See? Boring as hell. We're just meetin' up to talk is all."

"You wanna drop me off at the arcade, then?"

I smirk. "Why? So you can go hook up with your weed dealer? I'm tellin' ya, if you've gotten into drugs ..."

"Weed isn't a *drug*. It's a *plant*. And I *don't smoke*."

"Alright, alright." I shift in my seat, growing more and more anxious the closer we get to town. "And for the record, I do care about ya, and I do want to hang with ya."

"We should play football sometime," he suggests with a shrug. "You and your friends do all the time. I wanna play with you guys, too."

"Next time they're over, you'll be on my team."

"I wanna try out for football in the fall," he says.

I chuckle. "Oh, yeah. Mama told me. You wanna be the next Spruce Juice, huh?"

"Nah. I'm gonna be better." He grins at his phone, which makes me laugh again.

"Set your mind to it, you can do whatever you want, Jimmy. I don't know what Mama and Papa are fillin' your head with, but you don't gotta do football just 'cause I did. You can be a painter if you want. Or a ballerina. I ain't gonna judge you."

He scoffs at me, fighting a laugh. "Ballerina."

"Don't be so quick to mock it, man. In college, I saw some guys in the dance department. Dude, those fuckers got legs twice the size of mine. Dance ain't a joke. It's a damn sport just as grueling as football."

"If you say so."

"Oh, I say so."

"Are you gay?"

I nearly run us off the road, dazed by his question so badly that I almost miss a turn. Righting the wheel, I have a solid ten seconds of simply denying that he'd asked the question at all. I stare at the road, grip the wheel tightly, and press my lips closed.

"Is that a yes?" he finally prods, a solid minute after he'd asked.

"Huh?" I grunt, like I'm actually going to play off that I didn't hear him in the first place.

My throat is dry. My heart is hammering in my neck. I can't seem to breathe right. *How the hell did he get that idea into his head? Who's been talking to him? What'd he see?*

"It don't matter," he says. "There's this guy at school who was in my Shop class. We had to make these picture frames for a project, and his was the best of the whole class. It had, like, dragon heads at either end of it. He even painted the whole thing."

"What's your point?" I spit at him.

"He was gay. And I'm cool with it. Reverend Arnold says—"

"I know what Reverend Arnold says," I say, cutting him off tersely. "We're all born equal. Love your neighbor. Blah, blah."

Jimmy gives me a frown. "The hell's wrong with you? If you're gay, I don't give a shit. You're still my brother."

Why aren't his words comforting me? Why can't I thank him and appreciate the branch he's extending me? Is my own fear of people knowing so intense that I can't even stomach my own brother hearing the truth?

"Fine, Jimmy," I say flatly, staring at the road.

There's a long moment of silence when we finally hit the main streets of Spruce, the farmlands falling behind. A red light stops us cold. Just the sound of my pickup's old engine rumbling fills our ears.

"So are you and Billy doin' it in the butt?" he asks.

I clench shut my eyes. I'm not sure I can deal with this right now. "Shut your mouth, Jimmy," I say evenly.

"I was just askin'."

"Shut your damn mouth."

"Alright."

I open my eyes.

The light turns green.

I pass right by Biggie's Bites. I take a turn, then stop in front of Billy's house. After killing the engine, I just sit there in my seat staring at the steering wheel and slowly trying to calm myself down one deep breath at a time.

"Didn't mean to piss you off," Jimmy finally says in a tiny voice.

I shake my head. "You didn't piss off nobody."

He shifts in his seat. "I ain't gonna tell anyone. Not even Mama or Papa. I just wanna know."

"We. Are. *Friends*," I state, punching each word while keeping my head facing the wheel.

"Friends?"

I feel the sting of a tear in my eye. I won't let it out. I don't know if it's from fear, or frustration, or if it's even a tear at all. I don't know why it's so difficult for me to say it. Maybe it's a product of twenty-one years of building up some false idea of who I am that's fighting me. That persona, that alpha dog, that lady's man ... he's pushing me like a bully, cornering me in a dark room of my mind. He's laughing at me.

Suddenly, I want to laugh at him right back. *You're a joke*, I'd tell that fake version of myself. *All your girlfriends knew. You're a joke. You're a liar. You're in denial.*

"Boyfriends," I hear myself say before I even realize the word came out of my mouth.

"Cool." He shrugs nonchalantly. "I'll wait out here."

I turn my face halfway towards him. "Huh?"

"So you can have time alone with him or whatever." He slouches in his seat and starts playing a game on his phone. I hear the little chimes and dings coming from it as his thumbs tap along the screen.

I frown at him. "Shit. Should I have dropped you at the movies or somethin'?"

"Nah. I'm cool here. I just needed to get outta that damn house." He looks over at me. "I love Grandma, but she's a bit much."

"She *is* a bit much," I agree, letting on a little smile.

Jimmy slouches further in his seat, returning his focus to his game while I pull out the keys and hop out of the pickup. With a slam of my door, I head on down the path to Billy's house, my legs shaking the whole way.

He opens the door before I'm halfway down the path. He's wearing a tank top and sweatpants cut off at the knee, which is about the most dressed down I've ever seen him. *And it's sexy as hell.* Already, I have to fight the urge to grab him and kiss him until everything's alright again.

Then I meet his eyes and see the sullenness in them. Reality smacks me over the face like a cold, dead fish.

I speak first. "Hey."

"Hi," he returns.

My hands are in my pockets suddenly. "Can I come in? Your mama said she was stayin' at the diner late with your papa, so I guess we, uh ... have time."

"I'm pretty sure she knows," says Billy, biting his lip all cutely.

I wanna bite that lip, too. "My brother kinda just figured it out. Sorta."

Billy lifts an eyebrow. "Seriously?"

"He just up and asked me. Just now. On the ride over."

After shutting the front door, Billy peeks out one of the windows. "He's sittin' out there?"

"Yeah. Kinda insisted on coming along just to get out of the house. Had to oblige. Well, I was kinda forced to by my mama and my grandma. She's in town already, by the way. Showed up early. Took my room from me."

Billy nods, his eyes scanning down my body slowly and taking me in. Then he snaps out of it and gives me a beckoning wave of his hand.

I follow him through his living room, which is pretty minimal with just a couch, an end table, and a TV by the front window. The kitchen is just off of it, radiating with waves of delicious aromas that pull at my stomach in an instant. Spices. Apples. Chocolate. Vanilla. I'm suddenly starved for a hundred different things and I haven't even seen what he's making yet. The counters are cluttered with tons of boxes and mixing bowls and egg shells. There is a dining room table filled from one end to the other with pastries and cookies and other edibles lined up like little doughy armies.

"You ... have been *busy*," I state, wide-eyed.

He chuckles dryly. "Yep," he mutters as he checks on something in the oven. "Test run before the real thing."

After another nervous glance around the kitchen—and a second of staring at his cute butt when he bends over the oven to survey its contents—I say, "Hey, Billy?"

"Hmm?" he grunts.

"I ..." I sigh, feeling myself tightening up inside. "I just wanted to say ..."

He straightens up and faces me. Though he doesn't look like the happiest guy in the world right now, at least he appears to be receptive to whatever it is I have to say.

And really, I don't have much. I'm not good with these sorts of things. "I just wanted to tell you that I'm sorry if I made you feel like you were this ... *thing* I had to hide in front of my friends."

Billy's eyes detach from mine, staring at my chest. He gnaws on his lip as he listens.

"I mean, I guess we both sorta wanted to hide," I go on. "At least, at some point we'd decided it was for the best, didn't we? It's just ... now, it doesn't feel right."

"Maybe I put too much pressure on you," says Billy suddenly, still not meeting my eyes, his mind working. "I shouldn't ... hold it against you that you don't wanna tell your friends."

"I *do* want to tell my friends," I insist.

"You're just scared to."

I open my mouth to argue with him, then realize that he's right. I know I've always been afraid of what could happen, but I think I may have severely underestimated just how scared I really am inside. I'm downright terrified.

"It's alright," he goes on. "I'm scared, too."

I let out one dry chortle. "The hell you gotta be scared about, boy?" I ask, lifting an eyebrow. "The town knows already, don't they? I mean, people here pretty much just make their assumptions. No one's thinkin' otherwise."

"Maybe. Maybe not."

"Listen. I wanna, like, walk down Main Street holdin' your hand and be able to take you to the damn movies without hidin' in the back row. I wanna do all the things I've done with girlfriends before. I wanna kiss you wherever the hell I like. I want ..." A heavy sigh escapes my lips. "I want to tell people how I feel about you. I'm so fuckin' proud of it, Billy ... of us ... of *this*."

He gives me a short, patient nod. "I know."

"You just ... gotta give me time," I finish.

Billy meets my eyes again. We stare at each other for a very long time. Every muscle in my body tenses with the fear that Billy could decide not to put up with any of this and break things off right now. I know that's a very real possibility I must face.

"Please don't leave me," I suddenly beg him. My eyes are welling up. *Fuck, don't cry.* "You're the best damn thing to ever happen to me."

Billy sucks in a bunch of air, then lets it all out. I see some lightness enter his face as he appraises me. Then, after too long a time, he says, "Shit, Tanner. Don't start cryin' like a bitch in my kitchen."

I let out a laugh. I feel a tear or two in my eye, but the sadness quickly turns to joy when Billy closes the space between us and wraps me in his arms. I let my head fall on his shoulder as I hug him back, my face nuzzled into his neck. We hold each other in the middle of a warm, richly scented heaven filled with deliciousness in all directions.

"You just came over for my baking," he mumbles into my ear. "Don't lie."

"I totally did," I confess. "I just want to eat up all this stuff and not let any of our guests have a single bite."

He pulls away to look at my face, smiling. I grin back, elated. This small moment has made all the torment and agony of Sunday night and Monday without Billy worth it.

"Well, it *is* a test run," he points out. "Your guests *won't* be eatin' any of this. In fact ..." Billy slips away from me, going to a cabinet and pulling down a paper plate, which he quickly fills with an assortment of his treats. "Here," he says, handing it to me. "You and your brother can be my taste-testers."

I stare down at the plate, eyes wide. "You'll probably become Jimmy's new best friend."

"I hope they turned out alright."

"Shut up. You know they're perfect," I tease him.

He lifts a softened expression at me, and then the two of us stare long and hard at one another, as if suddenly recalling all the words we just shared a moment ago.

"I'll give you time, Tanner," he tells me. "As much as you need. Even if ... we never tell anyone about us, I don't care. This ..." Billy takes a quick breath, then finishes his sentence. "This ... is enough for me."

I stare into his hazel eyes, which glow with longing. Something about his words saddens me, despite his effort in trying to do the right thing.

Right thing ... *What is the right thing?*

I set down the paper plate full of treats on the nearest counter with a papery slapping sound, then shut up all my worries by bringing his face in for a kiss. I didn't realize how much I've missed Billy Tucker's tender lips until my own are touching them. From the way he tugs at my hips, he has too.

CHAPTER 15
BILLY

"Triple fudge brownies," I announce, "with roasted walnuts and white chocolate chips."

"Ooh," moans my ma, wide-eyed.

I give a nod at the next set of plates. "Mini pecan pies and apple tarts."

"Those are *so* adorable."

"Next to them, raspberry-swirled custard-filled cream puffs with chocolate ganache on top. I'm especially proud of those," I point out. "The custard was a bitch."

"Really, though, you're stopping my heart with the descriptions alone," my ma insists, a hand to her chest. "Junior, these are just ... titillating."

I smile, proud of the work. "All I've got left to make is the vanilla bean cupcakes, topped with my homemade marshmallow cream frosting. Oh, and I nearly forgot." I give a nod at the freezer. "Three flavors of my ice cream—chocolate, strawberry, and vanilla bean—for the do-it-yourself sundae station we talked about, complete with an assortment of toppings, including caramel pecan sauce ... and my signature hot fudge." I glance back at her, finding her in a frozen, half-swooned state with her jaw dropped. "Tanner loves my hot fudge."

She snaps out of her stupor and gives me a sharp nudge with her elbow. "Oh, I bet he does."

I grin. "I'm gonna need a taste-tester, y'know."

"I still can't believe we're catering a Strong Ranch party," she murmurs, slapping a hand to her cheek. "You realize they've had at least fifty or so different events and gatherings out there and not *once* have they considered using our food to feed their guests? This is huge, Billy. This is really, really huge. Your father's beside himself. I mean, these Strongs, they pay, and they pay *big*. That Nadine ain't foolin' around."

"All thanks to Tanner insistin' on using us," I point out, then suffer a pang of emotion as I think on him and the look on his face when we stood in my kitchen at home just a few short days ago. Since then, we've exchanged many texts in the midst of my being totally occupied in baking and his being totally occupied in managing something of a war between his ma and his grandma. *I can't wait to see him tomorrow at the party.*

"That Tanner boy really is somethin' else," sings my ma, then suddenly hugs me. "And so are you, Junior."

"Aww, Ma."

"He's treatin' you right?"

My eyes shoot through the kitchen window, as if to spot anyone who might be hearing this, but then realize that we're closed and have been closed the past two days, since we're using all our resources to cook up everything for the party tomorrow. No one's here but me and my parents.

"I know you're probably keepin' it all down-low for his sake," she goes on, "or maybe you just don't wanna say. That's fine, that's fine. I won't pry. I just wanna know that my son's happy, like any good mother."

"Your son's doin' just fine," I say to the counter, then find myself folding my arms and leaning against the nearby fridge.

She studies me for a moment, likely not buying my statement one bit. "Good," she says anyway, though her voice is distant and reeks of that *we'll-come-back-to-this-later* undertone.

A moment later, I'm in the front laying out my pans and plates of pastries on various tables to cool, since I've run out of counter space in the kitchen. It's oddly comforting, having no customers at any of our tables in the bright, summery sunlight of a Friday afternoon. I've had to address a number of folk who stop by our doors and tap on the glass, apparently unable to read a simple sign posted at the front.

Right as I'm setting down another pan by the booths, my pa comes barging out of the kitchen, his eyes crazed and a hand up at his chin, pulling on the skin there. "The hell did I leave the dang pepper?"

I lift an eyebrow. "Black pepper? Or the cayenne?"

He looks down at his hand, tightly gripping a canister of pepper. "Oh, shit. I'm holdin' it."

I shake my head. "Pa, you need to take a break."

"I'm fine, I'm fine." He stares at the pepper for a long while, then sits down at the table closest to him and bites his lip, staring up at the glass windows and appearing to daydream.

I decide to take my own advice and grant myself a break, joining him at his table. "Overwhelming, huh?"

"Never produced an order this big," he says sleepily. "Can't remember the last weekend we actually closed. So many things can go wrong. Twice now, the back smoker has given out. It isn't used to smokin' this volume of food at the same time."

"Same goes for you, I think."

He looks at me, then gives a wiggle of his mustache as he pulls his face back. "You sayin' I really need a break?"

"I think I know how to smoke pork butt," I tease, knowing how to cook every damn thing on the menu. "Let me take some of the load off your shoulders."

"Nah, Junior. You got enough on your ..." He waves his hand in the air, searching for the word, then gives up. "Just keep doin' what you do. I'll be fine."

I frown. "Last time you looked the way you do and said what you just said—"

"I collapsed in the kitchen—knockin' my head on the door of the oven on my way down—and got rushed to the hospital for a heart attack. Yep. Well aware, son."

"So let's keep ourselves paced," I tell him softly, "and maybe try to ... avoid havin' that happen again ...?"

He smiles at me out of the side of his face, twitching his mustache, then gives me a short, tired nod. "I'll ... take breaks. I'll take it easy."

"I'm serious," I tell him, my eyebrows pulled together. "I don't wanna be in Florida and get the call that you've dropped from another heart attack. You gotta take care of yourself and keep this dang place open. For Ma."

He frowns with thought. "Sounds like the kind of speech _I'm_ supposed to be givin' _you_."

I grin. "I'm just lookin' out for you, Pa. We're a team."

"That's right. I bring the savory ... but you bring all the sweet. Those Strongs are gonna want you to cater all their parties after they get a taste of what you got to bring." He nods at the tables behind me filled with all of my creations. "They're ... _We're_ going to miss you. Shit. I'm havin' doubts about you goin'."

"It's just Florida," I point out.

"That's halfway across the country!"

"I'll be livin' with your brother. You guys talk every day, almost."

"Just not ready to see you go."

"I'm still here a few more weeks, about."

"I'm so used to havin' you around every day, Billy." He shakes his head. "It's not gonna be the same."

"Dang! I ain't gone yet!" I finally shout with half a laugh. I lift out of my seat to give my pa a big hug. He returns it halfheartedly, still lost in his thoughts. "And ... Pa?"

"Yeah?"

"You really gotta stop smokin'."

He eyes me, not saying a word. Then, after a long moment, he finally shuts his eyes and gives a slow nod. "Alright, alright. It was just a lapse. I know."

"You gotta stop. For your heart. For Ma."

"I know."

I give him another hug, this one a bit tighter. Then I freeze. "Uh ... I'm smellin' meat. How close to bein' done is it?"

"Shit."

My pa's out of the chair and rushing back into the kitchen to check on the meat.

I stand there in the middle of the diner surveying all the tables. I pull out my phone and take a picture of the confections, then shoot it over to Tanner. Crossing my arms, I lean against the nearest window, staring out at our tiny, empty, sun-bathed parking area. My phone vibrates. I glance down and find a selfie of Tanner with his tongue hanging out and a message drawn across it in blocky pixel art that reads: OMG FEED ME. That makes me chuckle.

When all the prep work and baking is finished and the sun is gone for the day, Mindy spontaneously stops by the diner to see all the hard work. "Nope," I tell her, stopping her at the door. "Can't see it. Gotta come out to the ranch tomorrow to—"

"Like hell," she spits out with a cocky smirk, pushing past me and perusing the tables. "I'm privileged people. I get to see the behind-the-scenes. Ooh." Her eyes light up. "Is that chocolate puddin' ...?"

"Ganache, actually, but call it what you want. Tastes like heaven in your mouth either way."

"Well, aren't you confident," she teases flatly.

I chuckle, watching as she continues to be dazzled by all the sweet, delicious fruits of my labor. As she goes on browsing, I'm suddenly reminded that she was supposed to have a date tonight with Steven Baker. She'd finally decided to ask him out after running into him at the grocery store. He actually said yes, which surprised me, since I thought he was flirting with that usher at the movies.

"You already back from your date with Steven?" I ask. "Or ... has it not happened?"

"Ditched that man-whore a-hole," she says with a roll of her eyes. "He's already jugglin' three different girls as it is, if in fact the rumors are right. I ain't gonna be a fifth wheel, if that's what you call it."

"Are you sure you don't wanna quit here and get a job at the movie theater?" I prod her. "He seems to have a thing for employees of the cinema."

"Funny story. The girl usher you're talkin' about," she says, tilting her head, "her and I compared notes. He's a big ol' liar, that Steven. Everything he said to her, he's said to Virginia at the pawn shop and to Elissa at the corner store."

"You still talk to Virginia?" I ask, incredulous.

"Shush. Not the point. We're formin' a bit of a plan, her and I. We've planned a little revenge-flirt to put that sucker in his place. Once he commits to a date with one of them, they're *all* gonna show up to give him a piece of their mind." She cackles once, proud of herself. "The player's about to get *played*."

I'm not sure whether to be proud of her or concerned. Either way, I give her a nod of encouragement. Then I shake my head. "Still can't believe, after what Virginia did to you, that you're talkin' to her."

"I know. Same ol' story. She stole my man. Backstabs and lies. Blah, blah. Friends turned to enemies. Why do I need to hold a grudge?" she asks, wrinkling up her face. "It happened junior year. Sometimes, we just need to get it off our chest, forgive, and move on."

Get it off our chest. Forgive. Move on.

My eyes detach as I think about what Tanner's doing right now. Did I really get it off my chest, what he did to me Sunday? Have I really forgiven him, if there's even anything to truly forgive?

And what would it mean, in this context, to move on?

With the summer passing by so fast, and the arrival of fall meaning that I'm hopping into an apron in Florida and Tanner's gearing up for another season of football, I'm not sure I like what "move on" sounds like.

"Billy."

My eyes snap back to Mindy. "Yeah?"

"You ain't listenin' to a thing I'm sayin', are you?"

I blink. She was talking still? "Sorry. My mind went someplace. I got a lot on my mind," I confess, slapping a hand to my cheek and shaking my head.

She nods, her eyes surveying all my desserts again. "You really do. Get it all sorted before tomorrow, pal. You are gonna need ... a *shit* lot of attention span. Those parties at the Strong Ranch are no laughin' matter. Just think of a busy Saturday night rush here at the diner ... except times ten."

"Thanks," I tell her dryly, not wanting to imagine it.

She puts a hand on my arm. "If anyone can handle it, it's you." She gives me an encouraging squeeze.

I smile, appreciating her support. "Thanks, Mindy."

"I'll see you tomorrow." With that, she's out the door, the bell chiming with her exit.

I glance back at my tables full of baked goods. I think about my pa handling this place when I'm off in Florida and whether he'll really take my advice in keeping it calm and not overworking his heart. I picture my ma giving him lengthy shoulder massages to calm him down while she's secretly tallying up numbers and figures in her head, picking up the work I usually do with the books.

That night when I'm in my room and I've brushed my teeth and the house is so quiet that I can hear the wind brushing along the grass in the front yard, I listen to my own breathing. It sounds lonely. Nothing quite compares to the sound of someone else breathing next to you. It's almost magical, the way two people can connect when all they hear is their own breathing. It's so intimate. It's so human. It's so vulnerable.

And I miss Tanner's breathing. I miss his body next to mine in a bed. Some strange fear keeps waking up inside me, a fear that I'll never have that again.

Tanner is the perfect guy. He's beautiful inside and out. Yes, he's afraid. Yes, he's shown his flaws. But that just makes him more attractive to me. He's real and raw and as unpretentious as the rough, chaotic sheets that envelop my body right now.

The house is empty, but my heart's emptier without him.

I pull my phone off of my desk by the bed, then stare up at the screen as it spills its light all over me. Should I shoot him a text? Is he staring at his phone right now, wondering the same thing? Is there a possibility that he's as miserable as I am?

Tanner's ruined me for anyone else I could possibly have. No one will compare to him. If I want to be happy, he's my one and only shot.

Damn you, Tanner Strong.

CHAPTER 16

TANNER

I leave the bathroom full of steam after my morning shower, clad in just a towel around my waist. I'm poking through the closet in the guest room for something to wear when Grandma's voice at the door makes me jump.

"Thanks, but no thanks."

She's standing in the doorway with a tissue that has something small dangling out of it between her pinched fingers, outstretched. I squint, not understanding. "Sorry, Grandma? You need somethin'?"

"I said thanks, but no thanks." She gives the thing a wiggle.

I take a few steps toward her, then freeze.

It's a condom.

Billy's unused condom from when he was over. My buddies showed up and interrupted us and I shoved it in my nightstand drawer.

Can I seriously act like I have no idea where that came from? "Uh ..."

"I mean, it was awful considerate of you," she goes on dryly, "to leave me a gift in your nightstand when I was just lookin' for the Bible. But seein' as it's out of the wrapper, I doubt I can make much use of it." She flings the thing at my bed. It falls short and lands unexcitingly on the carpet. "You can have it back."

"Uh ... Grandma ..."

"And this, too," she says, producing a tube of lube.

Oh my fucking God.

"Grandma ..." I'm sweating and my face is burning. "I don't even—"

"Don't get me wrong. Strawberry's a nice flavor," she says as she sets the tube on the dresser by the door, "but I'm much more of a *chocolate* girl. So *no thanks* to that as well. Is this anal lube?"

I shut my eyes and slap my face. I can't even make thoughts right now. I feel pins and needles of anxiety all over my body.

"I don't really want an answer to that," she decides. "You know I'm just givin' you a hard time, Tanner. I don't give a horse's heinie what you're doin' behind closed doors and it ain't none of my business as long as it's consensual." Grandma wrinkles up her face. "But really, Tanner. Strawberry?" She shakes her head as if gravely disappointed, then leaves.

What a way to start my day.

I put on a short-sleeved red plaid shirt that has roll-up tabs on the sleeves, which I button, giving them a crisp and clean look despite them tightly hugging my arms. I wear a nice pair of shorts with a belt. I let my hair drift in lazy short strands to one side, giving it a faux-parted look with some rebels sticking up in the back.

When the Tuckers show up, it's only Billy's parents at first. I help set up the downstairs of the house with Jacky-Ann while several of the farmhands set up the portable gazebos in the yard with tables and chairs where the guests will sit to eat. My papa talks to Billy's father about what the arrangements will be like outside for his buffet.

I keep turning to them, distracted, since I haven't really taken the time yet to get to know Billy's father. He came to all my games, too. That thick mustache of his has seen the existence of dinosaurs. He seems like a fun guy with a lot of wisdom under that Biggie's Bites cap on his head, squishing down whatever hair he has. My father looks so clean-cut and baby-faced compared to him, despite being a foot taller.

I slip through the glass doors to find my mama with Billy's mother at the tables under the big gazebo where the food will be served. "Billy's right behind us," explains Mrs. Tucker. "He had extra things he needed to attend to before headin' on his way, so he'll be comin' in my car. Nadine, you have such a lovely place out here! Oh, your chafing dishes are so *fancy* ...!"

My mother, of course, doesn't know how to take a compliment. "Oh, really, well they just aren't a big deal at all," she says, wrinkling her nose and giving a dismissive wave of her hand at them. "Did you say he was bringing two desserts or three?"

"Six," says Mrs. Tucker, wiggling her eyebrows.

I leave the mothers, stand calmly on the front porch, and lean against the railing. I'm not much needed inside, since they're finishing up with all the decorations and have the furniture pushed to the perimeters of the living room, leaving plenty of space for dancing and loitering.

The DJ my mama always hires shows up, a man about forty years old named Lyle "The Boot Scooter", who gives me a dimply smile and a tip of his hat as he enters the house.

Ten minutes later, my mama's cohorts show up to criticize everything with sweet backhanded compliments. Cassie Evans and all her blonde curls of hair over her milky skin, Marcy Whitman and her waves of shoulder-length red hair, and Cissy McPherson with her tight black hairdo that hasn't a single strand daring to drift beneath chin-level. The trio of them arrive at once, as if finely choreographed, and saunter into the house one at a time, each of them giving me a sweet nod and a word or two of greeting. None of them ever had an issue with me, since I'm the sweet son and "Star of Spruce" who can do no wrong; it's my mother they grew up with. I had wished that after all this time, they would have become adults by now and learned to embrace whatever common ground they have, which by the look of it is actually a lot. I don't know anymore who's antagonizing whom.

Some of my buddies show up early, including Kirk and his girlfriend Bonnie, who is a cute brunette twig standing next to Kirk's big frame. Harrison shows up too and is immediately put to work by my mama, who catches him and has him help set up another gazebo-style tent that my little brother is having trouble figuring out.

It's about thirty minutes before the party starts that I see Billy's car—or rather, his mama's car—pulling up the long driveway and taking a spot by my pickup.

I'm already by his door when he steps out. He wears a long-sleeved green plaid shirt that's fitted, hugging his frame perfectly, with khakis cinched by a brown leather belt. I have no idea how he's planning to contend with the heat out here in that attire, considering I already see beads of sweat on his forehead, but damn does he look cute. His hair shows wet evidence of having been fixed, but still carries that sort of messy *I-woke-up-with-my-hair-doing-this* look he always seems to have.

"Hey, Billy," I greet him. "You look good."

"I'm an idiot," he blurts, popping the trunk, coming around the car, and fussing with large closed containers of his treats. "I'm gonna be a puddle before it's even time to put out my desserts."

"You'll be fine," I assure him, despite agreeing that he will, indeed, melt completely before the sweets are set up in the house later on. "Thank God for the shade."

"Can you help carry this?" he asks.

"Of course," I say, coming up to his side.

When our shoulders touch, it occurs to me very much that there's no one driving down the road, everyone is in the house or in the backyard helping with the setup, and not a single person's eyesight is directed our way. I breathe in Billy's scent, driven crazy in an instant because it reminds me of those nights when he'd fall asleep at my side. He has such a clean and inviting smell, even when he sweats. I'm all animal in an instant, feeling my cock stir and my stomach start to dance.

"Billy ..."

He lifts his eyes. I don't think he even realized how close I am until his face is an inch from mine, drawn by my uttering his name.

"Yeah?" he murmurs quietly.

There's something expectant about his eyes. He wants me to kiss him. His hands have frozen and he's not even concerned with his desserts anymore; he just wants me to move an inch forward— just one tiny inch—and bring our tender, hungry lips together.

Just one inch.

Just one small, stupid inch.

Then I hear the crunching of gravel beneath boots, and I pull away from Billy just in time to see Kirk appear. "Hey!" he barks out. "Gimme somethin' to carry!"

A flicker of annoyance passes through Billy's eyes before he faces Kirk with a smile. "Thanks, Kirk. If you can take these ..."

"I can take twice those! Stack them up!" He takes the load from Billy, then holds them balanced against his chest while Billy stacks a few more.

"Keep them straight, please," Billy calls out to Kirk as he heads back to the house. "There's a cooler in the back seat with ice cream, too!"

While I'm trying to meet Billy's eyes again, he hands me a short stack of wide containers before gripping the rest of them on his own.

He isn't looking at me anymore. "Billy ..."

"We gotta get these inside before they melt," he says coolly as he starts toward the house. "Can you get the trunk?" he calls out over his shoulder as he goes.

I sigh. *You're such a wuss, Tanner.*

I brace the containers I have against the back bumper in order to reach up and slam shut the trunk, then rebalance them in my arms and make my way to the house. In the kitchen, Billy and Kirk are working together to fill the fridge and freezer with some of his confections. I hand each of my containers off, watching Billy's expression the whole time and trying to discern whether he's pissed to all hell, or just super incredibly focused on making sure everything goes right.

Maybe it's a bit of both.

When the desserts are put up, Billy is called away to the yard to help with his father's food setup, and he goes without another word to me. And like the big waste of headspace that I am, I just stand there in the kitchen like an idiot and say nothing. My shirt is wetted slightly by the condensation from the containers I was just holding and my eyes are locked on Billy, watching him through the glass doors as he walks around helping with the setup and looking so damned cute.

I'm going to lose him if I don't do something soon. If I don't find my balls and stand up to my own stupid fears, he's going to get tired of me really fast.

He said he'd be patient. He told me in that kitchen of his that he wanted to give me all the time I needed, but I don't think he knows what that means. He's going to be off to Florida come the fall. I'll be back in Oklahoma trying to keep up my reputation of being the big football star everyone wants me to be. I'll have to face my classes, the grades of which I'm barely holding on to.

Who am I kidding? Billy's going to be the best damn thing at his school in Florida. He's gonna wow all of his instructors. He'll do well because he's studied and he's a quick learner.

And he'll cook alongside lots of other cute guys. He'll meet some other sweet budding chef with a goatee who asks him to taste his sauce. Then that'll lead to aprons being torn off and *other* sauces being tasted. Then they'll fall in love and open a restaurant together and ...

And I'll be returning to Spruce like the loser I am. No one knows how much I struggle just to pass my classes, or how hard I have to fight to keep my spot on the team, since there's always some new up-and-coming hotshot every year that could take my place.

Everyone assumes the best. I can't open my mouth to let them know otherwise.

I back into the kitchen island, staring out that glass door and watching Billy among the tents and smiling at the others who are helping him. I feel so detached from it all and downright helpless.

When the guests start to arrive, I don't have any more time (or space) left to feel sorry for myself, so I put on my party face and mingle, greeting all the townsfolk who come by name. Marybeth and Jack. Lee and Gene Marvin who we do business with. Kirk's mama Clarice. Quincy, Penelope, Michael, Martha, and Charles. A lot of former teammates that I haven't seen in years—having missed seeing them even last summer—show up. So many of them have changed, but not a single one of them pursued football the way I did. I hear the same thing over and over, how much bigger I look, how much more confident I look, how strong I look. They tell me their versions of how they think my life must be like up in college, how I must have a million adoring fans, and comparing the sounds of the enormous college crowds to Spruce High's stands of screaming fans and cheering.

I take it all in with a smile. I don't correct any of them. I let them believe in the fantasy of what my life's like. It stings a little, to know what they think about me while also knowing what it's really like and not wanting to say a word in my own defense. I can't bear to destroy the spark of inspiration and joy in everyone's eyes.

The DJ is playing some seriously beat-driven country music, with a speaker or two blasting the music to the backyard. Plus, the doors to the deck are open, so people are streaming in and out of the house constantly. I always seem to be standing in front of new people every ten minutes or so.

But I'm never standing in front of the one person who matters.

As the afternoon progresses, I catch myself staring at the back glass doors looking for Billy far more times than I can count. Once,

I catch him by the pool talking to Mindy instead of at the tents. He never looks my way, but I think that's because he's so focused on whether any dishes need clearing or food needs replenishing. It might be the only thing that truly warms my heart right now, watching him devote himself to making sure everyone's enjoying themselves. He takes part in so much of his papa's grilling and cooking, a pinch here and there of his own recipes and spices, that I feel so much damn joy surging through me. Like an antidote, it just washes out all of that nastiness inside my head.

This is why I want Billy in my life. He makes me worry less. He makes me feel like a better person.

Billy Tucker makes me feel at home in my own home.

I decide after a few hours in the crowded house that it's time to try and brave some proximity to Billy, the only damn person on these three-hundred-odd acres whose opinion I truly care about.

But just as I head out, he heads in, and we both stop at the doorway nearly face-to-face.

He doesn't say anything, his eyes hovering on mine. His pits are wet and there's streaks of moisture down his front. His face glitters with sweat and his cheeks are pink.

"You look like you need a cool glass a' water," I tell him.

He chuckles once breathily, then nods and says, "At least there's some shade."

"So how's it goin' out there?"

"Tastily," he says, flat-lipped.

There's such tension in him. I don't know how much is from the party and how much is me. I lean against the doorframe, studying him. "You look really good, Billy."

"I'm a mess."

"Well, you're sweaty. But you still look mighty good."

He gives a short shrug and the tiniest smile. "If you say so, Tanner."

"If you need a replacement shirt," I point out, "I got some more summer-appropriate stuff in my closet that might fit you. Polos. Short-sleeves. Another pussy-lickin' tee, if you prefer."

"That one was enough," he insists with a smirk.

Without thinking, I reach for his hand and start to unbutton his sleeve. He watches, his lips parted and his breath caught. Slowly, I fold up the sleeve of his left arm up to the elbow. Then I take hold of his right and do the same, gently unbuttoning the sleeve and rolling it up as neatly as possible. I take so much care to ensuring that every fold is straight and pristine. I even redo the cuff a couple times, just to be sure.

And yes, maybe I'm taking my sweet-ass time because I want to touch Billy so badly right now. Maybe I like the way my fingers kinda graze the tiny hairs on his forearm. Maybe I like him being forced to pay attention to me as I fold up his sleeves with excruciating attention.

Maybe this act will be all I get of touching Billy and feeling his skin graze mine, the first Saturday night I've spent in almost a month without Billy and I, alone, having the time of our lives.

When I'm finished, I look up into his eyes, then let go of his sleeves. He folds his arms, pushing the sleeves up a bit, then smiles tightly and gives me a nod. "Thanks."

"You're welcome," I murmur back so quietly that the thumping music almost drowns me out.

Then he passes by me far closer than necessary—his scent wafting off his body and intoxicating me—and I turn to watch him pull containers from the fridge. When he passes by me again, he gives me another little smile on his way back to the tents.

My heart fills up with just that tiny interaction, but it's not enough. *It'll never be enough.*

The party carries on, and soon the sun starts to bruise the sky orange as it runs away, taking the day with it. No one seems to have left the party. In fact, the house looks twice as crowded as before after the sky gently darkens. Lamps are lit up all along the yard, including paper lamps on the porch and tiny floating candle-like decorations in the pool.

Now it's Billy's time to shine. All of his desserts are beautifully displayed on the formal dining room table inside the house. People form a buffet line of sorts as they help themselves.

I flood with pride as I watch the guests. To put it simply, they are in awe. I see more wide-eyed gapes and dropped jaws now than at the most pivotal football games at Spruce High that I can remember. There is a constant murmur of delight thrumming through the crowd, who are salivating over the line of chocolaty, fruity, colorful desserts before them.

Billy outdid himself by far.

"Who in the *world* is responsible for this?" asks Mario Tucci, executive chef of Nadine's, who's holding a small plate with three different desserts in one hand and a half-eaten pastry in the other.

It's my father to whom he asks the question. "William Tucker," my papa answers. "He's my son's friend."

"William? You mean the owner of that burger-flipper near Wicker street?"

"His son," clarifies my papa. "William Junior."

Since I'm standing right there, I take a step right into the conversation. "He goes by Billy," I say. "He's a nice guy and a good friend of mine."

"I don't care if he's nice," says Mario in his brusque, stern way. "That boy can *bake*. This is *good*."

"He does the dessert menu at the diner," I go on like an excited puppy. If I had a tail, it'd be slapping the wood floors repeatedly. "Every Saturday, he has this thing called his 'Saturday's Sweet', which is a new, special dessert he makes from scratch, and they are to die for. I can't think of a single Saturday that he hasn't given me somethin' that's made me salivate."

Like his cock.

Like his tongue.

Like his hands when they grip my hair.

Like his lips when they suck on mine with force.

"I didn't know about this at all," Mario confesses. He speaks to us while staring at the dessert line, his whole grey beard wiggling as he chews the pastry. "His talent's being wasted here in Spruce."

"He's going to culinary school in the fall," I go on, catching Mario's attention again.

"Culinary school?" grunts Mario. "Where?"

"Florida. I don't know which school."

He shakes his head. "Damn shame. I have connections closer by. He should study at my alma mater. I could put in a word. Damn shame." He pops the rest of the pastry in his mouth, chewing with more force than before. Then his focus is pulled by his wife, a sweet-faced woman who drifts up to his side and steals him away.

My papa soon after gives me a nod and a wink and says, "He really stole the show, that Billy," then strolls into the crowd, vanishing.

After I've let enough people help themselves, I finally step in line behind Kirk, who's attached to Bonnie by the hip, the two of them unable to keep their hands off each other. She whispers something into his ear, and then he laughs. Watching the two of them together, their love and affection on display for the whole world, it fills me with yearning to have that kind of freedom for myself.

My plate is filled with one of everything. Billy is making his way around, checking on all the dessert platters and ensuring that none of them become empty before he can refill it with more. The do-it-yourself sundae station at the kitchen island is my next destination after I finish my plate, treasuring every sweet, flavorful bite of Billy's tasty confections.

I seriously could help myself to five more servings, but I don't, kicking back with Joel as he goes on about that Mindy girl and how he can't stop looking at her. "Go for it," I tell him, despite his protests that she already seemed dismissive toward him. "She's wide open. She's eating in the corner by herself scowling at everyone and hating the world. Sounds just like your type."

"That's just it. She's not my type at all. But I can't stop staring. It's like ..." His eyes flash. "Is she a witch? Did she cast a spell on me?"

"Yep. That must be it."

"I'm serious, man."

"Why don't you go over and ask her? Ain't doin' you no good standin' over here chattin' with me."

"Just leave me alone for a bit," he says, giving me a shove of his shoulder. "I gotta work up to it. I need to gather up the nerve."

"Don't wait too long or you'll miss your chance," I tell him.

"Lots of good-lookin' guys here who are lookin' her way, too."

He shakes his head irritably. "Gotta work up to it."

So I leave him there to "work up to it", as he says.

Telling him that makes me realize I need to take my own damn advice. I've given myself enough time to "work up to it", haven't I? When am I finally going to tell Billy what he means to me and not give a shit who's around to witness it?

I make my way through the room, determined to find Billy. I have so many things I need to say to him and have been agonized all night with the words locked inside my stubborn mouth.

"Tanner."

I turn at my mama's voice. She's standing there with her posture so straight, you might think she'd just been spanked. "Not now," I tell her.

Her eyes grow double. I realize belatedly that she's flanked by Cassie Evans and Cissy McPherson, who just witnessed me curtly dismiss my mama.

I try to undo my little faux pas. "Sorry, that was rude of me. I just meant I'm ... headin' over to Billy to tell him somethin'. It's kind of important."

"Tanner, hon, that's exactly why I'm comin' to *you*. Everyone is abuzz about his desserts. You gotta seize the opportunity and make a statement to the room. Introduce them to the Tucker family—*namely Billy*—and lead them in a big ol' round of applause for our brand new caterers. *Even Mario is beside himself.*"

I freeze up. "You want me to do the congratulations? Isn't that what papa usually—?"

"It's your party. Everyone's here for you. *You* do it."

I glance up at Cassie and Cissy. The pair of them have a plate in their hands, delicately eating a pastry each. My mama must be riding a high of pride right now, showing off Billy like he's *her* find and *she's* responsible for all the deliciousness being enjoyed tonight.

But in that same breath, she's also wanting me to give due congratulations to him.

"Alright," I assure her. "I'll go do it."

"Better do."

I lean in close to her and lower my voice. "You sound like Grandma when you say that."

"Say that again," she warns teasingly, her voice just as low, "and I'll give her your room permanently."

Just then, I spot Joel over her shoulder. He's made it across the room—I guess having finally "worked up to it" enough—and he's chatting with Mindy, whose eyebrows are lifted curiously.

Staring at them, I say, "Sounds like just as much a punishment for *you* as it is to me."

My mama sighs. "Remind me when she leaves again."

"Tuesday."

"Lord help me."

I give my mama half a hug, then resume my pursuit across the kitchen toward Billy, but this time with a new intent in mind. He's leaning against the counter with his hands clasped as he quietly observes everyone.

He looks up when I approach. I don't like to say that the look in his eyes is cold or distant, but they don't carry the warmth that they usually do. It's like I'm just anyone else here approaching him to offer my compliments.

I'm about to remind him how *not* like anyone else I am.

"Billy," I say the moment I'm in front of him. "You're a hit."

The trace of a smile touches his lips. "They're really likin' the sweets," he agrees with a mild nod.

I melt into his hazel eyes. The fear is trying to reach up through my chest to choke me, but I'm going to be stronger than it. To earn back that place in Billy's eyes is worth all the terror I'm about to face and charge through.

"You're *my* hit, Billy."

His eyes flicker with confusion.

"I'm sorry," I tell him, "but you're gonna have to face the truth someday, that you're the most awesome person standing in this room."

He smirks, shaking his head and looking away.

I lean into his ear. "You're beautiful, Billy," I whisper.

When I pull back, there's a frustrated expression on his face. After too long a time, he finally turns his hazel eyes onto me, and they look fierce with emotion. I know this is bad timing, but when he's pissed, he looks so hot.

"I couldn't sleep a fuckin' wink last night," he growls.

Shit. He's growling. Again, bad timing, but damn that low voice is sexy.

"Me neither," I confess, "and I wanna do somethin' about it."

He lifts an eyebrow. "What do you mean?"

"I wanna do somethin' big. Really big. You just gotta promise me one thing."

Billy wrinkles his face all cutely, confused. "What the heck am I promisin'?"

"Not to get mad."

"Mad? Mad at what? At you?"

I throw an arm around his back, startling him. I pull him into my side like a buddy. "Are you ready for this?"

Now it's *him* with the fear in his eyes. "F-For what?"

I pull him along, my arm still over his back. I won't let him slip away, and he makes no move to get away. He comes along with me, his eyes curious as I drag him along. People part for us as we cut through the room to the corner where there's a lifted platform upon which the DJ is working his audio magic. We step up onto the little stage. My mama is right there to tell the DJ to cut the music for my little congratulatory speech.

The music quiets. So does the room. My mama gives me a tightened nod.

I turn towards everyone. A hundred faces look up at me. Most I know, some I don't. Kirk is in the back with Bonnie. Joel is near the stairs with Mindy. Harrison is in the crowd. So's Robby with his girl of the week. And my papa's there too. And Mario. And even Coach Adams. And dozens of others I knew from Spruce High. And, of course, Grandma.

"Thank you all for comin' out," I say to the crowd. "I know, lookin' out at all these faces, I'm in a room full of my best friends. And we've all enjoyed some seriously good food today, thanks to Biggie's Bites. If you liked a lick of what you enjoyed tonight, stop by their diner and have yourself a nice, tasty meal. Open 'til eight weekdays, 'til eleven weekends, closed on Sunday like the rest of the town. You and your stomach will thank me later. I personally recommend the Tackler, which about kicked my ass *and* my mouth in the best way possible."

A small chuckle of appreciation runs through the room, in which I also happen to spot Billy's papa near the couch. There's a twinkle in his eye that I daresay looks like a tear. His mustache curves with his smile.

"And if it isn't enough that they make tasty, belly-lovin', comfort food ... they have a dessert chef right there among them, who's responsible for all the delicious sweets you're enjoying tonight." My arm still rests over Billy's back, and I give him a squeeze the same way I would a buddy I'm especially proud of. "They speak for themselves, but dang it, let me just say a few words. Those desserts are not only so delicious I could cry tryin' to find the damn words to describe them ..." The crowd titters lightly. "But they are also ... works of *art*. The meticulousness put into making each dish. The plating itself, how he presents all his work. The artistry. Shit, listen to me. His desserts are makin' me say words like 'artistry'."

Billy is so flushed right now. I take a moment to peer into the side of his face, appreciating what all my praise is doing to him. His eyes flit nervously to me and he raises an eyebrow.

"So let's give a toast. With whatever you got. A plate of chocolate heaven. An apple tart. A sundae. Give a nice, mouth-thankin' toast to our dessert chef, Billy Tucker." I look his way. "My boyfriend."

Billy's eyes snap to mine, flashing.

I press my lips to his.

CHAPTER 17
BILLY

Well, I guess that's one way to do it.

I hear nothing, know nothing, and feel nothing else but Tanner Strong's lips against mine. I don't hear the gasps. I don't hear the scandalized murmurs. I don't notice heads turning and jaws dropping. I don't hear Tanner's little brother shout out, "Way to go, man!!" And I definitely don't hear a spattering of half-confused and half-appreciative applause.

Fuck it. Yeah. I hear all of that.

And whether they're applauding our field goal kiss, or my talent as a dessert chef, I don't know. Tanner's consuming me in front of the world, and I let him. Then, quite suddenly, the one and only thing I hear is his hot, jagged breaths as they beat against my face in feverish explosions. Those breaths speak a million words. He's liberated. He's determined. He's scared. He's brave.

And I'm right here with him.

I bring my hands up to his face, engaging myself in the kiss as much as he has. The touch to his face makes him calm, as if he had been reaching across some great, scary chasm for me—muscles quivering, eyes glassy with fear, fingers outstretched—and I just accepted his hand.

Our lips detach. We look into each other's eyes.

Now let's try not to fall down that chasm.

Tanner faces the room. Then, as if the kiss and his declaration didn't just happen, he lifts his hand. "C'mon, people! Give your dessert chef here and Biggie's Bites the round of applause they deserve!" He lets go of me and starts clapping.

It's Kirk in the back whose deep voice booms over the room. "Hell yeah!! Best damned burgers and desserts in Spruce!"

"Biggie's Bites rocks!!" cries out Joel, making Mindy laugh.

Then others shout their own versions of excitement, and soon the room is exploding in the joyous applause that Tanner was trying to summon a minute ago.

Y'know. Before he buried his tongue down my throat in front of the whole town of Spruce.

With the room applauding and cheering, the DJ takes a cue from his own intuition and resumes the music. Tanner looks back at me, a sweaty, red-cheeked look of happiness exploding across his face, and he reaches for my hand. "C'mon," he tells me with a wink. "Let's make the rounds to all your adoring fans."

"Tanner," I murmur unblinkingly. "What did we just do?"

"We just told the world how amazing you are."

"Tanner. Y'know dang well that's not what I'm talking about."

But before we can carry on our own conversation, we're descended upon by face after face from the crowd. Each person wants to offer their praises to me for the wickedly sweet way I worked everyone's tongue tonight—and not just Tanner's. Some people ask me for my recipes. Others just want to know how I came up with some of the desserts, especially the raspberry-swirled custard-filled cream puffs. I have to improvise coy responses on the spot, telling them just enough to pique their interest while also retaining some of the mystery. What's a chef, after all, without a secret ingredient or two?

My head is spinning by the time Tanner and I slip out of the room and end up by the pool, where there's a few people still mingling. The shimmering reflection coming through the water from the pool lighting dances across Tanner's face in waves.

"Wow," I mumble. "I ... wasn't expecting—"

"So much praise? Dude, I'm gonna make you believe it someday whether you like it or not, how awesome—"

"Tanner." My eyes are set on his. "You just came out to the whole town."

His face tightens a pinch, he thrusts his hands into his pockets, and he shrugs. "I did."

"And?"

He lifts an eyebrow. "And what? You're worth it. I couldn't stand another second of everyone *not* knowin' what you mean to me, and ..." He sighs, gazing down into my eyes in that way that makes me weak in the knees. "Billy, I've hated this past week."

There are so many things happening in my body right now that I don't know what to pay attention to.

"Me too," I admit.

He slowly runs a hand up my arm, his eyes following thoughtfully, until it comes to a rest atop my shoulder. After gazing into my eyes for a moment, he gives my shoulder a squeeze, then pulls me into him for a hug.

Comically, the country music playing inside the house turns into some two-step slow-dancing tune everyone's heard before.

Tanner, heeding the music like his cue, takes my hand and gently leads me into a slow dance. The few others who are still out here mingling and eating from small plates filled with my desserts have stopped their conversations to pay witness to us.

If my face wasn't on fire before, it sure as hell is now.

I get my mouth close to his ear and whisper, "People are staring."

He glances over his shoulder. Those who were staring quickly look away, returning to their own conversations as if they were never looking at us.

He faces me with a grin. "Who's scared now?"

"I ain't *scared*," I say, pulling away slightly from him.

He doesn't let me, his hand gripping mine tighter and his other holding me firmly at the small of my back, keeping me trapped in this sexy slow dance he's obviously enjoying. Our hips never disconnect.

He grins down at me superiorly. "You're mine, Billy."

I quirk an eyebrow. "Can you say that in a creepier, deeper voice, please? I didn't quite feel enough of your possessiveness."

A growl rumbles in his throat and a wickedness enters his grin. "You're ... *mine*."

"Perhaps you might like to say that at three in the morning while tapping on my bedroom window from outside," I suggest.

"Don't lie. You'd think it's hot."

"And creepy."

"Besides, I won't be *outside* your bedroom."

"Okay, that's better."

He grips me tighter. "Damn it, Billy, I just don't wanna let you go at all now. Can you forgive me for bein' a total dick in front of my friends a week ago?"

I lay my head against his chest, which also happens to remind me of precisely how he looks without his shirt on. "If you can forgive my neuroticism. I kinda said I'd be okay with us keeping things a secret one minute ... then *wasn't* okay with it the next."

"Shit. My parents know, now."

I lift my head off of his chest. His eyes are wide as they reel onto me.

"Havin' second thoughts?" I murmur.

After a moment of staring at me, he giggles. Then he lets out a laugh, as if someone just tickled him.

I wrinkle my brow. "You ... losin' your mind right now or somethin'?"

"I think I'm in shock," he confesses. "What ... W-What did I just do??" he asks as he fights the grin happening on his hysterical, dimpled face.

I can't help but laugh myself. "What *did* you do??" I throw back at him. "What's your ma gonna think?"

"She's probably spinnin' it however she can to her friends, I'm pretty sure. Pretending she knew. Or actin' like ... Oh, hell, I have no idea."

"Do you need to go talk to them?" I ask. "I mean, I'm gonna be here. I can just hang out while you—"

"Nah," he decides suddenly, pulling me against his muscular chest and resuming the slow dance. "They can wait. Tomorrow, I'll have a chat with them. Let my mama have a meltdown. Watch it all go to hell with my grandma makin' things worse and my papa just ... watchin' it all with that clueless look on his f-f-f-face," he titters, breaking into laughter again on the last word. He shakes his head. "If you'd bet me a hundred dollars that this is how tonight would go down ..."

"I'd be a hundred dollars richer," I mumble against his chest. The sound of his chuckles vibrate through my ear. "Honestly, I'd probably be out a hundred, too."

"Did you hear my little brother?"

I grin against his chest. "I totally did."

"And Kirk? Shit. He definitely knew already."

"Definitely."

When I glance over my own shoulder, I realize that everyone else has gone back inside. We're the only ones out here, swaying in the summer night breeze by the glimmering reflection shining from the pool.

Tanner was really brave to do what he did. I know it. He must know it. Of course, I might've picked a far less *dramatic* and *in-front-of-everyone-and-their-mother* method to tell his family and all his friends. But now it's done. And now we don't have to hide what's happening between us.

I feel like I can literally hear the page crinkling as we enter the next chapter of ... whatever this is.

And since Tanner faced his fears, perhaps it's about time I faced my own. "So, like ... now that everyone knows about you ..." I start to say.

"I was thinkin' the same thing," he grunts.

The ear pressed to him is filled with his heartbeat and the vibrations of his voice. "What thing?"

"Now that the big gay cat's out—all official-like—other boys will follow suit. You're gonna have nine hot dudes ringin' your doorbell askin' you out on a date, and you'll cast me aside ..."

"Hey, hey," I try to interject.

"Yep, I can see it now," he goes on, holding me tighter and not letting me pull away. "You'll get yourself a cute ol' butt boy from down the street, and he'll be all smart and sensitive in all the ways that I'm not ..."

I finally manage to push away from him enough to get a look at his face. When I do, I find him smirking.

Oh. All of that was a joke. I cross my arms and lift an eyebrow. "And what if that *does* happen?" I ask him with all the sass I have left in me. "What's the big bad college jock gonna do about it?"

He lifts his eyebrows, stunned at my attitude. The way he stands there—poised for a fight, his biceps flexing all on their own, his pecs rising and falling with each of his breaths in that tight shirt of his—he looks so fucking hot.

Then he lets out a laugh. "You wanna know what I'll do? I'll tell you what I'll do. I'm gonna beat down every fucker who thinks they can get their paws on you before I have a chance to *really* steal your heart."

"Steal my heart?"

"And," he goes on, ignoring my question, "I might *actually* pull out my dick and have a measuring contest. I'm pretty sure I got everyone in Spruce beat. I mean, I've taken showers with half the dudes here throughout high school. I know what most of our graduating class was packin', whether I wanted to or not."

I stifle a laugh, turning it into a snort. "You were such a homo back then, checkin' out your teammates."

"Nah. Just checkin' out my competition. And I win, hands down," he says, then grabs his crotch and gives it a firm jiggle. "You're one lucky man."

"Wow. Someone's full of themselves tonight," I tease, trying very hard not to grin despite myself.

"Confident," he corrects me, taking a step forward and reclaiming me with his hands slipping around my back. He pulls me in tight, our hips meeting. "I'd like to say I'm confident."

I feel his cock flex through his shorts.

Damn.

I look up into his eyes. Something about the way I look at him must sober him right away, because I watch as his sharp, cocky gaze slowly softens. Then he tilts his head slightly and smiles, almost sweetly.

Fuck. This man has his claws in every single part of me. He makes me hard as a rock. Then he melts my heart with a single gaze into those rich brown eyes.

"What're you thinkin', Billy?" he asks me gently.

I didn't quite get my fears out earlier, since he sort of hijacked the point I was about to make. "Well. I was just thinkin' ... now that the town knows about you ..."

"Yeah?"

"I was ... actually thinkin' about *you* getting nine or ten dudes ringin' *your* doorbell." I shrug. "I guess I sorta feel like ... maybe I was just your default choice. Maybe, if you had a broader selection, you might—"

"You wanna stay the night?" he asks, cutting me off.

I blink. Is that all this man thinks about? Sex?

"Why?" I ask him.

He brings a hand up to my face. His fingers softly run through my hair, then grip the back of my head. "So I can show you why you're my *only* choice."

My lips part.

And for the second time tonight, he surprises me with a kiss that claims every bit of breath within me.

CHAPTER 19

TANNER

Billy's peacefully sleeping face is the most satisfying thing a man can open his eyes to in the morning. His tush makes two cute and nearly irresistible humps in the bed sheets. His backside is smooth and firm as he clutches the pillow, his face pressed into it with a look of peace as he softly takes in each breath of air, then lets it out slowly.

Okay, maybe I am a bit of a creep, but I can sit back and watch him like that for hours. Yeah, it's also a kind of torture, since what I'd *really* like to do is wake him up and repeat a little bit of the "body aerobics" we performed last night. It involved a lot of muffled moaning, butt-grabbing, my cock on his lips, his cock in my butt, and strawberry lube. Not to mention the sensual shower we took together before dropping into the bed, exhausted.

When he finally wakes up, sunlight is pouring all over his body, and he smiles into it when he sees me. *I hope I always have that effect on him.* "Babe ..." he moans groggily.

Babe. There he goes with that word again. "I think I smell some breakfast," I tell him.

He lifts an eyebrow, then takes a big whiff. "I don't smell anything."

"You sure about that?"

He squints sleepily at me, confused.

I decide to "unconfuse" him by slipping right under the sheets, swimming between his legs, and devouring his stiff morning wood. I get the private pleasure of feeling his leg muscles tense up and his fingers claw into the bed sheets, gripping tightly.

I don't come up for air until *he* comes.

It doesn't take long.

Sliding out from the sheets, I grin down at him cockily as I survey the breathless state I've invoked in him. "Can't say I've ever enjoyed a 'protein shake' like that so early in the morning," I groan at him.

He's out of breath for a while, unable to respond. "You're ... somethin' else," he finally gets out in that deep morning voice of his. Then he chuckles, unable to wipe the smile off his face. I love that I do that to him. "Fuck. *Now* I'm starved."

"Me too."

He gives me a wink. "I'll make some breakfast," he says, then hops out of the bed.

I give him a swat on his ass before he can get away from me. It makes the best sound in the world, second only to the throaty giggle he lets out as a result. "Yeah? Maybe it's *my* turn to make *you* breakfast."

He quirks an eyebrow. "Please. You couldn't even boil an egg."

"Oh yeah? Is that a challenge?"

"Double dog dare."

"You're on!"

Of course, by the time we get dressed and downstairs, Jacky-Ann is already in the kitchen starting the coffee for the household. When she sees us, a coy sort of grin comes over her face and she says, "Hi, boys," before starting the coffeemaker.

I come up to her side and give her a playful bump of my hip.

"Hi there, Jacky-Ann. You're gettin' the mornin' off. Breakfast is on *me*."

"Is that so?" she asks, giving teasing eyes to Billy.

"You just kick back and relax, sweetheart," I assure her. "I got this."

Half an hour later, I totally don't got this. Billy leans against the counter with his arms folded as he watches me try to make pancakes with his lips sucked in, firmly trying not to laugh at my endeavors. Jacky-Ann is leaning against the kitchen island with a mug of coffee, watching purely for the entertainment, if I had to guess.

"Can I take over yet?" asks Billy.

"Like hell," I spit back, despite the mess of flour and eggshells and strings of egg white that didn't make it to the bowl.

"You're literally gonna kill us with your pancakes," he lets me know.

I smirk at him. "How 'bout you get your tush over here and teach me?"

Billy grins, as if having won some game I didn't know we were playing, then starts to teach me the proper way to make pancakes—plus a little secret or two of his own to make them fluffier, melt-in-the-mouth, and perfect. By the time he pours the first pancake from the batter, my stomach is inside-out with its urgent growling. I can't wait to bite into these crispy-yet-soft pieces of heaven.

Soon, my little brother's down the stairs and joining us at the table for some Billy-caliber pancakes. He sits next to Jacky-Ann, who we've demanded to sit down and enjoy some breakfast with us. There's an assortment of scrambled eggs, bacon, and sausage on the table, thanks to my clumsy hands that were carefully guided by Billy's soothing, patient instruction. I burned one side of the sausages, but no one complains. Eating breakfast with Jacky-Ann, Jimmy, and Billy feels so strangely natural, it's almost weird. Jimmy keeps asking Billy questions about cooking and what he does at Biggie's. Jacky-Ann listens with a constant look of curiosity in her eyes. I sit at the end of the table like a king, enjoying it all.

When my parents descend the stairs, soon followed by Grandma, the dynamic of the room takes a turn for the awkward. My mama can't stop staring at Billy like he's a damn Martian and wondering why he's still here. My papa acts like he always does: oblivious to everything and smiling at everyone.

And then there's Grandma. "You have to install some soundproof walls in this dang house, Paul," she says. "I can hear everything, and it ain't doin' any favors for my sleep apnea."

Jimmy snorts mid-gulp in his orange juice.

Billy and I share a look across the table, and I get to watch him fight a blush.

"Hon."

It's my mama's cool, detached voice I hear. I swallow my bite of pancake and lift my chin. "Yeah?"

"We need to talk later. You and I."

I lift an eyebrow. "About what?"

"Just us. Later on."

After a glance at my papa's airy face, I squint at her. "Is this about last night?"

"Later, hon."

"You can talk to me right here. We were all there last night," I press on. "If you got somethin' to say ..."

"Dang it, Tanner," she blurts out, setting her fork of eggs down on the plate so hard, it rings out like a bell and fills the room. "If I knew you wanted a comin' out party, you shoulda told me beforehand so I could have planned accordin'ly!"

I blink. That wasn't quite what I was expecting.

"Colors and themes, hon!" she goes on, her eyes wide and incredulous. "I have a gay hairdresser in Fairview and he coulda come! Hell, he probably woulda had fabulous ideas for decorating! My nails." She lifts one of her hands, as if accusing me of its dullness. "I would've done my nails differently. Rainbows or some glitter. Great, that chance is gone too, now." She slams her hand back down. "I woulda gotten a different DJ. I woulda set it all up and then gotten the chance to gloat to those insufferable McPhersons and Evanses and—*ugh*—those Whitmans!"

"I ... don't exactly understand what you're all in a tizzy about, mama," I confess blankly. "Are you mad that I'm ...?" I choke on saying the word, so I try again with an easier phrasing. "Are you mad about Billy and I?"

She tilts her head and narrows her eyes. "Obviously not, *Tanner*. What—"

"Not that obvious, but please, go on."

She takes a breath, then resumes in a much gentler tone. "You were my only chance to have a ... *gay* party. Shit, I know I ain't gonna have that option with Jimmy here. I've caught him with more boobs on his phone than when I put the wrong dang words into Google."

"Mama!" Jimmy shouts out, all red-faced.

"I sure as hell don't got a problem with you and Billy. Reverend Arnold says we're all born equal and the gays are God's answer to a lack a' fashion sense."

"Pretty sure that's not what he said," I mumble.

"But if I'm gonna keep the upper-hand over the girls, I sure as hell can't be blindsided *at my own party* by your ... antics." She huffs again, puts a hand to her hairdo as if to make sure it's still there. Then, after a breath, she says, "But regardless ... I thought that your words about Billy's family were kind. And right. And well-spoken." She gives him a sidelong glance. "And ... very well-deserved."

"I meant every word," I say, shooting a look at Billy, who just smiles and buries his flushing face into a sip of orange juice.

That afternoon, I pull Billy out into the fields with a football to give him a little introduction into *my* world. He resists at first, but then can't seem to help himself after I put on a particularly tighter pair of gym shorts that I've outgrown, plus a skimpy tank that hides nothing. I give him some clothes to borrow for himself, which amuses me since he fits perfectly into my high school shorts and tees.

"Grip it like this," I show him, placing his fingers correctly over the laces on the football. "Then throw it like this." I demonstrate with an invisible ball, showing him the arc. Billy's first try fumbles out of his grip and lands in the grass with a sad thump. His second try soars across the field with perfect balance, causing us both to gape at the enormous distance he achieves. "Lord, boy. Maybe you should've tried out way back when."

"Nah," he says, brushing off his shoulders and playing the role of a cocky athlete. "Wouldn't wanna outshine you or nothin'."

I tackle him to the grass, inspiring a throaty giggle from him as we wrestle for a while. The bodily maneuver ends up with me on top, pinning him by his wrists to the ground. We both breathe heavily, staring into each other's eyes. Then I descend on him, taking charge of his mouth as we kiss with force and jagged breath.

The sound of my brother calling out from across the field interrupts our joy. "Where the hell are ya?" Jimmy's shouting.

I stare down at an out-of-breath Billy. "Looks like someone wants to join us," I groan.

"We can put a bookmark in this for later," Billy assures me.

We're off the ground quickly, inspiring Jimmy to snort and roll his eyes, not having missed the fact that we were on top of each other. "I can come back later," he tells us, already turning around.

"You wanna throw some ball or not?" I shout back at him. "Billy done thrown it halfway across the world. Go get it for us, Jimmy!"

Jimmy grins, then races across the grass to go for the ball.

Billy stands by me, watching. "A mini-Tanner."

"Nah," I say, shaking my head. "He's gonna be better than me. I doubt he'll stick with football. Maybe he's more of a baseball kind of guy."

"Or a software developer," Billy muses. "He could be the next millionaire app designer."

I chuckle, turning my face to Billy's. "I don't think so. Not with all those *boobs* on his phone."

"He could code an app for boobs."

I pull Billy against me, then plant a kiss on his sweaty forehead. "I feel like I'm just gettin' to know you, and yet I feel like we've known each other our whole lives."

"We *have* known each other our whole lives, dummy," he shoots back, wrinkling up his face in that cute way that makes his hazel eyes sparkle.

I growl. "You look good in my clothes."

"I feel good in them, too," he admits.

"Bet you'd feel great *out* of them."

His eyes turn sinister. "Likewise."

"You've been starin' at my ass in these shorts ever since we came out here. Don't lie."

"Those shorts barely contain it." His eyes drift to my chest. "Not to mention what that shirt does to your pecs."

I give each one a bounce. "What're you talkin' about? These ol' things?" I flex them a few more times.

Billy grips me, then lets his hands slide down my back and onto my ass, gripping firmly and not letting go.

That is, until we both realize Jimmy's returned with the football. "Uh, alright. Yeah. I'm definitely comin' back later," he announces, tossing the ball in our direction—it lands near our feet—then heads back to the house. "Later, love birds!"

I chuckle, then give Billy a swat on his ass. "You ready to play some catch?"

"Bet your tight-shorts-wearin'-ass I am."

With that, I grab the ball and toss it into his hands. He catches it like a natural, then prepares to throw.

"Go long!" he shouts as I run to make distance before he lets loose the ball.

Going long with Billy. *That's exactly what I plan to do.*

After an hour or two of throwing the ball and getting sweaty in the field, we toss our shirts aside and hop into the pool to cool off. Today and yesterday look like a lot more sunlight than Billy's used to, if the red sheen across his neck and face is any indication.

"We're gonna have a really busy week at the diner," Billy notes, his elbows propped up on the ledge of the pool next to me. "Thanks to the promo your little *speech* gave my family and I."

"The food spoke for itself," I tell him, putting a wet arm around him, drops of pool water dripping down our faces from our hair. "Didn't need no sponsorship from me. And I'll be a fool if I don't go and try another Tackler."

He smirks at me. "You think you can handle another? Really? You cried like a baby."

"Maybe 'cause someone made me an *atomic* version of the Tackler. Did the cap fall off your cayenne pepper or somethin'?"

"Cayenne?" His face turns all superior as he enjoys teasing and taunting me. "Don't go usin' big words you don't understand."

"I'm gonna miss the fuck outta you."

His expression changes. He looks at me, his face just an inch from mine. "Tanner ..."

"Sorry." I shrug and let myself drift some distance from him in the water. "I don't wanna get all clingy. We got, like, a month of summer left."

He drifts along the water, too, following me across the pool toward where the volleyball net is usually set up. "I definitely don't wanna think about runnin' off to Florida. Everything's so different now."

"Hey." I stop him right there with my tone. "Don't you go thinkin' about *not* going to Florida. You are gonna chase them dreams of yours, Billy. And I don't want you stoppin' until—"

"Tanner."

"Lemme finish," I say, coming up to him in the middle of the water. "I don't want you stoppin' until you're the owner of that big ol' bakery you always wanted."

He smiles, his eyes glimmering in the sunlight.

"You're gonna achieve those dreams, Billy Tucker. I won't let you fall short on account of a little flutterin' in your heart."

He tilts his head forward, smirking. "You know damn well, Tanner, that you are more to me than just a little *flutterin'* in my heart."

My arms slip around him in the water. Then one of my hands decides to misbehave, slipping under his shorts and catching a firm hold of his cock.

"I suppose I'm a bit of a *flutterin'* down here, too," I tease.

He grins and doesn't respond—unless you count the way his cock starts to respond to my grip.

Then, quite suddenly, I find myself seeing more in Billy's cute, shimmering eyes. The timing is awfully strange, but suddenly I'm not thinking about how horny he makes me, or how hard I'm getting, or how sexy he looks all wet from the pool water.

Now, I'm looking into his eyes and I'm seeing the boy who wanted to do something with his life that made others feel good. I'm seeing the first dessert he ever made that caused someone to moan with pleasure as they put the first spoonful or forkful past their lips. I see the teen who grew up in his papa's diner absorbing all the lessons he possibly could. I see the dreams in his eyes of a future where he's respected and renowned for his talents. I see his aspiration in the firm setting of his jaw. I see his determination. I see his brilliance and his intelligence and the deeply personal way in which he pours all his love into everything he does.

My hand has already slipped out of his shorts and found its place around his back, pulling him close. Sure, he's sexy and can turn me on in a heartbeat, but he's so much more than that. "Fuck," I murmur thoughtfully.

He tilts his head a bit, studying me. "Yeah?"

"Was just ... realizin' a few things."

Billy gives me a soft kiss on the cheek, then lifts his eyebrows expectantly, waiting.

All the smile's gone from my face now as I look upon his. "Billy Tucker, I think I'm fallin' for you."

His eyes light up. The words stun him, but I don't see fear in his eyes; I see longing. *He wanted to hear that.* The realization fills me up with a warmth I've never had.

"And shit," I blurt, "we ain't even had a proper first date!"

"You askin' me out, Tanner Strong?" he asks softly.

I smile despite my racing heart. "Well, dang. I guess I kinda am." I take a breath. "Billy Tucker, will you go out with me?"

He answers with a kiss.

CHAPTER 19
BILLY

After I rush home from Tanner's to shower and get ready, he picks me up at six that same night for a seven o'clock reservation in Fairview, since the town of Spruce is effectively closed all day Sunday. He takes me to a place he hopes I'll enjoy: Nadine's.

"Tonight, *you're* the one bein' treated like a king," he says when he holds the door open for me.

"You really don't gotta go through the whole chivalry thing," I assure him, feeling myself blush. "I'm just—"

"You're my date, dang it," he sasses me, giving my ass a little swat. "Let me treat you like I wanna treat you and wine n' dine ya if I want."

"Fine, fine," I tease, playing along.

We're seated in the middle of the room at a quaint, tiny circular table complete with a candle and a flowery centerpiece. This place is fancy-schmancy and then some. I can't stop looking around at all the glittery décor and glass shimmering from the chandeliers. Everything keeps catching my eye.

But Tanner Strong, who sits across from me, steals the show. The fitted red button-down shirt he wears hugs every contour of his broad shoulders and thick arms. He wears black slacks with a belt and a fine pair of shoes, making him look all cleaned-up and proper. I'm in a baby blue polo, but I've dressed it up with khakis.

After the server gets our drink orders, Tanner looks me over. "You were wearing that the first time I brought you to my ranch."

"You mentioned that on the ride over here." I give him a nod. "That's a new shirt, huh?"

"I've had it. You just haven't seen me wear it before."

"Looks great on you." *Understatement of the century.*

He props his elbows up onto the table, then brings his hands up to rest his chin on. The gesture makes his biceps bulge ridiculously in those tight red sleeves. Of course, my eyes go there, distracted and perpetually horny as ever when I'm in his presence.

What's going to happen when I'm *not* in his presence? What's going to happen to us when I'm in Florida and he's in Oklahoma and all our correspondence converts to just texts and goofy selfies and ... longing?

There's only so much comfort clinging to empty bed sheets can give you.

"So tell me about yourself," Tanner says with a cute, dimply smile.

I chuckle. "We're really gonna play this out like a first date, huh?"

"It *is* our first date," he explains innocently. "I don't know what kind of beautiful bod you got under that polo of yours. Maybe you're crazy hairy or have a weird scar."

"I *do* have a weird scar," I point out. "Someone must not have noticed it yet, or—"

"The one on your upper thigh? Yep, seen it. What's it from?"

I gawk. I *did* notice once that he's observant. I have a feeling I'm going to continue underestimating exactly how observant he is for quite some time.

"Kitchen knife when I was a kid," I explain. "Dumb mistake, and my pa blamed himself for the longest time."

"Aww." He tilts his head. "You just couldn't keep out of the kitchen even way back then."

"Nope. I was born curious."

His foot knocks into mine under the table. With the tablecloths and dim lighting, I don't suspect anyone can see, but I still blush—especially when his foot starts to rub my own a touch more deliberately, toying with mine.

I snap my eyes to him like a warning.

He lifts a brow, looking all innocent. "What?"

"Why are you playin' footsie with me, dude?" I throw back at him lightly. "We just met."

"Oh yeah. We *did* just meet. This is our first date, isn't it?" He doesn't stop playing with my foot.

"Tanner ..."

"Can we maybe pretend this is our second date? Or maybe our third or fourth?"

I chuckle to myself and shake my head. "I swear ..."

"I just wanna guarantee that we're at *least* gettin' to third base later."

"You ain't gettin' to no bases if you don't behave."

"Can I at least score a field goal?"

"Now you're crossin' sports analogies!" I say laughingly.

"Wow. You ... actually *know* the difference between baseball and football?" he asks with mock astonishment. I kick him under the table. He gawps, recoiling his legs. "I was just sayin'! Didn't know a stud like you would know your way around a pair a' all-American sports."

I cross my arms on the table and lean forward. "Guess I must look awful dumb to you, huh?"

His teasing face softens. The corner of his lip lifts up into a smile. "You know," he says gently, "you look far from dumb to me."

"Do I?"

"You're smart. You're gonna freakin' annihilate that institute in Florida with all your smarts and cleverness."

Bringing up culinary school casts a very unwelcome shiver down my back, but it's a reality I need to face in a couple weeks. Maybe I should quit being afraid of it and start keeping a straight spine about the subject.

"What's your favorite thing about Oklahoma?" I ask him.

The question seems to cast the same discomforting wave through him, but he holds a smile on his face almost admirably. In fact, his smile strengthens as he observes my face with his sexy brown eyes. "I don't have my sweet and loving and ... *naggin'* mama on my back."

I chuckle. "What else?"

"Other than the independence, I guess ..." He glances to the side, considering it. When he returns his gaze to me, it's sharper. "If I'm totally honest with you, Billy, I get pretty damn lonely up there in Oklahoma. I haven't made a lot of friends. Everyone in college is so damned serious. I thought I was walkin' onto a campus full of frat parties and alcohol, but ... it just ain't like that at all."

"So it's boring?"

"I just feel ... twenty steps behind everyone. I'm kinda strugglin' in most of my classes. Shit." He laughs lightly, looking away for a second. If I'm not mistaken, his eyes seem to be watering over. The emotion is subtle and he's trying his damnedest to mask it, but it's there. "I haven't admitted this shit to nobody."

"You shoulda told me it was that bad, man. I could be, like, tutoring you or something. I'm pretty decent with math. I do the books at the diner. Oh, Lord help me, I can't think of the nightmare of my ma takin' that over while I'm gone."

Tanner grasps at my little joke like a straw, chuckling.

I reach out and take his hand. He stills, staring down at our clutch. The look in his eye is so soft, it reminds me of when he's drifting off to sleep and he looks so sweet and vulnerable. My heart is wrung out in an instant as it races and warms.

Then he moves his thumb, gently rubbing the top of my hand. Tanner lifts his eyes to me.

This must be our first truly honest moment, when we drop the little shields we didn't realize we were holding up and dare to look at our true selves.

I guess that's what inspires me to say my next words.

"I oftentimes wonder if I should resent my parents," I murmur. "It wasn't my pa's fault for havin' a heart attack, but I get kinda mad sometimes that I lost my chance to head off to college after high school. It's so damn selfish. I hate even thinking it, let alone saying it out loud. But ..." I bite my lip, looking off and thinking it over. "Maybe it was meant to happen this way. I wouldn't have gotten my associate's in business. I wouldn't have gotten three years' experience in restaurant management and bookkeeping. I wouldn't have—"

"This might not have happened."

I meet his eyes, pulled out of my thoughts. I smile, then tighten my grip on his hand.

Just in time, we're greeted by the large-bellied, big-bearded presence of Mario Tucci, who appears at the side of our table with a big smile (buried somewhere in that insane beard of his, I'm sure) and setting down our drinks. "Welcome to Nadine's!" His eyes are on me, getting to the point. "You're William's son. You're responsible for the delicacies I had the pleasure of enjoying."

"Yes, sir," I affirm, feeling my cheeks redden.

"Damn fine work," he says, extending a hand. I let go of Tanner's and clasp Mario's, then regret it when I realize how strong and brutal a handshake this hulking man gives. *Does he wring his pasta into submission for a living?* "I'm Mario Tucci, executive chef here at Nadine's. Tanner told me all about you."

"Oh? He did?" I peer at Tanner with a lifted eyebrow. He just gives a coy little shrug.

"If you ever considered venturing out of that diner your father owns, you ought to consider working for me as my dessert chef. We could meet sometime and talk about it, William."

"I go by Billy," I correct him politely, "and thank you for the offer, but I'm going to be heading off to—"

"School in Florida," he cuts me off. "Yeah, I heard. Why Florida? Is that where your father went?"

"No. My father's self-taught," I explain. "My Uncle Aaron lives there, and tuition's affordable. I had to carefully find a culinary school that fit into our budget, and going to Florida takes care of my housing, so ..."

"No scholarship? A talented young man like you?"

"No, sir."

He scoffs at that, as if that bit of information was the most offensive thing he'd heard all week. "You deserve better, William.

I'm gonna put something on the table. Take it or leave it. I have contacts at *my* alma mater. It's closer. It's affordable. And if those desserts are any indication of your talent, you might even be eligible for financial assistance." He fishes something out of his shirt pocket, then slaps it on the table: his business card. "Give me a call if you change your mind. Talent like yours shouldn't be ignored by any school."

"Wow." I take his card, give it a look, then squirrel it away. "Thank you, Mr. Tucci. Truly. I'll consider it."

"Mario. Just Mario. And you ought to go by William," he tells me with a twitch of his beard. "Suits a young man. Billy's a boy's name." He gives us a short bow. "Your server will be with you shortly. You'll want to try the special," he says with a wink, then departs.

I look at Tanner. When I see a superior sort of smirk on his face, I find my mouth parting. "Was that the plan?"

His smirk vanishes. "What do you mean?"

"Your ulterior motive? To introduce me to Mario and make me *not* go to Florida?"

"No, no, no," he assures me, reaching out for my hand again. Then he freezes. "Well. Yeah, actually."

I stare at him for a solid ten seconds. Then I shrug, fight a smile, and say, "It might have worked."

"Really?"

"I ... need to think about it."

I rub his hand, enjoying the feel of his smooth skin. What if I actually don't have to say goodbye to him in a few weeks? What if I went to a school close enough to home to visit Tanner on the weekends?

"You know where his alma mater is, right?" prompts Tanner. "I did a little research after Mario approached me last night at my party."

I meet his eyes. "Where is it?"

"Oklahoma."

My heart skips a beat. Is this real? A scholarship to a culinary school that's not only closer to home by over fifteen hours, but also close to Tanner? A scholarship that may, in fact, cover my whole tuition? Am I even awake right now, or is this all some elaborate dream?

"Billy. You look like you're about to pass out."

I rise from the table.

"Whoa. Billy."

He rises too, alarmed.

I rush around the table to Tanner and embrace him, burying my face in his warm, muscular chest. My body fills up with an element that's somewhere between love and helium.

"Babe ..." he murmurs quietly.

"Thank you," I whisper back. "It's all because of you. All of it, Tanner. It's all you."

"It's all *you*, babe."

"All of it ..."

"I'm ... pretty sure of it now," he whispers as his arms take me in, wrapping around me and holding me tightly against him.

"Sure of what?"

"I've fallen for you," he answers, his lips against my ear. I tilt my head back to get a good look in his eyes. He's smiling. "Ain't nothin' gonna come between you and your dreams now," he whispers. "Not even me."

"Dang." I bite my lip. "I think I'm fallin' for you, too."

"So ... does this mean that I *do* get to score a field goal with you tonight?"

"Oh, shut up," I tease, laughing.

And he kisses me. Though neither of us are under the impression anymore that this is really our first date, the way he kisses me sure as hell feels like our first real kiss.

Maybe it is.

CHAPTER 20

TANNER

One Month Later.

It's the last Sunday of summer break. The air is like a soft breath from mother nature herself and the sky is smiling on us through the web of branches overhead.

I lie down on the end of the dock that juts out into the lake. Billy rests by my side. Neither of us have said a word for what feels like forever.

Finally, he turns his face towards mine. "I don't know what's next, Tanner," he murmurs softly, "but whatever it is, I'm excited for it, and I can't wait to do it with you by my side."

Lying next to each other on the end of the dock, our shoulders are pressed softly together and our fingers are entwined, rested between our thighs. I could lie here for the rest of eternity for all I care, as long as Billy's there.

"Billy, I got a confession."

"What?"

I hear him breathe while he waits for my confession. Each breath is a cute little brush against the tiny hairs in my ear. "I'm scared," I tell the sky.

"About what?" he asks right away.

"College. Life. Future. I kinda thought I had this vision when I was in high school of how things would be like. I'd marry the girl. I'd have kids, maybe. Throw footballs in the yard while my wife bakes ... biscuits or some shit. Then I blinked and ..." I blink for real. The world vanishes, then comes back right away. "And now it's all different."

"You tellin' me you wish you had a girl here instead?"

I let out one breathy chuckle, then let go of his hand to grab his crotch. He totally lets me, issuing a cute grunt when I squeeze. "Nah," I mumble. "I think we're good."

He puts a tiny kiss on my cheek. "You don't gotta be afraid, Tanner."

"I always pictured myself with a bunch of kids around playin' football. I always wanted to lead them, show them how it works, train 'em. Know what I mean? It was always part of the bigger picture."

"That ... and biscuits," murmurs Billy.

I reach with my other hand and give him a little pat and a rub on his belly. "I think I got that part covered."

He giggles when my belly-rub turns ticklish, causing him to buckle a bit and turn onto his side, throwing his arm around me. I turn too, bringing our faces an inch apart. I'm staring into his eyes now. It's the safest place in the whole world, those shiny hazel eyes of his.

"*I got a confession, too,*" whispers Billy.

"*And what's that?*" I whisper back at him loudly, mocking his sudden decision to whisper.

"*I have a boner in my pants and I don't know what to do with it,*" he hisses, his forehead wrinkling with alarm. "*Can you help me?*"

"*Shit. This sounds serious.*"

"*Really serious.*"

"*Why are we still whispering?*"

"I don't want the whole town to know about this," Billy explains. "Should we call a doctor?"

"I'm a doctor. Let me inspect it." I reach down between his legs and give it another squeeze. Billy's eyes rock back in response and he bites his lip. "I just saw an adverse reaction on your face when I touched it."

"Uh-oh."

"That can't be good. I better do it again."

I grab hold of everything he's got down there and squeeze again, harder this time. I watch as Billy's whole face scrunches up adorably while he tries not to whimper. His cheeks turn pink and his lips part.

"I think I have your diagnosis."

He opens his eyes, recovering from the squeeze, then whispers, "Give it to me straight, doc. No sugarcoating."

"Your diagnosis is: you're horny."

"Shit. What should I do about it?"

"You need to put it in my butt. Like, pronto."

"Wow, doc. You sound like you know what you're talkin' about."

I slip into my pocket and pull out a condom and the tube of strawberry lube, wiggling my brows. Billy grins, breaking character. He snatches it and undoes his pants. He can't get them off fast enough. I do the same, yanking off my shorts so fast they fly into the water.

When our bodies join at last, there's without a doubt something different about the energy bouncing back and forth between us. He clings to me more. My grip on his shoulders is something like a caress. I'm sitting atop him and riding my boy as he works his way deeper and deeper into me. He holds my cock and jerks me in rhythm to our movements, driving me wild. Our eyes never disconnect.

It's the most intimate sex we've ever shared.

And over this summer, we've shared a lot.

His fingers slide up and down my torso. Gripping him as I am, he's enjoying all the fruits of my flexed arms and my tightened pecs. His constant touching of my body only adds to the sensitivity of him pounding into me from beneath in time to my rocking hips. We've perfected a sort of rhythm. Sometimes he takes the lead. Sometimes I do. And sometimes, there's an unspoken intuition that fires between us, inspiring perfect synchronization.

Today is one of those intuitive days, from the feel of it; we know what the other craves at every moment.

"I want you to kiss me when I come," he moans.

"Every time," I promise him.

"I'm close."

"I know."

Just when he pushes over the edge, I lean forward and put my lips to his. My hips never stop moving, keeping a perfect pace with his thrusts as he empties into me. He bites on my lip while he groans his agony of release.

God, I love when he does that.

My cock is hard as steel when I sit up and place my hand over his, guiding the way he jerks me off. He's still inside me and I'm still rocking my hips, working him even after he's spent. Billy loves when I do this, turning him into my rag doll after squeezing every ounce of orgasm from him.

With his cock still flexing within me, it doesn't take long before I get close myself. I lean forward and slap a hand on the dock next to his head, bracing myself as I stare down into Billy's eyes, jerking harder and harder.

"I love you," he whispers.

My eyes flash.

Cum rockets out of me, dressing his chest in ropes of my unprecedented ecstasy. I've never felt release quite like this. Even the perfect fantasy and a cooperative mix of right-hand action, lube, and the privacy of my room can't get me to the high I'm feeling right now. Staring down into Billy's eyes, I'm swimming in the sun.

And then his words repeat in my head. "What did you just say to me?" I blurt.

Billy licks his lips. His eyebrows are lifted. His cheeks, flushed from the heat of passion. "I said I love you."

I crush my lips against his, consuming him. My hands hold him down as our bodies press together with no care in the world of all the stickiness and *sex* that's between us.

I pull from his lips. "Say it again."

"I'm in love with you."

Another quick and furious kiss is pressed into his lips, feverish and animal. "Again."

"I'm in—"

I wrap my arms around him and pull him up as our mouths crash together. I'm basically sitting in his lap, straddling him, while I hold him tightly against me and take full command of his sexy lips.

Then the kiss turns gentle as I tilt my head, then pull away to get a good look into his eyes.

"Love you too, babe," I say back.

The way he smiles at my words, it's so vulnerable and sweet. My future looked so bleak not long ago, thinking I was heading back up to Oklahoma all alone. Knowing that Billy will be there at my side makes me feel like I can brave anything that comes my way. Football. No football. Tough classes. Cold peers. Competition. It doesn't matter. I'm invincible with Billy on my team, and I'll never lose.

"I've really gotten used to this place," murmurs Billy thoughtfully, his eyes taking in the lake around us. "It's so beautiful in the morning. And afternoon. And evening."

"You should see it when it rains," I tell him, giving a wiggle of my eyebrows.

He gives me a little kiss, then says, "You realize my dick's still inside you, right?"

"Yep."

"Not lettin' go yet, huh?"

"Nope."

"Gonna stay here on my lap 'til I can't feel my legs no more?"

"Probably."

He grins and shakes his head. "I guess I'm all yours to do with as you please."

Billy really knows how to pick them words. "And maybe if I do this right, I can get you to come to all my games."

"You think I'd miss a single chance to see your *tight end* in them hot spandex pants?"

I lift right off of him, wrap him up in a towel, and throw him over my shoulder as he yelps with a laugh and a protest of, "Hey!" I slap his ass as I carry my boyfriend—my everything—back home.

EPILOGUE
BILLY

Three Years Later.

The T&S Sweet Shoppe is busier than ever. It's not only a Saturday, but it also happens to be New Year's Eve.

I smile at a dozen customers a minute, it seems like. Every single one of them is a friendly face I've come to know over the decade I've spent in my pa's diner. They've seen me grow up from a clumsy, curious teen into the focused, dessert-shop-owning man I am today.

Focused is a bit of an understatement. At times, my peers think I'm too focused, watching me like a curious anomaly in the night sky as I stand at my station in the back and cut every piece of pastry with precision. I know they watch me sometimes, but it doesn't pull my focus a bit. Sometimes, I even invite them to come closer, then explain what I'm doing and why. Watching the eyes of my employees light up with curiosity as they learn is one of the most thrilling feelings in the world.

My time in culinary school has sharpened my skills and taught me new techniques. Apparently I've been cracking eggs wrong my whole life. Who knew?

Yet there are other techniques I've been employing all these years by instinct that apparently have names. I had an instructor peer over my shoulder once and ask me where I picked up my technique of—*I forgot the strange French term he used*—and I stared at him blankly and said, "You mean it ain't just called mashin' it up with the flat of my knife?"

The look he gave me, I wish I could frame that and put it above my cooking station. It still makes me bust a gut.

We close early today, so I make sure to get everything wrapped up and handled on time for all of my employees to head home to their families while the sun is still setting. After the last person is gone, I lock the door, then peer through the window at the sunless street to ensure that no one else is coming. Once certain, I hurry to the back and pull out my secret project for tonight. I give it a last looking-over with undistracted eyes to make sure everything is perfectly in place. Then, I pack my surprise into a small cooler and bring it with me to the car along with the cupcakes for the party, locking up the shop behind me.

The drive out to the Strong Ranch feels like nothing, now that I've had the experience of driving all the way from Oklahoma to Spruce and back again—several times, I might add. The secret is having good music to listen to along the way. *And good company.*

I pull into my usual spot—right next to a certain someone's beat-up pickup he loves so dang much—and grab the cooler and the box of cupcakes before hopping up the steps to the front door. I put the cooler on the ground before giving it a hearty knock.

Nadine answers the door. "Well, there you are, you sweet *thang* you," she sings out with a little waggle of her head that makes her hoop earrings dance. She then gives me a kiss on either of my cheeks and pushes open the door. "Come on in, you!"

Yeah, Nadine's changed quite a bit over the years. I can't explain it in any other way except to say that she's been infected with the "gay bug of fabulousness". Ever since Tanner came out to her three years ago right in the middle of his midsummer party, she's become gayer than either of us. She did weeks of online research, joined a local chapter of PFLAG (by "local", I mean three counties over), started having tea dates with her gay hairdresser in Fairview, and memorized Cher's complete discography. Tanner and I were helpless to stop her. Now her outfits always have some sort of glitter in them and, if anything, she's become thirteen times sassier than before.

My parents are already here chatting it up with Paul, Tanner's father, while drinking beer in the kitchen. My ma rushes up to me and clutches my face to give me a kiss, as if she hasn't seen me in ten years. They still see me every dang day, considering T&S's Sweet Shoppe is just three blocks down from Biggie's. But I guess without having me at the diner or their house anymore, it isn't quite the same, and she gets all clingy and excited when she sees me. My pa still has his mustache, and it tickles my neck when he pulls me in for a clumsy hug, clearly on his fourth or fifth beer already. He better slow down; the sun's only just set an hour ago and we have a handful of hours left until midnight.

I find Jacky-Ann by the dining room table setting up the finger foods. I hand her the box of cupcakes to be added to the table, then quietly ask, "Can I bother ya to find a place for ... this?" while indicating the cooler in my hand. Being in on my little secret, she gives me a wink, then says, "Consider it handled," before stealing the cooler from me and hopping over to the fridge to make room for it where it can't be seen.

"He made a run for soda," Nadine tells me, obviously having caught my eyes darting around the room looking for my better half. "Oh, and fireworks. He went with Kirk in his minivan. He'll be back soon, hon."

"Thanks, Mom," I say with a smile, and she giggles and strolls back to the TV, always tickled pink when I call her that.

Before the guys come back with soda and fireworks, others show up at the door. Twelve teens from the Spruce High football team show up for the party. Each of them asks where the coach is, but they're quickly distracted by the ridiculous spread of food and snacks on the dining room table, which they descend upon at once. A few moms and dads came as well, staying to chat with Nadine and Paul and my parents, chatting away about this year's season and how accomplished the team has become ever since Coach Adams retired two years back.

Despite it being the south, a cool front blowing in tonight is keeping everyone inside, the warmth of the house being far more preferable. Bonnie, Kirk's wife, is picking through the food and making a plate for their little one, Kirkland Junior, who has taken a liking to hiding behind people's legs, even when he doesn't know the person whose legs he's hiding behind. "Get over here, you little turd," Bonnie calls out with half a laugh. "Kirkland! Don't you wanna try some sweets? Aren't ya hungry?"

I join the others in the kitchen when my ma shows off the newest claw mark she's earned. Shortly after I left for culinary school, she filled the void in her heart by finally bringing in the stray cat who lived on our porch. My pa was against it at first, but ended up paying for the vet visits to make sure the cat was healthy—*he was*—and then they named him Timmy Tackler and the rest is history.

Except for the claw marks. "He's really awfully lovin' and sweet," my ma insists, "even if the only person he ain't ever hissed at is Billy."

It's true. Little furry Timmy Tackler loves me. I can't explain it. Even when I was gone for months at a time, he'd race up to me, headbutt my leg a hundred times, and purr like a little engine the moment I came home.

I hear a car door slam. Call it intuition. Call it being utterly unable to be separated from him for too long. Call it whatever you want, but I know it's Tanner.

I open the front door and watch them climb out of Kirk's minivan with two cases of soda and a big box of what I can only assume are fireworks. Kirk's put on about sixty pounds in the past few years—*he calls it his "daddy weight"*—and grew a big ol' lumberjack beard.

Then there's Tanner, who is fit and muscled as ever in his ass-and-thigh-hugging jeans. He's wearing a plaid shirt with the sleeves ripped off, beautifully showing off his inked guns, which bulge invitingly in his effort of carrying the cases of soda. A cockeyed cap squishes down his messy hair, which he's let grow out a bit over the fall.

The sight of his face, however, is what truly melts me. His rich brown eyes have grown hungrier over the years, like the more he yearns for me, *the more he yearns for me.* I'm pretty much addicted to him too, so I can't complain. He has a light stubble along his cheeks he's been working on, though he doesn't quite grow facial hair the same way I do, thanks to my pa's genes. It's kinda cute when Tanner tries to grow something. He always gives up and shaves it away, annoyed that he can't master the kind of beard that *I* could, if given a week or two.

He slaps a kiss on my cheek on his way into the house with

the soda. "Hey there, husband."

"Hey, babe," I murmur back. "Where's your jacket?"

"Shit. You think *this* is cold?" He snorts. Tanner acts like he's master of winter weather just because he lived in Oklahoma for three years longer than me.

"Get inside," I say, smacking his ass on his way in with a grin, then step back to give Kirk room.

Kirk lifts an eyebrow at me, the box of fireworks held against his chest. "What? No smack on the booty for me?"

I snort. "Get on in, Kirk! I'm freezin' just standin' here holdin' the door for ya!"

Inside the warm house, the party starts to pick up. The whole football team is all over Tanner—or, should I say, Coach Strong— the moment they realize he's arrived. Roars from the teenage boys fill the house as they start eagerly recounting their favorite moments both on and off the field when the team went to state. For it being only Tanner's second season coaching football at Spruce High, it's unheard of to have a team already go all the way to state. Even Coach Adams shed a tear, if the rumor's right.

Joel shows up late, as usual, and he seems to be in the middle of an argument with Mindy. From what I can gather through the noise already drumming through the room from the TV blaring, the football team roaring, and the parents squealing at one another's jokes over glasses of wine in the kitchen, Joel and Mindy are arguing about something to do with what music to play at their wedding. I doubt they've even set a date. Tanner and I keep placing bets on how many more times—*I say two, Tanner says five*— they'll break up and get back together before finally tying the tangled knot. "Our love is atomic," Joel told me one day when he dropped by the Shoppe for a "please forgive me" pastry I made for him to give Mindy, "but the make-up sex, man, dude, seriously, wow. That girl's tongue is outta this world." It was more information than I needed about my friend Mindy, but I laughed anyway and gave him the pastry on the house.

Time really flies when you're spending it with friends and laughing so hard that soda comes out of your nose. Kirk's nose, to be specific. Robby is with his girl of the week on the couch watching New York's ball drop and countdown, which is an hour before ours. I notice for the first time that the girl he's with is actually the same girl as last week. Is he finally settling down? I guess only time will tell. Harrison, after working for years on Tanner's uncle's farm, is thinking of someday owning his own. According to Nadine, he's completely buried in his work and never dates, which I can more than relate to from my time at the diner before Tanner showed up and wrecked all of that. Nadine is convinced that he's gay and keeps pushing me and Tanner to hang out with him and find out if it's true, since she's desperate for someone to play matchmaker with now that she's basically Queen Bee of everything gay in Spruce. Some people just prefer to be alone, marry their work, and the company of friends and family is enough to fill their hearts. Who are we to deny Harrison that particular kind of peace?

Another set of headlights flashes through the window just an hour before the big countdown. The door busts open and in saunters the ever-cocky Jimmy, Tanner's little brother, who ain't so little anymore. He's brought three girls, though I am at a loss as to which one he's supposedly dating. Ever since he dropped out of football and joined the dance department—*yes, Jimmy took up the art of dance after he watched a show on TV and became obsessed with hip-hop and pop-locking*—there hasn't been a shortage of girls coming into and dancing out of Jimmy's life. A little Robby in the making, Jimmy seems to be romancing a new girl in the dance department every week or two. Tanner keeps calling Jimmy his ballerina brother, which is apparently some inside joke between them that I don't get, but it always makes Jimmy throw punches at Tanner's arm.

With jackets on and sparklers in our hands, we stand near a fire-pit that's been erected in the field next to the pool and watch the boys light all the little wicks and fuses as the final seconds of the year tick away. The air rips open with rockets charging into the sky and exploding into colors and sparks and rainbows before our fascinated eyes.

I turn to Tanner, my husband, whose arm I'm clinging to for warmth despite my wearing a jacket. He faces me, the sparkle of fireworks reflecting in his eyes, and he smiles. The wicked way his lips curl, showing those cute dimples of his, melts me to the core.

"Happy New Year," I murmur to him.

"Right back at ya, babe," he says, and then our lips join together in holy matrimony, much like they did on this day one year ago when we first got married in front of Reverend Arnold and the whole town of Spruce. He pulls away and softly whispers, "Happy Anniversary."

"Here's to another year."

"And many more."

The world explodes all around us as everyone shouts and roars. The football boys play and roughhouse one another. Kirk and Bonnie share a tender moment with little Kirkland staring into the sky with his tiny mouth agape. Robby and his girl are ... nowhere to be found (probably "exercising" behind a tree). My parents are drinking champagne with Tanner's parents, already laughing about something fun and scandalous, probably related to Cissy, Marcy, and Cassie's big New Year's Eve party they've supposedly thrown somewhere in town. Nadine doesn't associate with them much anymore ever since her priorities have changed and she's become buddy-buddy with my ma. Oddly enough, the lack of having Nadine to compete with has made the wicked trio of Cissy, Marcy, and Cassie less of an issue at all, the three of them minding their own. I spot Joel and Mindy with sparklers in hand, pointing at the sky and laughing with Jacky-Ann and Harrison at their side, their feud from earlier forgotten.

Being in the presence of so many friends and family tonight, I feel warmed to my fingertips and toes with love when Tanner and I finally decide to make our rounds of goodbyes and goodnights. With a gasp at the door, having nearly forgotten about it, I hurry back inside the house and grab my cooler from the fridge, smartly hidden by Jacky-Ann behind the cases of soda. Tanner asks what it is and I shrug him off, saying it's nothing at all.

Of course he doesn't believe me, but he's smart not to push. *He'll find out soon enough, anyway.*

The party carries on as Tanner and I make our way across the field toward the lake, where the house we live in was built a year ago, right by the dock. The lake is so peaceful this late at night, and its smooth waters reflect the sparks and light that still explodes in the sky from distant, belated fireworks going off.

After I take the cooler in and Tanner lights up the fireplace, we hang out on the porch and cuddle up under a blanket his grandma crocheted for us, which is red and pink. "Strawberry colors," she told us last Christmas when we opened the present together. "Even though I'm a chocolate girl myself," she added with a wiggle of her eyebrows at Tanner. He explained to me the inside joke about her finding that unused condom of mine and the infamous strawberry lube when we first started seeing each other. Yes, my face burned a whole new shade of red that Christmas that I didn't know my cheeks were even capable of.

Tanner takes hold of my hand under the blanket, drawing my eyes away from the sky and onto his. He's staring at me with one corner of his lip cutely curled, hinting one of his dimply smiles.

"You starin' at me like a creep?" I ask him softly, a teasing edge to my voice.

"Can't get enough of ya, babe," he says back. "And I'll stare at you as much as I damn well please. You're just too dang pretty, Billy Tucker."

"Billy Tucker-*Strong*," I correct him sassily, poking his ribs beneath the blanket. "There's a reason it's T&S's Sweet Shoppe and not just *T's* Sweet Shoppe. Tucker & Strong. Both of us. If it weren't for your family's help ..."

"You woulda found the money yourself," he tells me, insisting the same thing he's insisted since the day I opened the Shoppe. "We just sped up the process is all. Hmm." He tilts his head thoughtfully. "I still prefer the name Tucker's Tasty Surprise."

"That sounds like what my grandpa would name the flask he hides in his coat," I spit back. "No thanks."

He laughs at that, the sound ringing across the lake and disappearing into the lightless woods and fields that surround us. "If ya say so, babe."

"I do say so," I sass back. "Besides. I *do* got a tasty surprise for you. And ..." I suck in my lips, shutting up and shifting my eyes.

His forehead wrinkles up as he stares at me. "Billy, did you lie about what's in that cooler of yours?" I don't answer, trying not to giggle. "Did you *seriously* make me somethin' for our anniversary, after we said we ain't doin' nothin' big at all?"

"It ain't anythin' big," I tell him.

"Well, shit. Don't keep me waitin'!" he says, pinching my nipple under the blanket and causing me to yelp out and giggle, fighting to get away from him. "C'mon! Let's see it, babe! Besides, it's cold as shit out here!"

"Oh, *now* who's complainin'?" I sass at him.

We pour into the house, shutting the door and locking ourselves in with the warmth coming from the fireplace. I sit Tanner down at our little dining room table by the window that overlooks part of the lake and the field, across which you can see the ranch. With a little swipe of a match, I light a candle at the table, then go to the fridge to unveil my surprise to him.

The cake I set before him is small, just for two people, and it's my sweetest creation yet. It's a triple-layer cake: vanilla bean on the bottom, strawberry in the middle, and chocolate on top. Glazed over it is a fudge frosting that's paired with dollops of strawberry sauce. Stripes of vanilla bean icing create laces across the top of the cake, which is, of course, shaped like a football. On the side of the plate is two perfect balls of my homemade vanilla bean ice cream.

"Dear Lord!" Tanner cries out, staring at the cake with his sexy lips parted and his eyes unblinking.

"Football Sundae Cake," I present him, taking a seat by his

side. When he meets my eyes, I shrug nonchalantly. "Can't part with our Sunday tradition, babe."

"I'm one lucky son of a bitch," he mumbles before his mouth covers mine in a feverish, heated kiss that steals away all the air from my lungs. "What," he kisses me, "did," another kiss, "I," kiss, "do," kiss, "to," kiss, "deserve you??"

"Calm down, babe, it's just a dang cake," I say through a giggle to his incredulous, shimmering eyes. "I know it ain't much, but ... your *other* anniversary gift is waitin' for you in the bedroom, and it's only somethin' I can give you with my, uh ... body."

I steal a move of his and grab my own crotch, giving it a firm squeeze and a jiggle.

He snorts, lifting an eyebrow as he glances down at what I'm doing. "You need some work on that. I'll teach you how to perfect the leerin' crotch-grab. But," he says, lifting his eyes back to me, "first things first. We're gonna dive into this cake, and then you get *my* gift."

Now it's my turn to look surprised. "Gift? I thought—"

"Shit, Billy, really? You think I ain't gonna get you anything? You're too cute." He picks up a fork, then stares at my cake, frozen in place. "I don't wanna wreck it. It's so damn beautiful."

"I already took a pic of it at the Shoppe," I confess, then slap him on the arm. "Go to town, babe."

"Still don't wanna wreck it." He pokes his finger into a smear of strawberry sauce and brings it to his lips. His eyes rock back. "Fuckin' heaven."

"I wanna see this gift!" I tell him, popping him on the arm again. "I didn't think you got me anything!"

He purses his lips, studying me. "You really want your gift?"

"Yep."

"Like ... *really* want it?"

"You want me to beg you or somethin'?" I say, tilting my head and giving him my attitude I know sets him off down below.

As I thought, Tanner growls with wicked pleasure—something in his pants likely stirring to life in one quick instant—but he behaves despite himself and says, "You got it, babe," then leans his body to the side and pulls out a white envelope from his back pocket. Tanner slaps it down on the table between us. "Happy Anniversary, babe. I got you an envelope."

I look down at it. Has he been carrying that in his pocket the whole night, or did he just grab it from somewhere in here while I was setting up the cake?

"I'm ... suspecting there's a gift card or somethin' in that envelope," I say, quirking an eyebrow at my husband. "You takin' me to Nadine's again?"

"It's just an envelope. I got you paper. That's it."

"Is it dinner reservations to that other fancy Italian place? Or that French restaurant? Oh, oh!" I start hopping in my seat. "It's, like, a full spa treatment or somethin'! You wanna pamper me, huh?"

He laughs at my excitement. "Billy! Will you just open the dang envelope??"

I grab it off the table and, after one last squinty look at Tanner, I finally tear it open. I pull out two slips of paper. Firm paper.

Tickets.

I read the destination.

My jaw hits the floor.

"I got you paper," he says. "Wasn't lyin'."

I can't breathe. "Tanner ..."

"And maybe you were kinda right, too," he says as he watches my expression, giving me his cocky smile. "Italian restaurants. French restaurants. Hell, Billy, you'll have reservations at *all* the restaurants ... when we fly over to Paris, France and taste our way across Europe."

I'm in tears. I can't even read the ticket anymore nor can I close my mouth.

I hear his soothing voice. "Babe ..." He puts an arm around my back, his hand rubbing up and down. "Did I do alright? Isn't that what you wanted?"

"I can't ... I c-can't even ..."

Suddenly I laugh, a couple tears spilling from my eyes as I clap a hand over my mouth, staring at the tickets. Then I lift my blurry gaze to Tanner. Not being able to see his face is simply not going to do, so I wipe the tears from my eyes and look upon the bright, cocky, proud-of-himself face of Tanner Tucker-Strong, my love, my husband, my heart.

"*There* you are," teases Tanner, grinning. "Ain't you ready to hop on over to France? I know we gotta wait until the summer obviously, but shit, I can't wait to see if *they* got anything on *your* brand of cuisine." He lifts an eyebrow. "And I *will* be picky. I mean, you basically spoiled me already, babe."

I throw my arms around Tanner's neck, pulling him in close. "I can't begin to thank you," I finally manage to say, my voice quivering with excitement.

"Aww, hell," he mumbles. "It's just as much a gift for me as it is for you, really. I can't freakin' wait to take a big ol' bite out of

Europe again. It just ain't fair that I've already been there and you haven't."

I press my lips to his, then shake my head as I pull away. "Tanner, you're damn wrong. *I'm* the lucky son of a bitch. Pinch me. Just fuckin' pinch me."

"Last time I tried that, I bruised your butt," he reminds me.

"We're goin' to Europe," I murmur, still in disbelief.

"We are," he affirms, the smile returning to his face before he leans forward once more to kiss me.

The world spins and it's all Tanner's fault.

Life has never felt so full of possibilities than it does now. Our future is in the big oven, baking high, all the right ingredients sprinkled in, and the heavenly aroma that feeds my nostrils is intoxicating. I'm anxiously waiting at the glass door, watching as our happiness rises and browns. I can't fucking wait for the oven to ding at me, indicating it's ready to feast. I just can't fucking wait for that ding.

After Tanner and I finish the Football Sundae Cake, we hold each other as we gaze into the crackling fire, cuddled on the couch with the blanket and kissing softly.

He chuckles. "You remember three years back ..."

"I was just thinkin' about that," I say. "It was the last Sunday of our summer break ..."

"And we laid out on that dock outside and talked about our futures. Didn't you tell me how much you loved the lake? How it looks so damn good at all times of day?"

"And you were right. It's beautiful when it rains."

Tanner smirks. "Reminds me of another thing that *I* said. I pictured my future bein' surrounded by kids playin' football. Now here I am, surrounded by kids playin' football. Maybe I shoulda been more specific, huh?"

"I think your future turned out just how you wanted it," I murmur. "Those kids look up to you. You're still the Spruce Juice, babe. You're a damned legend."

"That makes two of us, Mr. Football Sundae," he says back, kissing me on the forehead.

Then he kisses my cheek.

Then our lips meet, and our breath deepens, and our hands start to explore.

"You said," Tanner speaks against my lips, kissing me through his words, "that there was another gift waitin' for me in the bedroom."

"Mmm-hmm," I moan against his mouth.

He keeps kissing me. "I'm ready for that gift."

I pull him off the couch, our mouths stubbornly refusing to let go of one another. A shirt is lost here. Pants are lost there. Shoes. A sock. Another sock. Our clothes come off in clumsy pieces. Then he picks me right up off the floor, making me giggle against his lips as he carries me straight to the bedroom to claim his gift.

And that's how the football star from my high school dreams did it: by strutting into my diner on that day so long ago, like the cocky man he is, and ordering the one dang thing I didn't know was on the menu: my heart. And it's his. It's all his. From now and until long beyond the ding of that oven, my love is all his to enjoy.

The End.

Made in United States
Troutdale, OR
05/17/2024

19963415R00166